Sophia's Diaries

BRONWYN J. TAYLOR

Synopsis

'Sophia's dairies' is the third book in the Clarence R. Smyth trilogy. These books are about psychic predictions, spirituality, historic facts and the elite few who really control the world. All are told in an interesting, amusing and believable way. The first two books are in the voice of the renowned psychic and physical medium Clarence R. Smyth; the third book is written by his similarly gifted granddaughter, Sophia Elizabeth Rothschild. They cover the span of the last century up to the present day.

The first book, 'The Diaries of a gifted Edwardian boy' begins Clarence's story, when at age six he was given his first diary. It takes Clarence from his early childhood with his family and tutor Mr Franks, a German, through his boarding school years from age eleven, to Berlin where he spent the duration of the first world war age fourteen to eighteen. The book ends with him as an Art student in Vienna on a scholarship paid for by the German Government, but with a different name.

As you will read, Clarence was no ordinary boy.... Sickly when young, but also very psychically gifted, Clarence was a bit misunderstood by his family. It took him many years to realise other people were not like him and how to control his gifts, as there were those he could trust and those he couldn't.

Clarence was born on an auspicious day, the 1st January 1900 in London, England, and he had an extraordinary life. He met many famous and infamous people of his era, some he influenced. And because of his accurate predictions more than one party were interested in him, so he was put on a 'watch list'. Clarence's father, a British diplomat, not believing war was imminent, took him to Berlin, just before the outbreak of the first world war. Clarence was fourteen at the time and already known in some circles for his psychic gifts. As a result, he was kidnapped and forced to work for 'The headquarters', a psychic branch of German intelligence, for the first half of the war.... For the second half he was interned in a P.O.W Camp. One good thing that came out of all of this for Clarence was that he met Maria, the love of his life at 'The Headquarters', as she was also conscripted.

The second book 'The journals of Clarence R. Smyth (physical medium), picks up where the first book finishes with Clarence aged twenty-one and about to marry Maria and embark on a life in New York. Clarence works there as a set designer, then a physical medium, and Maria a violinist with the New York philharmonic orchestra. After five years, some adventures and an attempt on Clarence's life, Clarence and Maria decide to go back to Vienna to live with their four-year-old twins William and Sarah. Clarence continues with the psychic shows he did in the U.S. and because of this and his gifts he is asked by British Intelligence to gather information, which he does whilst touring Germany.

Clarence knows intuitively to get out of Austria just before the start of the second world war so the family spend the duration of the war in Baden, near Zurich. But before they leave Vienna, Clarence is detained for several days by the gestapo. Fortunately, a former acquaintance of his saves his life. Once safely in Switzerland Clarence and Maria help refugees who have crossed the border and open spiritual centres called 'Beacons of Light' to counteract the evil happening around them.... They offer spiritual guidance and help many souls pass over.

The second book takes Clarence from aged twenty-one until his mature years. He has even more adventures and two attempts on his life, due to his work. And because he will not cooperate and join 'The Order', a secret society of the elite who have always monitored Clarence, who some may call, the Illuminati?

Clarence and his family return to New York to live after the war but not before his daughter Sarah marries into a wealthy banking family, who to his dismay, are also part of this elite.... In New York Clarence starts a psychic newspaper and bravely a secret society 'The White hats', to counteract the

Illuminati.... But after an attempt on his life and disillusioned with the U.S politics of the 1950s he and Maria decide to return to Zurich again to live. As do their adult children with their families.... Clarence and Maria are only there a few years when his health starts declining so they return to the U.S. to live, Los Angeles this time, for the climate. Sophia, Sarah's twelve-year-old daughter makes the move with them as her both her parents decide to get her away from her father's family and what they have planned for her.

'Sophia's Diaries' is the third book in the trilogy.... Born into a wealthy Swiss banking family who are also, part of the Illuminati. And gifted like her maternal grandparents, who are anti-illuminati, but without their temperaments.... Means, Sophia leads a complicated life. Her Poppa Clarence who is her main mentor and protector dies when Sophia is only sixteen so she must now rely on her own intuition. Her beloved Poppa does come through to her on many occasions giving guidance and making predictions. But ultimately, she must survive on her own and she tries very hard not to be a pawn in any Illuminati game. A task which proves to be impossible, as Sophia spends her whole life unsure who she can ever really trust. When Sophia is widowed for the second time, she realises she must now protect her children as two have been selected for special roles within 'the Order', just like she was.

The third book really begins with Sophia as a young model living in London. This is where she first encounters the extent of the power of her father's family, the Rothschilds. As a young woman she lives in both New York and Los Angeles following different career paths and with different husbands. But her life is monitored and manipulated by 'the Order', a name she prefers to use, and who she tries but also fails to protect her children from.

This book spans from the 1960s to present day. It is a combination of historical facts, psychic predictions, spirituality and conspiracy theories.

Contents

Sophia

October 2020

It has taken me nearly a year to do so, but finally I have put my years of scribbled thoughts into some- semblance of order. This is a record for the family only and it will surprise some of them. I doubt it will ever be shared with the public though.... But at least it has kept me occupied over this past critical year as writing has always helped me focus, calmed my nerves, and brought some clarity to my life. That plus meditation.

But today I am absorbed with waiting to see, who will be the next President of the United States of America, as the American people are now voting. The polls have only been open a few hours so it is too early to predict an outcome yet.... But we are all waiting anxiously to see if Donald J. Trump will do another term in office, or be 'trumped' by my son the Democratic candidate, Jonathon Clarence West. We should be able to tell in about six hours, unless it is close, then we'll have to wait for the special votes to be counted.

I doubt that will be the case though as my son is not in bed with the N.D.A. and has promised to finally do something about the gun laws in America. First, he plans to stop it being legal to purchase weapons that can shoot multiple rounds. As the American people have had enough of these all too- frequent mass shootings, especially in schools. And with the numbers of fatalities due to firearms increasing annually. Now in the U.S., more children are being killed in learning institutions by a lone gunman each year than U.S. soldiers fighting overseas, this is abhorrent.

Also, Jonathon's plans for the war on terrorism and his economic reforms are masterstrokes and what's- more he will have the support of good honest people to help implement them. And unlike Trump, Jonathon doesn't make constant gaffs. Who's ever heard of a President resorting to social-media, like 'Twitter'. Plus, with Trump's sexist and racist banter over the years, how did he even get elected in the first place? And look at his irrational and irresponsible comments since becoming the President. Not that I would have preferred Hilary Clinton as president. They had their time the Clintons and a fair share of scandals.

I must admit, in some ways Trump has given everyone a good shake- up and achieved more than I thought he would during his term. He has tried to keep jobs in America though with tariffs on Chinese made goods as too much of the world's manufacturing has gone to China. Although things are changing now with the world in the grips of this Corona virus pandemic.

This virus, which supposedly originated in the wet markets of Wuhan, China, and China's delay in alerting the world, plus their lack of transparency on the matter has resulted in many countries now boycotting their goods. But China has taken no responsibility for the pandemic which so far has killed nearly three million people world-wide.... Instead, they have bullied the countries they have financial interests in who have questioned their actions and even ceased some trade with them.

The majority the Americans polled think that Trump has handled the pandemic poorly because in the beginning he was far too casual. He should have locked down the country earlier, closed the borders to all but returning Americans and made them quarantine for two weeks. The countries who did this had far fewer cases and deaths. Although sadly many of these countries are now enduring a second wave. I have been amazed through this pandemic crisis that so many countries have put people before profit.... There is hope for humanity yet.

Over thirty million Americans have contracted the Coronavirus Covid 19 so far, with 600,000 deaths. But I feel these figures will only double before a vaccine rollout slows it down. As scientists around the world are madly working on a safe and effective vaccine.

With the pandemic out of control in the U.S. Trump blamed the World Health organisation, plus the Chinese of course, calling it the "China Flu" or "Kung Flu" Trump also did not handle well the fourteen- day riots and subsequent lootings in Minneapolis in June. These began with the death of an afro American man when a white cop had used undue force on him during an arrest. And these demonstrations went national, then global, with several other countries also protesting that 'Black lives matter'.... Once again Trump showed a lack of leadership.

He just kept saying everything was under control and again played the blame game, this time blaming the socialists. But this will continue to happen as racism in the police force is systemic.

Unlike the rest of my family, I think it is a good thing that Trump and Putin, the Russian Leader, appear to get on.... Better to have him as a friend than an enemy. Especially as tensions between China and the U.S. are now increasing. And I do not believe for one moment that Trump was in cahoots with the Russians at the time of his election. This was something fabricated by the F.B.I. and other U.S. intelligence services, and we all know who runs them....

And it appears that Putin will be in power for many years to come as all his opponents and critics seem to get eliminated somehow, sometimes with poison.

I have got to hand it to Donald though, as he is my age and has done well keeping up the pace with everything that has been going on in the world, plus the election. Both Candidates have been going head- to- head for weeks now.... But my son is going to win.... What's- more he will make a damn fine President, and the first Jewish one. Or should I say of Jewish descent, as he is non-practising.

Jonathon in fact is agnostic and thinks that religion should not come into politics at all. This could lose him some votes in the middle bible- belt states of Arkansas, Mississippi, Alabama, Tennessee, Georgia, Kentucky and North and South

Carolina; although he is still popular in these states. But at least Jonathon is honest about what he believes and does not pretend to be a Christian as I'm sure some past Presidents have done .... Although despite Jonathon's denial of any religious attachments, his DNA confirms that he is 90% of European Jewish ancestry.

Trump may be crowing that he resolved the threat of nuclear war with Kim Jong-un of North Korea. But it is China that North Korea fears the most as their sanctions and embargos are capable of ruining the North Korean economy. Plus, they fear their close military might even more. Kim Jong-un, is a tyrannical leader but if a U.S. and China conflict happened, he could side with China, plus Iran possibly....

My Poppa the famous clairvoyant Clarence R. Smyth, made many accurate predictions before his death in 1962.... Some of which were later channelled through me in 1980, as I am also a medium. And this channelled prediction of his may possibly be right.... By the late 2020's the world's leading currency will be the Yuan, as China will be the new world economic leader. He said that the U.S. will fall, like every great nation has done throughout history.... But I hope my son will be able to prevent this from happening.

Many countries have threatened to sue China over their handling of the Coronavirus pandemic, which has resulted in an aggressive reaction. China is confident with its plethora of global investments, as they own multiple key commodities in several nations. And they expect loyalty, especially from the poorer nations they have given aid to.... But this pandemic has caused a world financial crisis with many countries now in huge debt, which could greatly benefit China.... But then this could be all propaganda. Are we all being manipulated into hating and blaming China for this catastrophe. Did this virus even come from bats or was it man- made and leaked from one of the many Wuhan labourites? If it was then by whom.? The secret ruling elite who control the world I believe, as they have always tried to prevent the spread of Communism. And they are ones who ultimately benefit from the world being in debt to them. This is a big play for control I believe.

Poppa also correctly predicted that the 21ˢᵗ century would see a swing away from Communism, towards Capitalism. And that in Eastern Europe and Indochina, criminal gangs would rise- up to fill this power vacuum.... He said third world countries have always had corrupt governments and police, but this will spread more to first world countries, excluding New Zealand and Denmark.

China would also have its problems he said, due to off-shore speculating taking too much money out of the country. Plus, their economy would grow far too quickly beginning in the late 1990's, without a stable enough foundation (true). He also predicted that a deadly virus developed in China would spread to the rest of the world around 2020, and hugely impact the global economy.... Intimating that it was man-made. Poppa also said whilst the world was busy coping with the pandemic China would arm itself. *Thankfully, Poppa never said there will be a war with China and its allies and the U.S and its allies which is my fear. Note: these italic sections have been added 2021.*

Poppa predicted that during this century the Islamic countries who nurture terrorists would suppress their woman even more. The West he said, instead of dropping bombs needs to help the girls. Empower the girls and disempower the terrorists.... Unfortunately, Poppa also predicted that Afghanistan would again come under Taliban rule.... Surely the world would not let that happen.

Females world-wide need better treatment. This needs to be the century for equality as too many are dying in childbirth, of Aids, from lack of medicine and care, because they are simply not valued enough. Look at the despicable practises of female honour killings and female circumcision. Plus mass raping, sexual violation and murder of females are viewed weapons, weapons of war. Even in first world countries too many women are being murdered by men. This has stop....

Jonathon and his wife Julia want to work towards empowering woman, and they are more genuine about this issue than Hilary Clinton ever was.

Past Presidents, like Bush Senior and Junior, due to their Christian values reduced aid, such as the distribution of condoms to help combat Aids and unwanted pregnancies. This is because some of the birth control centres in Africa were permitting abortions, which went against the Bush's beliefs. Jonathon wants to increase this spending....

This is an issue I feel passionate about, along with the world-wide wastage of food, as a third of what is produced goes to waste. Even though 40% of the world's population survives on less than $2 a day and does not have enough to eat which is shameful.

Anyway, I need to get off my soapbox as I am digressing....

I am going to use this long day to write an introduction to my memoirs, as they are now complete.

But they will never be allowed to be published as they could affect my son's political career and be an embarrassment to not only him, but to others I hold near and dear. Putting their lives in danger even, plus mine, as I have written about some powerful people.

Of course, my son and his wife and both their respective families have been scrutinized by the media for months now, well years really, during his time in the public eye. First as a twice- elected State Senator and then as the Governor of California.... And it is public knowledge that his mother is a Rothschild, meaning, that it has been assumed that Rothschild money has funded his entire presidential campaign....

This is not entirely the case but pretty close to it, although his late father's brothers Zeke and Rueben West have helped Jonathon to grow his personal wealth over the years. But this did begin with a significant investment portfolio that he hates to admit he inherited from my late paternal grandfather, the wealthy Swiss banker Florian A. Rothschild.... As Jonathon does not associate with being a Rothschild.

Now that Jonathon's uncles have both retired, his cousin Solomon West is his financial advisor. And Jonathon has stated that he has a place for his cousin Seth West also if he makes it in to the White House. I hope he does, as Solomon and Seth are both honest and capable young men.

There has been no doubt though, that a faction of the Rothschild family has wanted to fund Jonathon's presidential campaign. And to control it. They also wanted him to use the name, Rothschild- West.... But Jonathon was not having a bar of it, or them. He has never needed the Rothschilds' he says and still blames them for the death of the man he believed for many years to be his father, Saul West, my first husband.... Saul, was a pilot who was killed when Jonathon was an infant, but that is a story I shall get to.

Jonathon would have been a fool though to entirely say no to a family worth an estimated 100 to 500 trillion.... as no one is exactly sure how much the Rothschild's are collectively worth, and they are certainly not saying. And a close friend of Jonathon's is the financier Benjamin Rothschild, who helped him to raise his election fund.... So, despite what Jonathon says, I'm not sure how indebted to the Rothschild's he actually- is.

One thing my son and President Trump do have in common though, is they have both put a significant amount of their personal funds into their presidential campaigns. Each raising around $800 million.... Trump is always crowing that he isn't beholden to anyone, as is my son, but there are some who obviously don't see it that way.

But I am getting ahead of myself again....

My story really begins with a significant event that shaped my life.... The death of my beloved Poppa, when I was just sixteen. This occurred in 1962, in Los Angeles, California. A place I had been living with my maternal grandparents for four years, for reasons I will later explain....

But before I relay my story, I need to record some of my family history first....

There is no doubt that my Poppa Clarence Reginald Smyth was an extraordinary person, but then so was his wife Maria Weiss, my beloved Oma, in her own way. And she remained an important part of my life until her death in 1995, aged ninety-five years old.

Both my maternal Grandparents were born the same year 1900. My Poppa in London, England and my Oma in Leipzig, Germany. And they met when aged fourteen in Berlin during WW1, when both were forced to use their psychic abilities to aid a branch of German Intelligence. Their job then was to try to predict what the enemy were up to.... A tall order really, for a couple of scared kids....

Now this may sound strange as I have just said that my Poppa was English.... But he was in Berlin, visiting a learning institution, as his father had studied in Berlin, when the announcement came that England had declared war on Germany.

Poppa was then tricked into getting in a car, supposedly to return to his father, British Diplomat Geoffrey Smyth, who was on the other side of the city. But instead, he was kidnapped....my Poppa believed by a rogue branch of the freemasons, the 'Illuminati', who had been informed by his old school friend's father, a mason himself, that he was in Berlin.... Even at fourteen my Poppa was a renowned psychic in many circles.

His captors under the guise of 'German Intelligence' had photographs of Poppa's family and threatened to hurt them all if he did not comply with their demands. Of course, Poppa's father tried for days to find him, but to no avail, so in the end he had to leave and return to England while he still could.

My Poppa had all sorts of adventures growing up, as he was outspoken from a young boy with what he saw and felt. This got him into trouble, especially with his mother Sarah, who never really understood her gifted son.

And once with the British Military, as he had channelled top secret weaponry designs when aged twelve, for a school project.... His then friend the famous author Sir Arthur Conan- Doyle, who was like my Poppa, a Spiritualist, had to come to the Military headquarters to vouch for his abilities. As the Military had suspected my Poppa, and indeed his father of somehow stealing these designs. This was a huge embarrassment for Poppa's father with his government position.

But unlike his wife, Geoffrey Smyth could not ignore his son's accurate predictions. That is why he took him to Berlin two years later plus he was considering sending him to the Steiner Institute there. Poppa's father truly believed that war with Germany and Great Britain was not possible due to the two nations strong alliance. This is how my Poppa got to spend the duration of WW1 in Berlin and how he met his future wife Maria, my beloved Oma, at the newly formed 'Psychic Headquarters' there which put his life on an entirely different path....

As a young boy Poppa had a comfortable middle- class upbringing in Kensington, London, with his parents Geoffrey and Sarah Smyth, an older sister Edith, who he was always crossing swords with and a younger sister Violet, whom he described as being 'most delightful'. Plus, his father's younger sister Aunt Fanny with whom he was always close.

Both Poppa's sisters grew up to have their own talents and successes. Edith as a water colourist and Violet was the author of several popular novels of her time.... Poppa was also creative and worked successfully as a stage designer in London, Vienna, and New York. But he more renowned as a psychic, in both the U.S. and Europe....

I met both of Poppa's sisters on several occasions and Violet lived until the grand old age of one hundred, passing away in 2006 and yes, she was a delightful woman.

From six years old Poppa kept a diary. I have those diaries from aged six until fourteen years, plus his writings of the time he spent in Germany, during WW1. He later kept a journal which he wrote in a few times a year or less, but it still gave a good indication of his life. As the eldest grandchild I have those diaries and journals of Poppa's.

Sadly, Poppa died at home in Los Angeles of heart failure in 1962, aged only sixty- two. He was born on the first day of the new century January 1st 1900.... He even predicted his own death date, 10th December, and had arranged his funeral with a friend who was an undertaker, to spare Oma the added stress....

I was unfortunately in Zurich, Switzerland, where my parents lived, for my brother Philip's Bar-Mitzvah, when Poppa died and not at home with my poor Oma.... A few days before he died though I had phoned my Poppa upset, telling him my dad was not letting me return home to Los Angeles. He was making me stay on in Zurich to attend a finishing school instead, as he and my mom were displeased with my rude and out-spoken behaviour. They had decided I needed to learn how to become a proper well behaved young lady.... All I'd done then was to stand up to my paternal grandfather Grosspappi Rothschild, who tried to bully me as he did everyone else in the family. Only I wasn't having a bar of it and told him so.

Poppa had told me, not to worry, I would return home soon. Which of course I did as I had to come back for his funeral.... And by being sixteen and an American citizen by Californian law, I was free to choose where I wanted to live. So, I decided to stay in Los Angeles with my beloved Oma, and thankfully my parents did not object. This turned out to be an important decision for me, as it kept me from the clutches of the Rothschild's a bit longer.... But of course, I could not change my destiny.

Before I record my own story, I need to talk more about the people that helped shape my early life, my maternal grandparents. They were by far the biggest influence on me, as it is from them I inherited my unique abilities.... These have been more of a curse than a gift and are the main reason I was singled out by one of the most powerful and sinister of cabals.... One who I know had always monitored my Poppa's life, then mine, and now my son's. And it took me years to admit that they really do exist, this cabal, this powerful secret society who some call the 'Illuminati'.

Now back to the family history....

Poppa was a sickly child with a weak chest and heart. He would never have been called to arms anyway, during both world wars, but did his bit in other ways. And because of his delicate health Poppa was tutored at home until the age of eleven. Mr Franks, his second tutor of five years, was a German Jew, he had believed in Poppa's abilities and became his confidante. And Poppa always teared-up when talking to me about him. (Sickly young children like my Poppa are more vulnerable to spirit interference as are prepubescent children)

At age eleven Poppa went to a boarding school in Kent with his neighbour and best friend, Henry Hargreaves, as his health had improved somewhat by then. He wrote regularly to Mr and Mrs Franks and tried to see them as much as he was allowed by his mother during visits home. This was before his fateful trip to Berlin in 1914 and the psychic work he did at the Headquarters and later at the Chartres hospital when only sixteen, during the first half of WW1. For the second half of the war Poppa endured hardship in a P.O.W. camp. There he became a spiritual healer and advisor as he was all his life wherever he went.

At the end of the war, Poppa believed his family in England would think him a traitor, since he had had no contact with them for four long years. This was because he had an assumed name, Wilhelm Brunnen, William Wells in German, which was Poppa's stage name as a child. He needed one so his mother wouldn't find out he was working as a medium. This was the main reason his father could not trace him in the P.O.W. records....

Instead of going back to England after the war ended, Poppa accepted a scholarship to study art in Vienna. Ironically, this was paid for by the German Government, for his services to the nation, as everyone thought him German, and he had papers to prove it. His only papers.

He and my Oma eventually roomed together as she was also given a scholarship to study music at the same university. My Grandparents unmarried co-habitation must have been frowned upon in the day. But Oma told me they were both nineteen and in love and everyone just wanted to be happy with the war now over. Poppa also worked as a Psychic as he always did wherever he lived.

Poppa did end up going back to England for over a year to complete his Arts- degree but he missed Oma too much so returned to Vienna for a while and worked as a stage designer. Poppa and Oma then both went to England for Poppa's 21st birthday, married and immediately sailed to New York. They thought this a neutral place to settle, being from countries that had been at war with each other.... And Poppa never again lived in his beloved England.

Poppa had a different childhood to that of my Oma. He was born into a comfortable middle-class life, was well-educated and had holidays away as a child.... Both his parents had inherited family money, as did he at aged twenty- one, plus his paternal grandfather's house. And a later inheritance that Poppa received from his mother's brother Rupert, was a god- send at the time, as it allowed my grandparents to leave Austria in 1938, before the start of WWII. My mother Sarah and her twin brother William were thirteen at the time and the family spent the duration of WWI, living in Baden near Zurich, Switzerland.

Once settled, my grandparents' helped refugees who had fled the war. They also ran their own spiritual centres called 'Beacons of Light'. Poppa said to counteract the evil happening around them. They trained others and had centres on the French and Italian borders as well. My grandparents and their workers helped many lost souls pass-over and offered spiritual guidance and healing.... What wonderful work they all did.

My own parents met during the war at university in Zurich in 1944, when my mother was nineteen and my father was twenty- three; but I will tell their story later.

My Oma was born Maria Weisschlegalsteinhausenbergerdorff, but shortened it to Weiss when she went to Vienna, so as not to be scorned. She had it changed legally at nineteen when she applied to become an Austrian citizen. Oma told me she had a strong feeling she should do the latter. I remember we always laughed when Oma told us her original surname.... In recent years I have met some of my German relatives, who amazingly have never shortened it.

Oma was one of seven children and was the eldest girl. She had two older brothers one younger brother and three younger sisters. I have seen a photo of my Oma's family, they were all white blond and handsome.

Oma displayed musical abilities from an early age and was fortunate that an elderly neighbour, a widower, taught her the violin in exchange for her mother's cooking. Oma's mother never minded her spending time practising the violin, as she still managed to help-out with the younger children and to do well at school.

Oma's father was a butcher who worked at the local Meat factory. He wanted his children to do better than him, which meant getting a good education. Frederick the eldest and Maria my Oma, got the best education, the other children all became factory workers. Their parents needed them to leave school and earn money as soon as they had completed their basic schooling despite their good intentions.

Frederick later became a Nazi as did Kurt the second eldest; they were both killed during the second world war. The youngest brother Rudi was a foot soldier and was injured but survived the war, as did Oma's mother and three sisters; but tragically she lost two nephews.... Poppa rescued the surviving three nephews from Allied work camps, through his military connections. He had volunteered to work as an interpreter and spiritual advisor for the U.S. Army immediately after the war.... Because of this, Oma's family always thought very highly of my Poppa.

Oma's family were fortunate really, my Aunt Katrine was the sole survivor of her family of seven from Dresden, Germany. Her parents and three siblings were killed when their house was bombed in 1942. A year earlier her handicapped sister was gassed by the SS, as part of their plan to get rid of 'undesirables'.... Katrine was Mom's twin brother William's first wife and the mother of close cousins Christian and Isobel Smyth, who were three and four years younger than me respectively....

My Uncle and Aunt had met in Dresden when he was stationed there with the U.S. army, immediately after the war.... She said she only married him because he was handsome and had food.

At school Maria, my Oma, had stood out because she was bright and a good guesser. And her school master Herr Fuchs noticed she often knew things were going to happen before they did. She also appeared to k now what ailed people and gave particularly insightful advice for a child. So, he believed she was a 'Hellseher' or 'Seer' and unfortunately for her he put this in a report.... Herr Fuchs was also apparently a freemason (I remembered his surname when Oma told me her story, as I thought it rather unfortunate).

In 1914, just before the outbreak of war, German Intelligence started the 'Psychic Headquarters' in Berlin and began recruiting children with abilities who could be trained. They were looking for six to sixteen- year- olds and Oma's name came up on a list.... She was then sent a letter to report to 'The Headquarters' as it was more commonly known along with a one- way train ticket to Berlin for the very next week.

Oma said she cried every-day of that week and for weeks after as she was so unhappy. Her family were upset also as she was too young to leave home and her mother relied on her help with the younger children.... Oma's mother worked long hours making and selling food condiments, Oma said that her mother's sauerkraut was the best in Leipzig.... Oma did however get an allowance during this time, most of which she sent home to her mother.

This is where my grandparents met and worked together for a year gathering 'intelligence', psychically. Both admitted to an immediate attraction to each other.

Poppa always insisted that he never once betrayed England but said it was very difficult to bluff. That is why he asked to go and work at Berlin's largest hospital 'The Chartres', to supposedly 'tune into' the soldiers coming back from 'The Front'.... He was surprised he had told me when 'The Headquarters' Kommandant had said yes....

This left my poor Oma to work with Martin Bormann, who years later became a high- ranking Nazi and Hitler's secretary.... Oma said Bormann was a cunning evil bully who even then had an interest in the dark side of the occult, as did most Nazis.... Poppa wrote about this in his journals.

Oma said that she missed Poppa dreadfully after he left, even though they were on different sides as Poppa was psychically relaying information to the Allies, through astral travelling. He even visited Winston Churchill himself, he said, which was difficult because Churchill was an insomniac.

Poppa said he knew he had to leave the Headquarters even though he didn't want to leave Oma. But he did good work at the hospital, first as an orderly, but soon was in demand as a spiritual advisor and healer with his unique abilities....

This is where my Poppa met Adolf Hitler once, when the future Fuhrer was merely another injured foot soldier and he made an accurate prediction for him.... Poppa told Hitler that he would rise to a position of power one day as he was a great orator. Poppa also saw an evil deity forming with Hitler, it was only small then, but he did not tell him this.... Years later when Hitler invaded Austria, Poppa who was in Vienna at the time, saw that the deity had grown to the size of a four story building, and was very menacing.... This is how my Poppa saw evil and good as deity's. He also saw good deity's like the one on Nelson's column protecting London, and those standing protecting Baden and Zurich, of which he did drawings of.

Fortunately for Poppa he was fluent in German, thanks to his tutor Mr Franks, so he simply became German during this period using his assumed name, which he was given papers for.... But Oma knew the truth, as did the Headquarters Kommandant Shultz, of course. He was the only one who did in the end as one by one all the original staff were deployed to 'The Front,' including the so-called doctors who did Paranormal experiments on the children.... Oma said they were all cold and uncaring except for the Kommandant and his wife. Shultz tried to protect Poppa as much as he could, possibly because he was a freemason himself, as was Poppa's father and grandfather.... But Poppa never joined the Order, or indeed any Order, even though he was asked to several times, for reasons I will later explain....

My grandparents managed to see each other most Saturdays whilst Poppa was working at the hospital, as he still had to report back to 'The Headquarters'. Poppa said he was fortunate at that time to have been boarded with a kind Jewish couple, David and Eva Emmanuel. He was English and she was German and they treated Poppa like a son.

Oma was boarded with a couple who just used her to do housework and look after their children and they would not let her practice her violin. Fortunately for the second half of the war she was boarded with a kind spinster schoolteacher who loved music.

But poor Poppa had to insist he be placed in a P.O.W. camp for his own safety during the second half of the war. As he was recognised at the hospital by an ex- Kent school pupil he once knew, Rudolf Hess, who years later became Hitler's right- hand man.... Poppa said that Hess was fanatical even as a teen-aged boy. Although this former association did save Poppa's life once, just before the start of WWII, when Poppa was arrested and questioned by the Gestapo....

It is amazing that Poppa met Hitler once, plus knew two of his closest comrades, but then Poppa had an extraordinary life and met many famous and infamous people of his time.

I did not mention then that the Illuminati funded both sides of the war, plus Adolf Hitler's rise to power. Or that his father Alois Hitler was the illegitimate son of a servant Maria Schicklgruber and Baron Rothschild. That is why Adolf Hitler was selected, because of his inherited oratory skills and hypnotic powers plus he always had an interest in the occult like most Nazis. Poppa also met the Austrian Chancellor Dollfuss before he was murdered by the Nazis. Dollfuss also knew about Hitler's true heritage which could have led to his demise.

After the war, as I have said, Oma and Poppa both went to The University of Vienna on scholar-ships paid for by the German Government. This was for their duties to the nation as recommended by Kommandant Shultz.... Oma said she would never have had the opportunity to study, get a degree or a position with the Vienna Philharmonic Orchestra, then later the New York Philharmonic Orchestra, if she had not done this work with German Intelligence. It had always upset her that she may have been responsible, even partially, for lives lost.... Although Oma did work with tarot cards most of her life doing readings, she never did develop her gifts as much as she could have. This was because of the responsibility they brought she had told me more than once.

Oma was always happy to play second fiddle to Poppa, which was ironic being a first violinist. She loved the violin but was not patient at teaching it I found out first-hand as a child. Indeed, this was the only time I remember her really losing her temper with me. Unfortunately, for me I never had her talent.

Oma's first love though was Poppa and then her children and grandchildren. She also helped her family in Germany as much as she could financially and was a warm, generous and caring person, all her long life.... Oma did not have Poppa's ego or indeed charisma, but she adored him and was always there to support him and he her, because of this they had a very happy marriage.

My Poppa was also a warm funny caring man, but like all the men in my family, he came first in his household. Poppa was nowhere near as controlling as my Grosspapi Rothschild though, my father's father, patriarch of our branch of the Rothschild family. He was an arrogant and domineering man, who could also be very charming.... My dad was like his father but less so, Mom saw to that.

Put simply, my maternal grandparents were warm and my paternal grandparents cold. Even the thirty- room mansion in Zurich, owned by my paternal grandparents was cold and uninviting .... I also know that my Grosspapi was an active member of the Illuminati.... I was never sure about my dad.

I never 'fitted in' with any of the Rothschild's growing up, except for my younger brother Philip. Indeed, I never fitted in with anyone really for many years, due to my gifts.

My gifts were the reason, why as a child, I needed the help and protection of my Poppa and Oma. And the reason why I had to grow- up and become responsible for myself at sixteen, when Poppa died.... Because of the threat posed to me by the Illuminati.... But let me go back further to explain what lead me to this point.

I was born on the 10th June, 1946, on my Mother Sarah and her twin brother William's 21st birthdays and in the very same hospital in Brooklyn, New York. My great grandfather Geoffrey Smyth was also born on this day, in England in 1872, so this was a popular birth date for the Smyth's it seems.... My parents had married in Zurich, Switzerland, the previous year on May 20th, two weeks after WWII had officially ended in Europe.

My Dad was Dominick Florian Rothschild, the eldest son of Florian Alexander Rothschild from the Zurich branch of the banking dynasty.... He said we were direct descendants of the founding father Mayer Amschel Rothschild, who had five sons. Each son then started a banking dynasty in different major cities being London, Paris, Vienna, Naples and Frankfurt; the last of whom we were descended from.... The Rothschild coat of arms with its red shield and five feathers represents this.

A lot of these descendants were then given titles and baronets, hence the German and Austrian Von Rothschild's and the French de Rothschild's.... The Rothschild's have always been a very wealthy and influential family. Over the last two hundred years there has always been much speculation about how much they are worth and what power they have wielded. And they have been accused of manipulating world events to their advantage, especially financially.... I am ashamed to admit, that to my knowledge, this is true.

My parents met at Zurich University where Dad was studying Economics and Mom was training to be a junior schoolteacher and they simply fell in love.... Although Poppa had always insisted that their meeting had been arranged by Dad's father, for reasons I will later reveal.

When my parents married, everyone just wanted to celebrate the end of the war, so Grosspapi Rothschild threw an enormous party with food and drink aplenty. Poppa said, there must have been at least three hundred people present, most of whom were not at the earlier small private ceremony officiated by a rabbi.... The Rothschild's you see were practising Jews, but hid the fact in Switzerland at that time, they even had a sozzled Catholic Priest at the party afterwards as a decoy.

My mom had to convert to Judaism to marry my dad which was a bit of a shock for my Poppa and Oma being then, Christian- Spiritualists. But anti-Semitism was rife in Switzerland also during this period.... After the war that they openly practised their Judaism again.

By the time I was born, my parents had just gone through what was to be the most tumultuous year of their married life. They had even been living apart for a few months, with my mom in New York with Oma and my dad remaining in Zurich with his parents.... My mom, with Oma's help had left him when she was unwell and newly pregnant with me. This was because my dad had changed and become very controlling, for some reason, like his father soon after they had married.... My mom told me this.

Poppa who had been working in post- war Germany as a spiritual advisor intervened and brought my dad back to New York with him.... But before this occurred, he had to confront Grosspapi and my dad and it had got pretty ugly causing my Poppa to levitate to the ceiling when he was physically threatened by my Grosspapi. Dad told me he was more respectful and a bit wary of my Poppa after that. He also said that going to live in New York with my mom and getting away from his father, was the best decision he ever made in his life.

Mom said one good thing about Grosspapi was that he encouraged his children to marry for love and did not insist that they marry within the extended family, like most Rothschild's do. Even so, his two daughters both married well, into prominent Swiss banking families. Anna, the eldest married Kaspar Mirabaud and the youngest Delphine married Erik Hottinger, both had three daughters each. (My Mom did not know at that time that she was related by birth to the Rothschild's also, through the illegitimate Collins side, as Poppa's father's mother was a Collins.... Oma was also from this bloodline apparently, and this is where our psychic abilities came from.

The Collins were responsible for bringing witchcraft from Europe to the U.S. in the 1700s, and my association with them was not destined to end there as you will later read.

My Grandparents decided to move back to New York after WWII ended having lived there before, and still owned a house in Brooklyn.... They knew Europe would be much slower to recover than America, post- war.... Plus, my Uncle William had fallen in love with American baseball, which he turned out to be rather good at and went on to play professionally.

My Dad came to live with my mom in New York, and fortunately they managed to work through their differences and stayed on. Dad of course had a prominent position with the N.Y. Rothschild & Co investment bank. My younger brothers Philip, three years after me, then Alexander two years later again, were also born in New York....

We lived in a spacious six-bedroom, five-bathroom apartment with staff quarters, in Manhattan overlooking central park which was owned by the bank. And we had a cook, a housekeeper and a nanny. Dad also had a driver.

Dad admitted to me once though that Poppa showed him how to be a loving husband and father. And it was just as well that my parents became a strong unit as they soon had a challenge ahead of them, namely me....

I was a difficult child for my parents, well indeed for anyone I came into contact- with. If I had been born into a different family I could have been institutionalised as autistic, or mentally disturbed as there was more than one professional who thought me so.... But fortunately for me my Poppa, Oma, and Mom knew different, they knew I was psychically gifted and was struggling with my gifts....

I remember the only way I could cope with the bombardment of spirit I constantly had around me was to shut everyone else out. But of- course I still needed looking after. I was only calm with my head was buried into someone, and my eyes tightly shut. This was usually my mom whom I'd then cling to and scream if I was put down, apparently.... My Mom admits she found this behaviour disturbing rather than comforting, as at other times I would scream if I was touched and was only calm when alone rocking myself back and forth in my cot chatting to my spirit friends.

And because of my awful behaviour, my poor parents had trouble keeping a nanny. This was why Mom and I never developed that close bond a mother and child should have, I feel, as she found me such hard work....

Mom told me I was so unpredictable and had these awful screaming tantrums where I would hold my breath until I turned blue if I was prevented from doing what I wanted. My poor Mom, as this behaviour went on for years really, even after I started infant school.... Oma and Poppa would help when they could.

I recall the main spirits I had with me would fetch me things and talk to me. I had Gretel and Jakob who were German, and Doris who was English.... Poppa would come and make them go away for a while, but they would always return. Jakob would tell me not to listen to my mortal family only my spirit family. They also blocked other spirts from coming to talk to me, including Poppa's mother Sarah, whom my mother was named after. Sarah was keen to be my guide, she did manage to tell me once.... Those were difficult years really, for everyone concerned.

I can recall the first time I saw my brother Philip.... I was three years- old and it was love at first sight. Philip is such a beautiful soul and I felt very protective of him, so I shut out the spirits myself, I just wanted to be alone with him.... We have always had a strong sibling connection.

I did not feel the same about Alexander though when he was born two years later. Indeed I always preferred my cousins Christian, who was two weeks older than Phillip and Isobel who is a year younger than him, to my brother Alexander. Mainly because Alexander has always been so Rothschild. Right from a young age he thought he was more important that anyone else and wanted his own way all the time.... And the others just gave into him, as Philip has always been easy -going and Christian just followed Philip and Isobel followed Christian. I was the only one who tried to put Alexander in his place and make him think of others.... This got me into trouble with the adults, plus the six silly female cousins on father's side, who used to indulge Alexander as well.

My Mom also adored Philip when he was born as she now had a calm contented baby and then a happy child who played well with other children and was funny and likeable, everything I was not. Philip has Poppa's charisma, as did my Uncle William, who after his baseball career went on to become a minor role actor, but rather successfully, as he was in many movies and T.V. shows.

This is who my son Jonathon inherited his charisma from. His oratory skills and hypnotic powers come from the Rothschild side.

Philip fitted in, where I did not, plus he did well at school, especially in sport and was always very popular. Even so, he did rebel as a teenager and did not follow the career path our dad chose for him, as I later record.... Thank heavens I wasn't the only one to disappoint our parents.

Now Alexander was always the model son for our mom and dad and did everything that was expected of him, especially academically. But he was never adored in the family like Philip, although he did end up marrying a lovely woman, a second cousin Marguerite de Rothschild, which no doubt would have pleased the majority of, our Rothschild relations.

Mom and Uncle William were always close, being twins, and mom befriended both his wives.... Katrine his first wife whom he came back from Germany with after WWII, was the mother of my cousins Christian and Isobel. After they divorced, she came out as a lesbian which was a bit of a shock for the family.... Selma, William's second wife, was from California and is the mother of his twins James and Patricia, my youngest cousins, who both followed their parents with careers in the film industry.... Selma is the only one of that generation who is still alive, at age ninety-one.

I have remained in contact with my Smyth cousins and their families over the years. Although tragically we lost Christian in a skiing accident, in 1976.... They have gone on to lead good and productive lives, Poppa and Oma would have been most proud.

Sadly though, my daughter Beth is estranged from me and the family and has been for many years.... But Alexander and I get on much better now. He has improved with age. No doubt he would say the same about me.

I never liked my Uncle Edmond dad's younger brother, as a child. He had lived in Israel most of his life and never married. Apparently, he preferred Arab house boys who tended to get younger each year we heard. He was accused of some dubious business practices as well.... Edmond died under suspicious circumstances, not long after my first husband Saul, in 1968.... But then I never really knew him.... Poppa had told me he was too clever for his own good.

Edmond was an active member of the Illuminati, and was probably gotten rid of because he didn't play by the rules.

Unlike my dad who had a strict controlling father who then sent him to a strict boarding school my Mom and Uncle William had a happy childhood with my grandparents.... Born in New York, they moved to Vienna Austria, when aged four, where they lived for nine years. The next seven years they resided in a pretty town called Baden near Zurich, Switzerland. Poppa knew to get out of Austria before the start of the WWII.

Mom was a lovely sensitive soul, but a strong woman as well and she tried not to be controlled by the Rothschild family which was not easy for her at times.... She loved my dad and he loved her and besides the first rocky year they went on to have a happy and successful marriage....

I feel sad now that I wasn't as close to my parents as I should have been, growing up.... We did become much closer, but not until I was in my thirties.

Now because of my psychic peculiarities and Grosspapi's statement to Poppa when I was a child of only ten.... That I had a part to play in the plans of 'the Order' as was my destiny, and there was not a damned thing that he, Poppa, could do to stop it.... Which confirmed for Poppa and Oma that Grosspapi was part of the Illuminati, as they had always suspected. Plus, my dad knew of his father's association too of course.... So, with my mom, they all agreed that I would be safer away from my Grosspapi and his cohorts.... That is why I went to live in California with my grandparents in 1958, when Poppa's health was declining, and he needed a warmer climate.... My parents feared for me, but knew the one person who could protect me was my gifted Poppa, Oma too, but Poppa more so, and of course, they were right....

I never told anyone, but I often felt 'watched' as a child. This was usually by men wearing dark suits and sunglasses who worked in pairs and nodded to each other when they saw I had spotted them. And often people at Rothschild family functions made cryptic remarks, which were not lost on me.... I knew I was being monitored somehow.... I always thought my dad knew a lot more than he let on about this secret society and the men who watched us. I never asked him if he was a member of the Illuminati and of course he never said, no-one ever admits to it.... But instinctively I knew as a child to watch what I said, which was just as well, with one grandfather Illuminati and the other anti- the Illuminati....

Poppa started the 'white hats' in New York in 1928 and their objective ever since has been to work against the Illuminati.... They are now active in several countries and have done good work averting catastrophes such as company take overs and recessions, by exposing the truth. They have even helped bring some people to justice who were involved in greedy corporate cover-ups that have caused deaths or risked people's lives.... An example of this is the 'Flint water crisis' of 2014, which President Obama made such light of. They were also involved in exposing Fannie Mae's financial irregularities, which played a major part in the financial crisis of 2008. Plus, way back the downfall of Joseph McCarthy in 1954; to name a few.

I am now back to where I started from, being aged sixteen and the death of my Poppa and main protector.... Poppa told me just after he died (in spirit) that he trusted my decisions and I would be alright.... I recall holding onto those words. He also told me that the Illuminati would do everything within their power to win my trust to convert me to 'the dark side'.... So, I decided then that this was not going to happen and I hatched a plan to take control of my life, which is reflected in my journal entries of that time.... I was so young then when Poppa died, and there was so much I did not know or understand about the ways of the world and what the limitations of a young woman like me were in the 1960s.

I only started a journal in June 1962, when Poppa gave me one for my sixteenth birthday. His only words were "keep it safe".

This is my story as told chronologically from journal entries, letters and memory. *Reminder: the italic sections have been written by me this year, 2021. I have also inserted sections from Piers Huxley's diaries at my request, because his life has run parallel to mine and our connection will be revealed.*

Sophia
1962

June 13th

This is the start of my new journal. Poppa gave it to me for my sixteenth birthday and said that he hoped I would enjoy writing down my thoughts as much as he has done over the years.... I said I was sure I would, as for some reason I feel this year is going to be a significant one.... Maybe because Saul keeps holding me close and kissing me. He also insists on walking me home at night which is silly as I only live next door. That is, when he is home as he is mostly away now training to be a pilot and I miss him soooo much. But he is home now for two whole weeks, yah! so we are trying to see each other as much as we can.

Saul gave me a gold neck chain and plate with my name engraved it for my birthday. It is so pretty. I love Saul, he is my best friend. Oma thinks we are boyfriend and girlfriend because we hold hands and kiss.... But I have known Saul and his younger brothers for four years as our neighbours so they feel more like brothers to me. Emotional replacements for Philip I think who I have missed so much living here, Alexander also, but not as much.

I never wanted to leave Philip, but I had to come to America to get away from the Rothschilds. He understands this, he knows the females in our family are dominated by the males, especially by Grosspapi. I do hope Philip comes to live here too when he is older though, but he is talking about joining the Swiss army when he finishes school. He likes sports and physical challenges as does our cousin Christian who he is thinking the same way.... Poppa said they will both change their minds when they do national service at eighteen. I hope so.

I like living in L.A. with my Poppa and Oma, but sometimes they can be a bit Oldsville and flip- out over nothing.... But my school is cool, and I am more popular than I ever was at junior school.

July 31st

Jaqueline Kennedy is so stylish I love the outfits she wears. When I grow up, I shall wear little fitted suits like her and cute pillbox hats.... I get bored with my blouses, straight skirts and pumps. I don't think I will ever be able to wear high stiletto heels though as I am already taller than the other girls, and most of the boys my age. But I am not as tall as Saul, so I hope I don't grow any taller.

I love clothes, but Oma says if I buy any more with my babysitting money, I shall need a bigger closet. But I can sew. Poppa bought me a sewing machine and I love to make clothes that are different that no one else has. My home economics teacher thinks I am quite skilled. That is my best subject, and history surprisingly.

How tragic Marilyn Monroe has been found dead from a barbiturates overdose, she was only thirty six. Why does this involve the President, John F. Kennedy and his brother Robert, but I feel it does. Oma says she was a bit of a tortured soul.... I don't believe she meant to kill herself, it was a cry for help, Oma agrees. Poppa said there will be much speculation for years about her death. He said there are some who want to besmirch the reputations of the President and his brother, because they are not playing 'the game'. I don't know what he means by that, but Poppa is usually right about most things....

Oma said that is all very well, but where there is smoke there is always flames. (She never gets any sayings correct and Poppa always teases her). She said the Kennedy brothers are 'ladies' men's' like their father and not faithful to their wives. Poppa did not disagree with her about this I noticed. I feel sorry for Jacqueline Kennedy if her husband is cheating on her as she seems so nice.

September 30th

Marty Chalmers from the grade above has asked me out on a date. Some of the girls think he's a swoon.... At least he is taller than me, but he has the most gross pimples. Anyway, I said no. I always know who fancies who at school because I see their pink flashing lights. No one has flashed pink at me yet. But the other kids think it's cool that I know who is going to ask who out on a date.

Some of the kids think I'm a bit weird though, especially after I predicted that Richie Valens was going to be killed in a plane crash three years ago, I even wrote to him warning him of this. It was terrible as Buddy Holly and the big Bopper were also killed....

I have predicted other things that have come true.... I warned my old classmates in Switzerland not to go on a ski trip and there was a huge avalanche that wiped out the ski lodge where they would have been staying. Fortunately, Poppa backed me up by phoning the headmaster....

I also warn my class when there is going to be a spot test, plus I'm good at guessing their grades. So well in fact, that my geography teacher accused me of looking at her ledger.

I never think to write in my diary really except for the end of each month. But that is something.

Poppa has not been well, he gets very breathless and goes a bit grey in colour. I often see spirit lights around him now.

October 28th

Once a month just before my menses I am very vulnerable to 'the other side'. This usually lasts a few days. It also makes me out of sorts and clumsy and things just happen around me, like alarms going off or clocks or watches stopping. And if someone really annoys me which isn't difficult then, they have a silly accident like walking into a door, slipping over, or dropping books. What makes it even worse is everyone seems to know it is me somehow, it is soooo embarrassing.

Lost souls visit me more then and I have visions, sometimes even during the day which is a bit annoying. Teachers accuse me of not paying attention and of daydreaming. Sometimes I go away to another place, like the character Walter Mitty does. One teacher even calls me 'Miss Mitty'. Poppa told me that I must ground myself by focusing on a solid object like a tree or hugging it. I also need to keep my blood sugars up by eating little and often he said. But I can drift off like I am falling asleep and go to different realms.... In history class I just have to think of a place and time, and I am there. I can then write huge descriptive passages which I embarrassingly have to read out in front of the whole class. And not everything I say is nice, as horrible, unjust and violent things happened in the past. One teacher said that I had a very vivid imagination, but another said I had an uncanny insight.

I am going to Switzerland in November for my Brother Philip's bar mitzvah; he will be thirteen. I am looking forward to seeing my family but none of the other Rothschilds particularly. Although Marlena is okay, she is the least silly of my six female cousins. I hope I shall like Alexander more this time, as I find him annoying. But I will also get to see my Smyth cousins, Christian and Isobel. They are such fun and so cool. I miss them living here but at least they come regularly for holidays to see their dad.

I am not happy about leaving Oma alone with Poppa as he is not well. Thank heavens for Carmen our housekeeper, she will look after them both, I'm sure.

December 21st

I have been too sad to write in my diary as I don't want to face it.... Oma's and my worlds have been turned upside down with the death of my beloved Poppa this month, on the 10th.... And I wasn't even here!... I had to come back with the rest of the family from Switzerland for the funeral. Everyone is sooo upset.... Oma and Mom can't stop crying, or my cousin Isobel. All the family came over for Poppa's funeral, it was huge.

Poppa was well respected it seems as there were a few famous people there like Elizabeth Taylor, Judy Garland, Bob Hope and Joanna Woodward, to name a few as Poppa was 'Psychic to the Stars'. Uncle William did a wonderful eulogy which made us all laugh; Poppa would have liked that.... I wanted to shout that he was still with us, as I saw him sitting in the back row and strangely everyone left that seat empty.... He looked at me and held a finger up to his lips, but I already knew not to say anything .... I thought he looked so well and strangely happy, it was everyone else who was sad.

Poppa had been to see me in spirit the night he died. He told me he was alright, and I would be too and said he trusted me to make the right decisions in life. He also told me he could not reach Oma at the moment as she was too distressed. So, I was to tell her that he loved her and to remind her that she has a lot of living to do before they met again.... He also said that this terrible grief we were all feeling would one day pass.... And warned me about the Illuminati, but I can't think about that now.

My great aunts Edith and Violet came over from England for the funeral. I also met Mom's cousin Marigold from Philadelphia and she brought her two sons. They are both younger than me but I 'saw' them in military uniforms one day and their lives in danger; but I did not tell them that. Both said they would like to be pilots like their father. Anthony the eldest said because he wanted to marry a pretty air hostess. For some reason I felt their father also liked pretty hostesses as there was a sadness around Cousin Marigold. Even so she is a beautiful woman who looks a bit like my Mom I thought.

December 28th

Saul came home for Christmas even though his family are Jewish and do not celebrate it. He was here for two weeks which was nice.... He said he was sorry that he missed Poppa's funeral. Both his parents and two brothers had attended.

Saul has changed, he is taller and seems more confident somehow. He told me that Aviation school was way better than high school, as he now gets treated like an adult. He also said when he qualifies he is not going to apply for the Air Force but instead wants to fly commercial aircraft to make more money.

I told Saul what my cousin Anthony had said, he laughed and said I would make a very pretty air hostess.... I was upset though after Saul left, as he seemed a bit distanced. It could have been me as I was so sad from losing Poppa. Plus, Oma was still very tearful, and I was feeling for her.... But Saul did not hold my hand or try to get me alone to kiss me which upset me.... Perhaps he has another girlfriend.... I must not think about that now, as I am sad enough.

We all tried to be happy on Christmas day which we spent with my Uncle William and Aunt Selma. My cousins Jimmy and Patty made us laugh though, despite our sadness.... Oma gifted me some deportment classes. She can read my mind I swear. And Uncle William is paying for me to have some professional photographs taken. Aunt Selma will do my hair and makeup she said.... I know they all mean well and are convinced that I am pretty enough to be on screen, especially now that I've had my braces off. But has anyone bothered to ask me what I want this is not why I want to do classes.... Honestly, old people can be so out of it sometimes.

1963

January 20th

I am back at school and trying to study hard so I can graduate and leave the place, as I am finding most of the kids my age so immature, especially the boys. Rita my best friend is trying to get me to go to parties with her to meet older boys as every weekend there is something on, she says. Now she desires to be a movie star, and wants me to introduce her to my Uncle William and his movie associates.... I said I would just to shut her up, as I'm so sick of her going on.

My friend Lori has never really forgiven me for embarrassing her and her older sister Cindy at that party by hurtling that creepy older boy through the air and into the swimming pool. But I didn't do it alone, I had help from my spirit friends. Not that I could tell her that, so I don't see much of her now as she probably thinks I'm some kind of freak.

Poppa told me that other kids used to think him a freak and he got called 'the Wizard' at school. He also predicted things before they happened, and odd things occurred around him as they have always done with me, he said.... Oma was also very intuitive at school and said that is why she was selected and sent away to do psychic spying during WWI.... This is where she met Poppa.... How cool though and scary, they were only fourteen, younger than me.... I miss Poppa so much.

The glamour of Hollywood does not impress me, even though I was asked by an agent to do a screen-test once, as I keep being told that I look like a young Grace Kelly. That is before she married Prince Rainier of Monaco and became a princess and a mother of course as now she is getting old. Uncle William said quite seriously that my height is a problem though at five foot ten inches tall. I told him I didn't want to be a movie star anyway, but that I had agreed to do some catwalk modelling for Macys department store. No one will be looking at me just the clothes I am wearing, plus, I don't have to say anything.

Uncle William seemed surprised by this, but I know Aunt Katrine his first wife was a model and shy like me. Not everyone is an outgoing chatterbox like him. He can't understand why anyone would not want to be in movies.... I also thought that deportment classes would help me to become an air hostess one day so I can fly and be with Saul, but I am not telling my family this....

Why does everyone have to have an opinion anyhow.... Mom is always on my case about something when she calls. Oma is the best she doesn't mind what I do, as long as I get good grades, so, I am learning to drive an automobile, and Uncle William is bravely teaching me that.... I hope to graduate school in another year and maybe go to university, but I'm not sure yet what to study. Well, that's what I am telling everyone, just to keep them off my back.

Mom has her own plans for me and wants me to 'come out' in New York society, which is silly as I don't even live there. But my parents are thinking of returning to New York so my brothers can attend the near-by universities, well Harvard.... Mom has high hopes for Alexander especially, who is a top student.... I don't think my parents are really interested in me getting a university education, being a girl, even though my mom trained to be a teacher but never ended up teaching, as she got married instead and had us children.

I do love the relaxed life we have in Los Angeles with the beaches and everything, but I am restless. I know there is more to life than this.... And because I have lived in Switzerland and travelled to Europe with my parents and can speak German, a little French and learnt Spanish at school and at home with our housekeepers, I am keen to travel and explore the world. But I want to go now.... One way I can travel the world is if I become an air hostess. Saul thinks I should apply when I am twenty, as they pick the tall pretty girls he said, but that is years away yet. Oma says no, I would be a glorified waitress and it would be a shame to not use the brain I have in my head.... I like to think I have a brain and I shall use it, but the academic world is difficult for us girls. As all we are really encouraged to do is fill in our time until we find ourselves suitable husbands.

Lori and Sandy say they are perfectly happy with this, and both want to get engaged to their older boyfriends as soon as they finish high school, like Lori's sister Cindy did, who is now married. This is not what I want though, I want so much more, but I am not sure what. I keep waking up and looking out my window in the early hours and saying to myself 'there is more to life than this'. But what is it I am excited about.... The possibilities out there in the world but I am scared also....

Then there is my gift, or curse rather, that I have worked so hard at shutting down as I just want to be normal.... Poppa told me I am normal, and that I can learn to live with my gift it doesn't have to be a curse, it is up to me.... I suppose it does make me a bit fearless in some ways as this is what happened recently.

The movie 'Psycho' has been in all the cinemas. Oma said that Poppa met the director Alfred Hitchcock once, in England, when they were both schoolboys on holiday. Poppa met so many famous people of his day. I miss him so much that my chest aches, as does Oma's of course.... Anyway, I decided to take a dare from my friends at school, and be one of the few people brave enough to sit totally alone in the movie theatre and watch the entire 'Psycho' movie. The theatre- staff nearly weren't going to let me do it being only sixteen, but as I appeared so confident, they probably thought I needed taking down a peg or two.

I went in and sat right in the middle of the theatre where I was told. Then it went pitch black except for the screen, but I knew that I wasn't alone. I sensed at least three people obviously all dressed in black creeping up behind me. I felt chilled air on me more than once and a slight shower of water when the lead actress Janet Leigh was being stabbed to death in the shower....

I didn't react much but instead decided to scare them, so I closed my eyes and asked some playful spirits to come and cause mischief.... Spirit faces soon appeared in front of these people, with five ghostly apparitions flying around.... Four people were soon running out of the theatre screaming and I was not one of them.

Very few people lasted the entire movie, most came running out at some stage screaming or crying. But I lasted, and what's more I got paid with free movie passes for six whole months. My friends were most impressed.... I knew that Poppa could conjure up playful spirits, but I was surprised how easy it was for me. From the stories I heard later the spirits must have stayed on and caused more mischief.... I didn't think to send them back.

1963

November 1st

Dear Diary, it is an age since I have recorded the events in my life and such a lot has happened....

I am now seventeen years old, living in London and working quite successfully as a model. I am fortunate really as I tend to get chosen for the photo shoots abroad. I think because of my blond Aryan good looks, plus the fact I can speak German. My French has also improved here as I am flatting with another model Veronica Plummer, who learnt French at a public school. She is mad about everything French so that is all we speak at home now.

Veronica and I met at the 'Lucie Clayton modelling and charm academy,' here in London eight months ago. I have never had a friend like Veronica. She is beautiful, very cool and quite smart. I am finding a lot of the other girls here 'as thick as bricks'. I also share with another model Alison Lovejoy, who is sweet but quiet. Alison can also speak French as can our friend Joanna Lumley, but she doesn't flat with us. We are all four saving up madly to go on a holiday to Paris together. I can't wait.

Oma was concerned about my coming to live in England alone being so young, but I have fared quite well. Mind you I was coming to a school as such. I could stay in the U.K. indefinitely because my Poppa was English, plus I have relatives here whom I am in contact with.... But I doubt that will happen unless I fall madly in love with some handsome, Englishman that is.

My Great Aunt Violet lives in Oxford, as does her son Sebastian and his wife Felicity, although they are a bit fuddy duddy for a couple not yet thirty. Aunt Violet is Poppa's younger sister and her husband Uncle Digby, was a friend of his from boarding school. They are all academics. Aunt Violet is sweet and funny like Poppa was but with a naughty twinkle in her eye.

Poppa's best friend though was Henry Hargraves, who I have visited, and he introduced me to his grand-daughter Carol. She is one year older than me and works for 'Births, deaths and marriages' in Kensington and lives not far from me with her family. Her Father Harry is a bit crotchety though. I suppose his gammy leg from a war injury has had something to do with that. But her mother Claire is sweet and so youthful looking. She was only eighteen when she had Carol so they could pass for sisters almost like me and my mom. Mom is still a beautiful woman for a thirty-eight-year-old. I feel sad and wish we were close like Carol and her mother are and I don't just mean geographically.

Carol and I share relations, as her Father's Uncle George married my Great Aunt Edith, Poppa's elder sister. Two of their daughters Daphne and Lilly, live near them in the South of England and they have three children each. The other sister Marigold, whom I met at Poppa's funeral, has two sons Anthony and Neville they live in Philadelphia. Lilly has carried on the floral names, with twins Poppy and Daisy, plus there are four more boy cousins, Roger, Arthur, Nigel and Charles. Carol also has a younger brother Fred. So that explains the family here, of which there are a few. Lilly and her husband Richard took over the family business of growing flowers a few miles from Tunbridge Wells. I'm so looking forward to my first Christmas day spent with the Smyth relations, at Great Aunt Edith's cottage in Tunbridge Wells itself.

Post Xmas day:

What a fun bunch they are, I can now see where Poppa got his sense of humour from. I think I fitted in quite well really. It was certainly less formal than the Rothschild's functions are. I even went to church with them all, they are Church of England like the royal family.

I'm not sure where I stand any more religion-wise. I may be considered agnostic as I am no longer a practicing Jewess, or a Christian Spiritualist, like Poppa and Oma were.... Even so I enjoyed the service and the singing especially. That evening we heard the Queen's message on the television and Great Aunt Violet can mimic her well.... Poppa was also a good mimic, as is Uncle William.

1964

February 7th

Veronica, Alison and I get invited to all the best parties. Photographers are always coming up asking us if they can take our photo. We have to say no though, as we are contracted exclusively to the 'Lucie Clayton modelling agency' which is considered London's top agency.... Of course, this is how I got into this business as my parents paid for me to go to her modelling and charm school last June, when I dropped out of high- school.

At charm school I chose to study makeup, deportment, fashion design, pattern cutting and dress-making. I'm quite good at the last three. I could have learnt cordon blue cookery or flower arranging but for what purpose I reasoned.... I think I may have some creative flair though as people are always complimenting me on my own dress style which is quite colourful compared to most. I spend far too much money on clothes and shoes though, especially boots and have several pair in various lengths. But so do most of the other girls I know, except for the practical Carol that is.

I was amazed that my parents even supported my decision to come to the U.K. alone, to learn about the fashion industry and try my hand at professional modelling. All of which I told them I was very keen on, even though I was not certain I was. I had just wanted to leave school.... This was instead of me attending a finishing school in Paris or Zurich, which is what they wanted me to do. Ironically though, I have been keen to improve my French here.

As for the school, well, I would have been better-off learning the business side of the fashion industry not just how to walk on a catwalk which is what I mainly did for six months.

My parents were probably hoping that I would emerge a charming, poised young lady, ready to find myself a suitable husband from within the Rothschild circles. But then this is not the aim of the school finding good models for the agency is.

My Oma was also surprisingly supportive of me coming to England. She thought I needed a change as I had not been studying much at high school anyway. She'd said I just wanted to go to parties and misbehave with my best friend Rita and were becoming a bit wild driving around in fast cars. She also said it was because I was bored and needed to expand my horizons. How wise Oma is.

And I did last the six months at charm school, after which I started getting some good modelling assignments. I was surprised though as Leslie Kark who now owns the school and agency with his wife Evelyn, said I was 'as awkward as a cow on a bike'.... I think that he has an awkward name, as when you 'kark it' you die. She's quite nice though, albeit a bit strict.

April 20th

Veronica, Alison and I are kept fairly- busy workwise, but we are certainly not the 'it' girls of the fashion industry. They are Edie Sedwich, Crace Coddington and Veruschka, the latter of whom is German born and because of this she always recommends me for assignments as she says she loves to talk to in her native tongue. Veruschka is my height and colouring but unlike me she is very sexy....

Joanna Lumley another model whom I am friends with is such a fun girl whom I adore, a real Miss Personality plus. I told her she should be an actress and she said that was a jolly good idea. At sixteen she has plenty of time yet, but I feel she will be quite famous one day....

There is also a big eyed fifteen-year-old named Lesley Hornby coming up in the ranks, who everyone calls 'Twiggy' because she is sooo skinny. She has the most god awful common accent though, which is so opposite to Joanna who speaks posh, but Twiggy is quite sweet. She has the modern short, bobbed haircut and is so fortunate as she can eat whatever she likes without putting on an ounce of weight. Such as fried eggs, bread and chips which the English seem to adore. Mind you I crave bagels, which I can't get here.

I have thought about having my hair cut into a bob but Vidal Sassoon our hairdresser says it would not suit me.

Jean Shrimpton 'The Shrimp' is the most sought-after model though, also because of her clever boyfriend, photographer David Bailey. There is no chance of any romantic attachments with him as they are madly in love, which is such a shame as David is so cute.

I do date boys or rather men, but I am not interested in any serious attachment. It's just a bit of fun. Sometimes I have had to wrestle with them on dates and been called 'a cock tease', as I will let them kiss and fondle me, but that's all. It's alright for them they don't have to worry about getting pregnant like we poor girls do. And Veronica says they don't always carry protection. They expect us girls to do that too.... How embarrassing to have to go and buy them. It's bad enough going to buy sanitary pads and having them wrapped in brown paper and slid across the counter.

May 10th

Once I have my high heels on I am over six feet tall. I try not to wear my hair up as I find myself towering over everyone as I have grown another inch and am now five foot eleven inches tall. Plus these false eyelashes I am made to wear probably aren't doing my real eyelashes any good. Neither is lacquering my hair, but at least I don't have to bleach it being naturally blond, like poor Veronica does. I also seem to be constantly hungry and get lightheaded spending time posing under lights with my hips thrust out, wearing a pouty big- eyed look. This is most unnatural except on Veruschka, who naturally looks like that.... Plus, on the catwalk we walk crossing one foot in front of the other it's no wonder I fall over occasionally. To be honest I am really a bit of a klutz, 'Kark it' is right.

There are lots of foods that I can't eat like bread and pastries, as I must stay stick thin, so I eat a lot of carrots. It's a wonder I haven't turned orange. I don't think this is a good state for me to be in for long. Sometimes I miss my period which would give me reason for concern if I was actually having sex like Veronica.

April 26th

I rang my Oma for her birthday today and caught up on all the family news. I miss her so much and have been feeling down in the dumps with the weather being so wet and miserable. So, Veronica and Alison are taking me to see 'Georgie girl' tonight at the pictures to cheer me up. They reckon I am homesick and I agree.... Although I have something to look forward to, as next Wednesday night I am having dinner with Saul. He rang me last week to say that he will be in London for one night only and said he has a surprise for me.... I haven't seen him in months, so I am a bit nervous.

May 4th

Great news! Saul will be flying to London on a regular basis. This is more than I had hoped for. It was so lovely to see him. We sat in the restaurant holding hands across the table and staring into each other's eyes, it was sooo romantic. Saul never tries to paw me like other men do he is a real gentle- man. How could I even consider dating anyone else.... I can't wait to see him again. He said that he's missed me so much and told me I was beautiful.

June 16th

I had a lovely eighteenth birthday. First, I had a long talk on the phone with my Oma, then I got a taxi to Heathrow Airport and boarded a flight to Paris. It was so exciting, and my friends were so envious. My parents had surprised me by arranging a four day trip staying with them at the Ritz. They had even got permission from my agency.... But I wished Saul could have been there also.

When I arrived at the hotel lobby Mom and Dad were waiting for me. They were surprised to see how grown-up poised and sophisticated I looked they said.... I must say I did turn a few heads where-ever we went, and French men are such flirts.... I had a lovely reunion with my parents as neither felt the need to lecture me for once, but it was strange without Philip and Alexander. I was a bit disappointed we were not all together again.

When I got back to London it was to some rather exciting news! Not only had Saul sent me the biggest bunch of red roses, which were now a bit wilted.... But photographer Antony-Armstrong- Jones, husband of Princess Margaret, no less, had asked 'Kark it' if I could pose for him. I told him I would, but only if someone comes with me, so Veronica has volunteered.

We girls try to never go anywhere alone, it is unwise to, so we tend to chaperone each other if we don't know anyone else on an assignment. This is because we are just fair game for a lot of men, of all ages, some old enough to be our grandfathers even. And Lord Snowdon does have a bit of a reputation with the ladies. Although some me like to tease and joke around and it is mostly just harmless banter. But I'd swear English men are taught how to chat up girls at school because they are constantly at it, which can be a bit annoying at times.

Now the other girls all thought ME a bit of a princess when first I arrived here, as I couldn't do a thing for myself.

They had to show me how to wash-out my smalls even, plus how to use the Laundromat....My parents always had staff and Oma a housekeeper, even if they were treated like part of the family, so I never learnt how to do anything domestic.

Veronica learnt cordon bleu cookery at our school, so she has shown me how to make delicious salads, dressings and omelettes, which is basically what we live on plus fruit, grilled fish and lean meats. We rarely drink alcohol, and don't smoke smelly cigarettes which we have banned from our flat as they stink the place out, plus our clothes and hair. It's just as well Oma can't see me though as she would say I am far too thin. But at least we eat healthily compared to most of the other models who smoke, to kill their appetites.

Most of the fashion photographers are great to work with. David Bailey is cheeky and such fun as is Richard Avedon, who has a real eye for spotting talent. He loves photographing Patti Boyd who is dating George Harrison from the Beatles, no less. Patti has the longest legs and great flippy hair, but her teeth aren't that great. She is lots of fun though, so I can see why the men adore her. Patti has been an absolute doll and got us free tickets to a few of the 'Beatles' concerts. We even met the fab four once and I'll swear Paul McCartney was flirting with me and he is sooo cute.

The Beatles are very popular. I feel they are going to become even more famous and give Elvis Presley some stiff competition in the U.S.one day.

I have also met Cecil Beaton he is a real gentleman and reminds me of my late Poppa. He told me Audrey Hepburn was his muse and he loved to dress and photograph her, "no one has such an elegant neck as she" he'd said. But he is getting a bit old and dottery now though.

The English have such funny expressions,'woopsie daisy' if you fall over, which I do a bit. But not David Bailey though he just says "whatcha doing on yer arse luv".

July 9th

How exciting! We have been questioned with regards to the Profumo scandal, as Veronica and I have attended a few parties at the studio of society osteopath and artist, Stephen Ward. He was hugely popular, but now is the opposite, it seems, as everyone is suddenly scrambling to disassociate themselves from him.... How awful, I've always found Stephen to be most charming.

Apparently he has been accused of 'pimping 'or living of immoral earnings....This is such nonsense as everybody knows Stephen earns a good living as a respected osteopath and sought-after portrait artist. He doesn't need to exploit the likes of Christine Keeler and Mandy Rice- Davies so what if they stay at his apartment sometimes. They've told the police that they are just good friends, but it seems to have fallen on deaf ears.

Stephen does like to surround himself with a lot of pretty, young girls though for a man of forty-seven. None of whom he's involved with, to my knowledge anyway. Veronica told me he's a voyeur, that is, he prefers to watch other people having sex rather than doing it himself, how odd.

Apparently, a lot of the less successful models are high class call girls we have since found out, but not the girls that we associate with. Veronica said she has always suspected as much.

Stephen's parties are always an interesting mix of people though with most being quite colourful and posh, some were even a bit shady I felt .... And I suppose the bevy of beauties there to adorn, were preyed upon, but then this was no worse than anywhere else.... I may have been a bit naïve though, as I now feel a bit used with what I have read in the papers, but I shall not tell the police this.

One interesting man that I met at the last party of Stephen's I'd attended, had an uncanny resemblance to my late Poppa, and I told him so. He even had a similar voice. His name was Peter Huxley. He was about forty-five and I felt was some sort of spy, as he was very cagey about what he did for the British Government.... But for some reason I felt drawn to this man and wondered what he was doing at that party, as he seemed out of place.

I found out years later that Peter Huxley was gathering information for British intelligence when he attended that party, amongst other things…. He never thought Stephen Ward was guilty of anything untoward either.

Anyway, this is how the scandal unfolded....

John Profumo was a forty-six-year-old conservative party politician when he first met the then nineteen- year- old, night club dancer Christine Keeler, at a party. This occurred in March 1961 at the lakeside cottage on the Astor estate of 'Cliveden', in Buckinghamshire, that the owner Lord Astor, let Stephen Ward use.... Profumo and Keller then started an affair and at the time she was also involved with a Russian military attaché Eugene Ivanov. Details of their affair eventually came to light and in March of this year Profumo lied about his association with Keller to the House of Commons, stating: "there was no impropriety whatsoever". This of course was not true and ten weeks later he had to resign, quote: "with deep remorse".

Ivanov himself had left Britain before the scandal hit the newspapers. But prior to this, Stephen Ward was used by MI5. They considered Ivanov a possible defector and sought Stephen's help in this giving him a case officer a man named Woods.... Stephen was later used as a back-channel through Ivanov to the Soviet Union, and was involved in unofficial diplomacy at the time of the 1962 Cuban missile crisis.... What an intrigue!

I feel that Stephen Ward is the scapegoat in this Profumo affair.

Victor, Veronica's boyfriend, found all this out, but told us to keep quiet for our own safety. His father Lord Coddington is quite well connected politically, and he had spilt the beans to Victor one night when he was drunk. I told the police that I found Stephen Ward to be a charming man and never once felt used by him. I said I had felt more unsafe on single dates, than at one of his parties. I also said that I wanted it on record that the police officers who questioned me were more lecherous than Stephen ever was.... I wasn't going to put the knife into the poor man or twist it like everyone else had. And it was true what I said about the policemen, they did make me feel cheap.

I felt at the time that Stephan Ward was murdered by MI6 because he was an embarrassment to the British Government and the royal family. He had numerous sketches of Prince Philip, the Queens husband, that had been kept quiet; the prince had also attended his parties.... Ward supposedly took an overdose of barbiturates on the last day of his trial for 'Pimping', of which he was going to be found guilty.... He was the fall guy, as although Profumo resigned, no one could prove or disprove his innocence or guilt in any political honey trap triangle. And Profumo fared well really, as he went on to work in Philanthropy and later received an O.B.E. from the Queen, for his work in 1975.

August 11th

I have seen Saul seven times now for dinner on his two-night stayovers. He is a co-pilot for Pan American Airlines, or PAN AM, as they are called, I am so proud of him. And he looks so handsome in his uniform being a six- footer.

The last time Saul and I had seen each other in L.A. was after Poppa's funeral and he'd made me feel like a young girl. This is certainly not the case now. He says I've turned into a beautiful swan.... I hope he didn't mean that I was an ugly duckling before, although I did have braces on my teeth for a couple of years there and was a bit gangly. I love seeing Saul, he keeps me in touch with home as I miss my Oma so much.

I do telephone Oma regularly I have to call collect and my parents and Saul, as I can't afford it.... Oma has never been confident speaking English on the telephone, so we usually speak in German, much to the horror of my flat mates.... *No one liked to hear German being spoken. It was still raw even then twenty odd years after the War.* My parents put funds into my bank account, but I try not to touch them. I don't want my girlfriends to find out my family are wealthy. They also have offered to buy me a car, but I've refused. I just want to be like everyone else and not a little rich girl and I am making quite good money by myself.

1965

January 4th

The first of January would have been Poppa's 65th birthday. I can't believe he has been gone for over two years now. I went to visit Great Aunt Violet as I was feeling sad. She cheered me up as she is so funny telling me stories about everyone she knows and mimicking some of them. We discussed the fate of poor Stephen Ward so I decided to tell her about Peter Huxley, the man who I'd met at Stephen's last party I'd attended. I said this man had reminded me so much of Poppa.... Aunt Violet surprised me then by saying that she had also met him once, after he telephoned her and made an appointment to visit. This was last year. Apparently, Peter Huxley was a big fan of Poppa's he said and had asked her a lot of questions about Poppa's life and work as a psychic.... Aunt Violet agreed that he an uncanny resemblance to her late brother. How odd.

February 10th

David's Bailey's studio has always given me the creeps and I've told him this. It often comes over all chilly despite the heating and David says he always feels like someone is watching him, when alone there.... Today I found out why.... I was by myself in the dressing room when a handsome young German officer appeared to me in spirit. He told me clairaudiently, that he had been tortured and made to confess to crimes he did not commit, which he had to sign a confession for. He was then consequently shot in this very room.... He told me many German officers were tortured and executed in this way.... I told him that was wrong, but many dreadful unjust things were done in war- time by both sides. I said that he needed to leave now and go to the light as his mother was looking for him as she had recently passed over.... He looked surprised not only at what I said but that I could obviously see and understand him.... I then asked my German guide Gretel to come and take him to his mother, which she subsequently did as they walked into a bright light together....

David and another model named Sybil were next door in the studio and heard me speaking in German so they asked what I was doing.... I told them what had happened and about the history of the building, which David said was correct. He'd been told it was used for military interrogations during the war but was surprised to hear about the executions.

Sybil just said "Ew! I don't want no dead Krauts perving at me when I'm dressing, thank God you got rid of him".

April 27th

I telephoned my Oma yesterday for her sixty-fifth birthday. After we both had our usual cry, she made me laugh by telling me that she has been asked out on a few dates. Some of the men at her country club who are still in their fifties, think she is their age. Apparently, they have a bet on as to who can get her out on a date? But none have succeeded as none have taken her fancy, she said. I hope I am like my Oma when I am her age, as she still has a trim figure and acts and dresses much younger. I told her that I would be happy for her if she found a nice male companion, but she said she never would.... I doubt that my charming Poppa would have remained so loyal.

May 30th

I have been living in London for nearly two years, so I was surprised when out of the blue I got an invite to attend an afternoon tea party at 18 Kensington Palace Gardens, no less. The owner one Lionel Rothschild II, whose father I was told, had done all the impressive renovations to this palatial Victorian mansion and its grounds.... The mansion was actually made of marble and its gardens were the most impressive I had ever seen at any residential property.... So, I was hob knobbing with the hob knobs, as David Bailey would say. David calls Joanna, Veronica and me 'classy birds' or 'a bit of posh', and he is partial to a bit of posh himself I've noticed.

I was glad though that I'd decided to take my posh girlfriends along with me to the party all dressed to impress, so at least I knew someone there.... The young men were all buzzing around us like bees around a honey pot (not an English expression).

We briefly met the charming Laurent de Rothschild and his younger brother Andre, the latter of whom just stared at me went bright red, then looked at his shoes. The witty Joanna soon had Laurent, who I think fancied himself as 'a bit of ladies-man,' quite tied- up in knots. But these handsome de Rothschild brothers soon had some stiff competition with all the Lord's this and Viscount's that, who butted in....They weren't going to let these charming Frenchmen monopolise the prettiest girls in the room, one said. None of the Englishmen sparked my interest though, and I could not believe how many of them lisped, was it affected? Surely their parents could afford speech therapists.

Later-on, I had one of those random statements said to me again, by a senior Rothschild totally unknown to me, when introduced to a family group by Lady Rothschild herself. He'd said....

"So, you're the one we've been told about, eh!"

To which I answered, clueless "I don't think so".... But it did unnerve me somewhat.

I also met Peter Huxley again, only this time he was with his charming wife Elanora and their rather dashing son Piers, who I'd say is just a few years older than me.... Again, I remarked to both the father and the son this time, how uncanny it was that they looked so much like my late Poppa.

Elanora is a Rothschild, she is the youngest sister of Baron Victor Rothschild, who was also at the party, but I met him only briefly. Peter asked me some questions about my family, the Smyth's- side that is, strangely not the Rothschilds whose party we were attending as I thought they may have been interested in some family connection.... But for some reason I was a bit guarded. I did notice though that Piers hardly took his eyes off me after we were introduced.

June 28th

I must confess that since I have turned nineteen, Saul and I have become lovers. But we're being very careful not to get me pregnant. I cannot go on the contraceptive pill yet as it is not available to unmarried woman, but one day it will be, I hope. Veronica insists I will be safe using rubbers as she and Victor do. She also told me that they avoid intercourse around her fertile time and do other delightful things instead, but I wasn't sure what she meant by that.

I like Victor but he can be a bit of a fool sometimes, he should never have told Veronica and I what he did about the Profumo affair. Even so, he is charming and handsome and drives a very nice red MG sports car, which he takes Veronica and I to all the best parties in. Even if I do have to fold myself uncomfortably into its narrow back seat.

I still date other men, but Saul is my only lover. I wanted him to be my first, as I trust him more than anyone else. At the moment, he flies to London once a week, but our schedules don't always allow us time- off together and then it is usually only an afternoon and an evening.... Saul is my best friend as I can be myself around him, but he doesn't know I date other men.... I do love Saul, but I am too young to commit myself to one man. But if I stay exclusive, I miss out on so much socially.

July 11th

I got another invite to a party of more English relations, on the Rothschild side. Veronica was even more impressed with this invitation she said, as she knew the estate. So, I decided to take her with me again plus Victor as our chaperone this time.... By now everyone knows I am from a wealthy family but it hasn't really changed anything.

The party was held at 'Waddersdon manor' in Buckinghamshire, which fortunately was not too far from Victor's parents' home, where we stayed the night. Victor's family home was nowhere near as palatial as the Rothschild mansion, nor the nearby Astor 'Clivenden' mansion, which kicked off the Profumo scandal, even so, I preferred it. And Victor's parents are so lovely and spontaneous, you can tell they are both into amateur dramatics.

I must say the Rothschild's certainly know how to throw a party. Present were so many dashing men and attractive stylishly dressed woman and the champagne was certainly flowing. The vast ballroom was decorated with huge ice sculptures and floral arrangements and a five piece band was playing on the stage above a large parquet dance floor. There were four sets of double doors open leading to a beautifully lit outside terrace with an impressive pond and fountain. It was all so perfect and romantic somehow, even though it was similar in style to my Grandparents Zurich mansion, which I have never really liked, but on a grander scale.

Veronica and I managed to cut a dash entering in our borrowed fitted sequined dresses, stiletto heels and bouffant hair styles. I felt taller than any other woman in the room and most of the men. Cecil Beaton was there and came up to me and said that he thought I was related to the English Rothschild's because of my bone structure.... He looked as dapper as ever, in his evening attire.

During the evening I kept switching between English, German and French. I was telling everyone I met a different story which had most quite confused as to which branch of the family I was actually from. But I didn't fool the elegant Countess de Rothschild from Paris though. She said I was a little minx, albeit a very pretty one, and knew exactly which branch of the family I was from. Apparently she knew my grandparents well and my parents a little, she said. She then insisted on introducing me to her two sons whom she called over.... To my surprise they were Laurent and Andre, de Rothschild.

We laughed and said we had previously met. Again, I thought they were the most attractive men at the party, being both tall, fair and handsome. Andre looked at me blushed then looked at his shoes. But Laurent was most charming and attentive to me on and off for the next few hours, even though he kept getting distracted by all the people he knew. More it seemed than at the last Rothschild party we'd both attended.... We had a few dances together and even stole a kiss outside in a dark corner of the balcony, which was quite delightful as he was a very good kisser.

Laurent was a few years older than me and worked in the luxury yacht side of a Rothschild owned business, based in Cannes, on the French Riviera he'd said. We spoke mainly in French, and he told me my accent was delightful, as was I.... Needless- to- say I didn't tell him I had a boyfriend but then I'd already figured Laurent for a play- boy, even so I was enjoying my flirtation with him.... Then Laurent came back with a drink for me around eleven o'clock and said he was sorry but he had to leave as he had promised to escort his mother home.... I must say I was a little disappointed.

Andre his younger brother just stared at me all evening, but never came and spoke to me again after his initial hello which I thought odd. But then he was only my age or even younger possibly and obviously, the shyer of the two.... I found myself thinking about both the de Rothschild brothers for days after that party and I don't know why, although they are both dashingly handsome.

August 2nd

What an exciting week Veronica and I have just had.... First, we were flown to Paris, then Cannes where we did a four- day fashion shoot for a nautical collection with a backdrop of luxury boats. And who should we bump into but one Laurent de Rothschild....Our agency was so impressed with what Laurent then arranged for the shoot that they let us stay on for three whole days afterwards.

During the day Laurent took us out sailing on his luxury yacht. At night he charmed and dined us then took us to wonderful parties. Andre turned up one night, hardly spoke to me again, but he did manage to disappear with Veronica for a couple of hours I noticed. Mind you I was engaged in some heavy petting with Laurent at the time.... Fortunately, he did not press me to go all the way as I don't know what I would have done, as I found Laurent so attractive and such fun to be with.

Veronica and I were on cloud nine for a few days after returning home. Obviously, she did not tell Victor nor I Saul about the partying, or about the charming de Rothschild brothers.

August 25th

What is it about this Laurent de Rothschild as our paths keep crossing? I recently went to a party at the studio of David Bailey, who has been trying to cheer himself up after his split from girlfriend Jean Shrimpton. And there he was again. Laurent.... David appears to have himself a new love interest already. A beautiful French actress named Catherine Deneuve and she had with her a group of French friends.... One of whom was

Laurent.... We locked eyes and I went over. I then spent the next few hours with this playful group, conversing in my passable French. They were all so charming and attractive. Laurent did not try to get me alone in any dark corners this time, but he did put his arm around my waist and was very attentive.... He always makes me feel special somehow.

Jean Shrimpton's sister Chrissy was at the party, she is dating Mick Jagger from the Rolling Stones, he is also a friend of David's. And David had a large photograph of a brooding Mick in a fur trimmed jacket, which was so cool, up on the wall.... I find Mick an odd- looking bloke, but in a sexy way. He certainly, has no shortage of female admirers though. The Shrimpton sisters grew up on the estate next to Victor's in Buckinghamshire and are close to Victor's two younger sisters: what a small world it is. As of course I went with Victor and Veronica.

Piers Huxley was also at the party. He came over to me and Laurent and said hello. Surprisingly he asked me to go outside with him where it was quiet. And I agreed for some reason.... Once outside Piers lit a cigarette, but didn't offer me one, as he knew I didn't smoke, he said. He then stated that he was surprised to see me with a playboy like Laurent de Rothschild....I didn't answer so he quickly changed the subject. We talked generally and then he asked me about my Poppa's work. He said like his father, he was also very interested in psychic phenomenon.

Piers was attentive, but not in a flirtatious way and when he asked me to join him and his parents for lunch the following Sunday, I saw no reason not to accept. I was curious about them. I could also make my own way there, as his parents lived only a short bus ride from me.... I liked Piers and his father and found their likeness to my Poppa comforting and wondered if we could be related also on the Smyth side.... Piers was an attractive man, but I could not read his interest in me.... Laurent was not pleased I could tell that I went outside with him.

August 30th

I've been invited to yet another party at yet another Rothschild Buckinghamshire estate. I am beginning to think that someone is arranging this like my parents or grandparents even. I hope one of the girls can come with me though.... I also wonder if Laurent will be there again.... I'm getting concerned as Saul is my boyfriend but I am spending too much time thinking about the charming, Laurent de Rothschild.... I have also seen Piers Huxley again and met his family including his grandmother, they are all such lovely people.... I was surprised though when I arrived at their charming home to see I was their only guest. Piers who seemed more relaxed this time, and his mother Eleanor, greeted me with a kiss on the cheek, the rest of the family a warm handshake.

Over lunch I decided that the Huxley's were huge fans of my late Poppa's, as they seemed to know an awful lot about him. Then I found out that Piers' grandmother Dulcie, had been in the same P.O.W. camp as my Poppa in Berlin, during the latter part of WWI and that she remembered him well.... Dulcie said he was a very special and gifted young man who had also been her very first boyfriend. After the war she and her family immediately returned to their home in England, having lost their Berlin factory when it was repossessed during the war.... Once home Dulcie took up with her childhood friend Gordon Huxley, whom she soon married. The Huxley's were close family friends.

Gordon was a soldier who had returned home from France sadly a bit disfigured and partially blinded by mustard gas. Dulcie married him a bit out of pity, she said, but grew to love him very much. And they had a happy marriage. Dulcie's father, Digby Dingleby was a wealthy importer, he set them up in a house, Dulcie said. She then went to work in the family business and surprised everyone, including herself, by discovering she a good head for business. When her father retired Dulcie and her younger brother Albert took over.

Despite his disabilities Gordon had been a successful sculptor who worked in clay, he had many pieces cast in bronze.... Peter was born the first year they were married, followed by two daughters Anne then Catherine two and four years later.... Sadly, Gordon had died several years ago she said.

I saw a photo of Gordon Huxley and thought his son Peter looked nothing like him. I told them I read all of Poppa's diaries and remembered him mentioning a Dulcie which seemed to please her. Dulcie said, although she and Poppa had exchanged addresses, she never wrote to him nor he her.

Peter and Piers both work for British Intelligence but didn't say in what capacity. I told them that Poppa's father Geoffrey Smyth had worked for British Intelligence, but they seemed to know this already.

Dulcie asked me a lot of questions about Poppa's life and about my Oma, so I told them all about the spiritual work my grandparents had done during both the wars and relayed some stories. They all seemed to find this interesting.... I never mentioned the word 'Illuminati' or told them about the attempts on Poppa's life, or about him founding the 'white hats'. I also never mentioned my own psychic abilities. But they seemed satisfied with everything I told them.... I noted that Peter Huxley was a Freemason as he had their insignia on his wall.

Piers walked me to the bus where I got another kiss on the cheek. I knew he liked me by the way he looked at me, but he seemed hesitant for some reason to ask if he could call me.

September 7th

I have been doing some fashion designs of my own lately which are quite bold and geometric. And I've even shown them to the designer Mary Quant....She said they were really- different. I've had to do something to take my mind off things lately and I've always enjoyed drawing.... That is all I am going to write down for now....

December 23rd

Shock horror! It's Christmas time and Saul being Jewish is working and not on holiday, just when I need him sooo badly.... As I think I am having morning sickness which lasts until lunchtime. I have also been feeling sooo tired.... I strongly suspect I am pregnant but haven't been to a doctor yet.... I've cried and thrown up every morning for a week now.... Maybe I'm just sick with worry. If I am pregnant there is no- way I am seeing a back street abortionist, which is what my flatmates keep insisting I do.... I shall be having this baby and keeping it. I know Saul will marry me, he loves me and I love him, I think.... But this is not what I had planned.... Not yet anyway.

Veronica is appalled at my bad luck and says that if we do get married then she insists on being my chief bridesmaid.... And now she and Alison are worried that they might get pregnant too, like it is contagious or something.... Honestly, I have had to swear them both to secrecy, plus Joanna.

December 26th

I am feeling a bit better, so I went and had Christmas lunch with Carol and her family yesterday as it was also her birthday; she is a Christmas Carol....It was a lovely day although I couldn't eat much and felt a bit rude. Carol's mother asked if it was because I was a model and ate sparingly. I said yes, but of course, it is not that.

Carol and I went for a walk after we had done the dishes. I am so pleased we have become such good friends. I decided to trust her and tell her what I suspected. She said "Oh my giddy aunt" a few times. This had me wondering if she was referring to me having to tell my great aunts, or if it was just another odd English expression.... Carol is very practical and said that Saul and I must marry here in the U.K., as soon as possible. Then inform our parents by cable and fly home well before the baby is due to avoid as much fuss as possible, for my sake. She said our parents would not be happy at first, but soon will be when I produce for them a beautiful grandchild.... I hope Carol is right.

Saul is based in Los Angeles but still flies to London weekly.... Now that I am in this fix, the thought of going home to my Oma, Uncle William and Aunt Selma is most appealing. I want to telephone Oma and tell her, but she will only worry. She won't judge me though.

I know Mom and Dad will not be pleased, and my paternal grandparents will be appalled, but what hypocrites they will be, especially after what's happened.... Well, Grosspapi anyway, because he was probably a party to it.... If only I could be honest with my parents and tell them the whole story about the wicked and manipulative Rothschilds....But I am far too ashamed and embarrassed, even though it wasn't my fault.... I was used. These schemers will never get their hands on my child though once he is born. I will make very certain of that....

And Saul's parents will not be happy either about our sudden marriage and I do care what they think. This is because a rabbi didn't marry us, rather than his choice of a bride, I hope. They will be happier once the baby arrives though, I'm sure.... What a horrible shameful mess, I could just die! But I know Saul's family like me as they have known me since I was twelve, and I like them too. Plus, I am looking forward to changing my name to West and being as far removed as I can from the British and European Rothschilds back in the U.S.... What was I even thinking, trusting any of them. I was seduced in more ways than one with my life here; how could I have been so naive.

1966

January 20th

Saul came over on the 10th we registered our intended marriage and got married a week later, January 17th....We chose our local registry office where Carol works, which is in the royal borough of Kensington and Chelsea. Carol booked the 'Brydon room' for us, but as she is not allowed to officiate yet, a nice lady called Heather did and Carol assisted her which was lovely.

Veronica and Victor were our witnesses and a few friends in the fashion industry came to the Savoy Restaurant where we had a beautiful meal, drank champagne and cut the wedding cake that Carol had brought for us.... I was far too embarrassed, to ask either of my great aunts, or their families. I hope they will understand. Carol said she would telephone them soon to explain the situation. And I wouldn't have asked any of the Rothschild relations anyway, not after what they'd done.... I would however have liked to have seen the Huxley's again before I left England, but that is not possible now either, under these circumstances.

My wedding dress was white, with a princess neckline falling below the bust to a length of four inches above the knee. I also wore a short veil. All of this was kindly loaned to me by Mary Quant. Mary commented on my enlarged breasts and said she would miss dressing me. I wasn't showing yet otherwise, but she must have guessed from the rushed wedding that I was pregnant, but was too polite, of course, to mention it.

I told Mary she was going to be a household name soon, with her new short skirts and set a new world-wide trend.... I said Jean Shrimpton would be her model. She laughed and said, "I wish" but told me she was going to name them after her favourite car 'a mini'. Mary has worked hard to establish herself as a designer. I think she is very clever and original, and I adore her shop in Carnaby Street. Mary took several photographs of me before the wedding for her catalogue. She was happy, and said she could not have got a more beautiful bride.... Any aspirations I once had to be a fashion designer were certainly dashed now with a baby coming....

Despite everything Saul and I enjoyed our wedding day. We then had a two- week honeymoon driving around the South of France in an old Citroen car, staying in pensions and having roadside picnics, it was wonderful.... I no longer had to worry about getting pregnant, that horse had bolted, so decided to try some of the things that Veronica had told me to do. Saul told me he was delighted not only with my increased C cup bosom, but because he had such a beautiful and sexy wife. But we knew the honeymoon could not last forever and we would have to go home and face the music. So, I sent my parents a cable telling them that Saul and I were now married and would be visiting them on our way back to L.A., to live.... I also cabled Oma with the news. I knew I would get too emotional talking to her on the telephone.... We then flew from Paris to Zurich.

I've never smoked and now the smell of it makes me sick. Fortunately, Saul doesn't smoke either, but I could have done with a cigarette then before facing my parents, to calm my raw nerves.... Mom was surprisingly calm, but my dad was angry, and looked as though he would have liked to of laid Saul out with a punch (if only he knew). The only good thing he said was at least Saul was Jewish and we were now legally married.... Saul, told them we were going to get a rabbi to bless the union when we got back home, not only to appease my father, but to appease his as well.

My brother Philip was embarrassed when I told him I was married and pregnant. At sixteen he didn't want to know that his big sister had been having sex. Philip said that he always liked Saul and his younger brothers from when he used to come over to L.A. for the holidays and we would hang- out together.... Blessedly, Alexander was away skiing with his school, so I didn't have to face his fourteen- year- old disapproval as well.

My parents insisted though that I had to tell my grandparents, so we all went over for dinner.... All Grosspapi said was that he hoped I would now settle down, like I was wayward or something. He then quizzed Saul about his lineage and said he was pleased to hear that his mother was a Bonfman. Saul told me later that he hadn't realised how wealthy and well- connected my family were. *Apparently the Bonfman's were a powerful Canadian Illuminati family I found out years later.*

February 1st

I hate to have to record this.... But I'm not actually sure who was the father of my baby is.... Charles Rothschild, or whoever he was, Laurent de Rothschild, although he denies it, or someone else possibly, whom I don't even know.... But I'm pretty sure it's not my husband Saul Aaron West.

The mysterious Charles had been most attentive and persistent at the party on that fateful night five months ago, when he'd been plying me with drinks. Was he responsible for what- ever I had ingested that made me so vulnerable.... I simply don't know the answer to that. Laurent had tried to cut-in and spend time with me that evening but Charles would not let us be alone.... What had I been thinking, allowing myself to be at the Rothschild's mercy and staying the night even, un-chaperoned, as Vanessa, Alison, and Saul, were not in town that weekend.... I should have asked Carol or Joanna to come with me.... Why had my intuition failed me? Or my Poppa in spirit, because he comes to visit me occasionally.... Where was he when I really needed him?

And was it this supposedly non- existent Charles who did the deed? I remember he told me he was the twenty–two- year-old younger brother of baron Rothschild, who owned the house where the party was held and where we all stayed the night.... He also told me, that he had no real interest in the Rothschild banking business. Rather than just making money, he wanted to do some good in the world, so was therefore keen to enter politics he'd said, which no Rothschild is encouraged to do.... I remember this clearly, this man does exist.... I can recall what he looked like of course. He was a bit like a dark haired and louder version of Andre de Rothschild, but with a plummy English accent. Although Andre had never really spoken to me much in either language. But then a lot of the Rothschild males look alike.... Dad and Alexander look Rothschild, Philip less so.

I am still disturbed by what happened to me later that night.... I have odd images of more than one person hovering over me and of a strange mask with horns and of feeling pinned down, reminiscent of the movie 'Rosemary's baby', when Mia Farrow's character is forced to have sex with the devil. That is what I would liken it to.... And I may have thought it just a disturbing dream, from some concoction I'd been given, except for the physical discomfort I had the next morning.... I knew I'd had sex....

What were these people thinking! That they could just do this to me and get away with it.... I wasn't some paid prostitute for the night.... The whole thing makes me so sick and angry. How dare they treat me this way! I should have gone to the police, but who would have believed me over the important and wealthy Rothschilds, and their equally important guests I'd reasoned at the time. But then I was a Rothschild too.... How could they let this happen to one of them, and under their very roof.... How completely wicked.... What made it even more disturbing was, the next morning at breakfast this Charles was not even present. And when I enquired about him everyone said they knew of no such person....

Apparently, Jacob, the now 4th baron Rothschild and the head of the British investment bank, whose house I was in, had only one younger brother Ashmel from his father's second marriage. And being only ten years- old Ashmel was obviously not at the party, so this Charles had lied to me.

Needless- to- say I was stunned at the time, and very confused, thinking I was going mad; then panic set in. As I knew the next morning when I woke up sore everywhere that I'd had sex the night before and someone had undressed me and put me to bed.... But who, had I had sex with? Supposedly I'd drank too much alcohol and passed out, everyone said....

I hauled Laurent to one side he denied emphatically having sex with me and admitted that he had passed out also.... How convenient.

All I knew was that I just had to act normal and get off that estate and never see any of these people again. I also knew that I should never have taken a bath I should have gone to be examined by a nurse at least, but I'd felt so disgusting.... This is still now, going around and around in my head.

Baroness Rothschild was most charming to me the next morning and kissed me goodbye and even got her driver to take me home. She'd said she hoped to see me again.... If the Baroness was party to anything untoward, she certainly didn't let on.... She insisted that two of her female staff had put me to bed after I'd passed out and said she remembered me talking to Laurent de Rothschild and David Astor mostly during the evening when I'd inquired.

I apologised and said that I hoped I hadn't embarrassed myself too much. She said I had not as everyone just assumed I was not used to drinking alcohol.

I remember wishing the next morning that Piers Huxley had been at the party or his parents as Elanora Huxley was the baron's youngest aunt. I would have felt safe with Piers or his father there for some reason, perhaps because they reminded me of my late Poppa.... I never saw the baron the next morning either and had only briefly met him the night before as he was too occupied with the forty or so other people who were present. The baron was a very well- respected man and a patron of the arts, I did not feel he was involved either with what had happened to me.

When I saw Saul two weeks later and after we had made love. I broke down and sobbed and told him what had happened. He was furious and said of course he believed me, as it had sounded so unreal, even to me. I also told him there were powerful people behind this and there was nothing I could do now but accept my fate....

Saul said I should have gone straight to a clinic and had a blood test at least to see what was in my system, plus been examined by a doctor. I said I know that now, but at the time I was too upset and embarrassed.... I didn't tell him then what I already suspected that I was pregnant as I was very late with my period. Not that it was unusual for me to be late, but I had other signs as well. My nipples had darkened in colour, and I was more sensitive to smells.... I also didn't tell Saul I suspected my part of the Rothschild prophecy was about to be fulfilled and that I was powerless to stop it.... Just as my Grosspapi had warned me as a child of ten.

What plan did they have for me if I hadn't had Saul in my life? Was it Laurent de Rothschild? Was he supposed to have seduced me and Mr Who-ever got in the way.... And was Laurent supposed to step in now and save me from ruin, as he seemed to be always popping up in my life.

I never told Saul about him, or that we had kissed quite passionately on more than two occasions or that I was disappointed we didn't get to spend much time alone together, at that fateful party. I wasn't a virgin when I went to the Rothschild party, as Saul and I were lovers. But with our busy schedules we had only done it about ten times, and to be honest I didn't really have the hang of it yet.... I didn't cry out in ecstasy as I heard Veronica doing with Victor in the next bedroom. Veronica says Victor is a wonderful lover and it sounds to me like he is.

But I knew this was not the case at the Rothschild party. I was not with a wonderful lover who turned me into what I became. I had been given an aphrodisiac of some sort, as I remember being very wild and uninhibited and not caring that there was more than one person in the room. I also remember feeling so high with sexual excitement and having a plateau of arousal that lasted for what seemed like hours and I'm sure with more than one partner.... I even had multiple orgasms and was screaming, no one else was. I was also the only one naked as the men present were dressed and masked; it was so surreal.... And what's more I'd had the physical evidence of this the next day, as I was so sore and swollen down there and had small bruises all over my body.

Of course, I couldn't tell Saul any of this, or that I had dreams recalling it, where I woke up highly aroused and covered in perspiration. The whole thing was a living nightmare and one I couldn't wake up from.

Saul told me that he had always loved me, so when the doctor confirmed in late December what I already knew.... that I was indeed pregnant, we agreed to get married. We never talked about that Rothschild party again or the fact that he was probably not the father.... Saul said he was my lover and he was more than happy to accept his fate.

Thank heavens I had Saul in my life, he was my saviour. Girls were ruined in those days for having babies out of wedlock. I had also warned my friend Joanna Lumley to be careful and she did have a baby to her photographer boyfriend, unmarried, one year after me.

I never got to say goodbye to the Huxley family before I left London, but our paths were fated to cross again.

February 10th

I never told my Oma I was pregnant, I didn't need to, as when we got home to L.A., she took one look at me and said "I think it's a boy", and I said "So do I" .... Oma was wonderful and didn't judge. She just said with Saul away so much we should live with her at least until after the baby is born and settled, to save up for a house of our own.

My parents and grandparents both offered to buy us a condo, but Saul and I refused. We didn't want to feel beholden to anyone.... They probably thought it was because we felt ashamed and that we didn't deserve it, but this was not the case.... Even so, it is the Jewish custom to chip in and help set up young couples so we received some generous gifts of money from relatives anyway.... Not that I feel very Jewish, but my new husband is and his family and mine for that matter and I respect that.... But I am not very good Jewess or daughter, I can only hope now to make a better wife and mother.

A Rabbi did bless our union, it was a private family affair. The long-sleeved lacy floor length dress I wore for that was so different to my Mary Quant mini.

I couldn't tell Oma the truth then, I was far too ashamed. But I would have liked to have had someone to discuss my sexual feelings with. As unfortunately it was many years before I sorted this problem out, which I now know was a sort of sex addiction caused by that fateful night.

February 24th

I was feeling well again and starting to get bored, so my Oma suggested I go to night school to complete my high school diploma. So, I enrolled back at my old school and because my grades had been good when I left, despite my slacking off, I'm aiming to get my diploma in five months.... Even though I will be having a baby in the middle of it.

I've made some friends at night school, l and no one knew I was pregnant at first as I wore short swing dresses or tops with princess necklines that fell below the bust with capri pants, all of which I sewed myself. I also rekindled my friendship with Rita, who now works as a film extra. She is newly engaged to a nice Fireman called Hank and they are planning on getting hitched next year, she said.

Rita is just the same and someone I can confide in, although I did not tell her about my baby's conception.

I feel ashamed to say this, but at night school there is a real stud called Hal. He's a truck driver trying to get a high school diploma, to better himself. And because Saul is away so much, and I am lonely and so horny being pregnant. I have been having sex with Hal every night after class in the back of his truck.... I'm not proud of this, but something has happened to me since that night at that Rothschild party.... Saul doesn't complain when he is home about my sexual appetite, he just thinks It's because I am pregnant with extra hormones or something. Fortunately, we have our own wing away from my Oma at her house.

June 30th

Jonathon Clarence West arrived fairly- quickly on the 6th of May 1966....Oma said he was in a hurry to get started in this life. Oma is now into numerology, and she said his 3 x 6s meant he is creative at problem solving, plus his 1, 5, 9, means he has an arrow of determination. I laughed at the 3 x 6s 666 the numbers of the devil, but Oma said look at his initials J. C.

Jono, what we've decided to call him, is a beautiful baby, fair like me and very alert and content. A month after he was born, I turned twenty.... Of course, Oma and I are now concerned that I have fulfilled the prophecy by giving birth to a baby boy in 1966, but at least he isn't a Rothschild. Poppa visited me one night, but just smiled at me and the baby and then faded....

1967

July 28th

I cannot believe that I am only twenty-one years old, a mother, and now also a widow.... Was it only last month that I celebrated my 21st birthday with family friends and our infant son Jono; it seems longer. And I was happy, really- happy, as my life seemed perfect for once. I had even got on top of my sexual problem, which was a big deal for me.... Becoming a mother had really settled me down.... Then tragedy struck when my beloved husband was killed in a plane crash.

After Saul died my love for my son is what got me through those first dark days otherwise I don't know what I would have done, I was crazy with grief. I sobbed until I vomited, then slept for too many hours then I was awake for too many hours.... I relived the horror of what my poor husband must have gone through, again and again, knowing that his plane was going to crash and there was not a thing he could do to prevent it.... Why did this have to happen!

My late husband Saul had tried to come through to comfort me (in spirit) but I was too consumed with grief.... He told me where the plane was located when I was still numb with shock and operating automatically.... Then realisation hit home when the wreckage and bodies were finally located. I wasn't allowed to see him either, one of his work colleagues identified the body, which made it even harder to accept. But he must have been pretty- mangled and burnt. My poor loving kind husband .... Why did he have to die so young and so tragically?

There were others on the plane also of course, Senator Doug McCall, and his secretary Joyce Nelson.... And I instinctively know that none of the families have been told the truth by government officials.

My Oma was wonderful and never left my side during the two weeks it took to locate the aircraft. She had some idea of the grief I was feeling having lost Poppa five years earlier.

As soon as I heard the plane was missing, I knew Saul was dead, well before that even, when I fed cereal to my infant son that morning I said, "only you and me now". This would have been about the time of the crash approx. 8 am e.s.t.... I knew something was going to happen.... Why didn't I try to prevent it.... But Saul had wanted to take that classified charter flight, he'd felt honoured he said.... I believe it was never meant to reach its destination, and what's-more Saul will get the blame. And I won't be able expose the truth either, well not for fifty years anyway until the files become public record.

I know in my heart that plane was sabotaged, and my husband sacrificed. I think it was one of those 'kill two birds with the one stone' scenarios and I have my suspicions as to who is behind it. But why? Why did my husband have to die? The Senator must have been one of the good guys who could not be turned or bought.... I feel he had evidence about the link between the Illuminati, the F.B.I. and the death of President Kennedy; as for Saul, he was simply dispensable.

I was officially told that the probable outcome of the enquiry would be pilot error and to prepare for that.... Even though the aircraft went down in the dense forest areas of Allegheny National Park, N.Y. State in dreadful stormy weather, which continued for another two weeks and hampered the search. The plane was enroute from Cleveland, Ohio, to New York City.... Why wasn't I more suspicious six months ago when Saul was head hunted to pilot and not co- pilot. This was too early after he had trained on this new smaller aircraft, plus the huge salary he was offered is also unusual.... *I always knew someone sinister had set this up, so Saul could be used and disposed of in this way.*

My Mom flew over from Zurich, but I only wanted my Oma and Jono. It must have hurt Mom that I didn't need her, but she stayed on and helped with practical things like meals and looking after Jono....During the search I had a lot of phone calls and visitors, everyone was trying to be positive but I knew Saul was dead and I just wanted the plane found.... It was a harrowing two weeks.

I wondered then why Philip hadn't flown over to see me. He told me later that he had been doing his compulsory military service and wanted to complete it. As he said he decided there and then to come to university in Los Angeles for the next three years, to be near me. He knew he said, that my grieving process would be a long .... How wise my brother is at only eighteen, bless him.

I found it difficult to see Saul's parents, as they had lost their beloved son and Jono was all they had left of him.... We couldn't comfort each other, and his younger brothers were also naturally devastated. They had lost their big brother, the one who always looked out for them.

Saul came through (in spirit) and gave me the co-ordinates to find the plane. He told me that it was sabotaged and he could not control it. And when I insisted the helicopter search that area after the clouds had finally lifted, there it was.... He also told me that he was sorry, but I wondered what for....

Saul confirmed for me that Mc Call did have some information with him that he'd been compiling about the link between the Illuminati, the F.B.I. and the assassination of J.F. Kennedy; just as I suspected.... He also said that there were plots afoot to assassinate Kennedy's brother, Senator Robert Kennedy, plus the Cuban President Fidel Castro....

Of course, news of the crash was in all the newspapers and on the television. It was just awful and when it came to light who my grandfather was, it was also announced that I had obviously inherited his psychic abilities by locating the aircraft.... Which brought me even more publicity as the media focused on this for some reason, which added to my distress.... My Oma was so angry about that.

Uncle William decided to employ a nanny/ housekeeper for me called Ruby. Ruby was a thirty- five year old Mexican woman who was very kind, practical and unflappable and Jono adored her. As poor Oma was worn out. Carmen had recently left us to get married and Mom had decided to go home a week after the funeral and return in three months- time she said.

My Dad and brothers came over for the funeral with my cousins Christian and Isobel. Philip told me he is enrolled and moving to L.A. to study, which at least was some good news. I am looking forward to having him close by.

September 1st

Oma has suggested that I continue with my studies, and I've decided she is right. I need to keep my mind occupied. I'm also concerned that my old problem had resurfaced.... As a couple of Saturday nights on consecutive weekends only a month after the funeral I told my Oma I was staying with Rita and Hank, to have a break.... Instead, I went to a bar got drunk and picked up any guy who was basically, up to the task of fucking my brains out all night in a cheap motel.... Fortunately, no one found out but Oma knew something was amiss with me, more than just grief.

September 30th

Like Philip I enrolled at U.C.L.A. in the fall, as a fulltime student. Philip is now living on campus and studying sound engineering. He is keen to get into the music or movie indestry he said much to the disappointment of our dad. Mom though, is a bit more understanding about his career choice as she knows Philip is not cut out for a career in banking.

I have decided to study for a degree in social services, to try to do some good in this world. Part of my studies the first semester in psychology involves addictions I read.... I should be able to relate to that as I am concerned about my need to be promiscuous.... Plus, I am still grieving so much, it is even worse than when I lost my dear Poppa.

1968

I shall recall this year as best I can....

My Oma and Ruby mainly saw to Jono as I still lived with them. Fortunately, Oma had a big enough house to accommodate us all, plus Saul's parents still lived next door. So, Jono had plenty of carers as I fully admit that during this period, I was not a very good mother.

I was fortunate that I didn't need to work due to Saul's life insurance, as I still wouldn't take any money off my parents or grandparents. I did however let Saul's parents buy me a car.... My parents gave me a generous allowance anyway after I was widowed which I hadn't touched. But then I started to dip into it, to pay for expensive recreational drugs, unfortunately.

I could have attended university, studied and still had plenty of time for Jono, but I was too busy being wild.... Some may have called it the 'first year crazies' which is not uncommon after the emotional upheaval of separation due to death or divorce. But it was more complicated than that, I know it also had something to do with what happened to me at that fateful Rothschild party.

I was by now a longhaired, braless, flower power hippie, who regularly went to anti- Vietnam rallies. I smoked pot but to be honest I preferred other drugs, the ones that enhanced my sexual arousal like cocaine, as I was into free love.... I knew I was beautiful with a beautiful body which I shared with many men, thanks to the new contraceptive pill, plus some women. Before that I had spent a few months picking up men in bars, having one- night stands, sometimes with two men in tow as one usually couldn't last the distance and satisfy me when I was high.

After that I moved on to group sex orgies and was often the one who instigated these. I chose people who I found sexually attractive then arranged a venue and paid for the drugs and drink out of my parents' account.... I think to spite them.... This wonton behaviour went on for about fourteen months.... I refused to tie myself down to just one boyfriend.... None of the men I slept with would have been any good for me anyway. *Thank heavens this was before the Aids epidemic really took hold.*

I know Philip and my Oma were very worried about me during this period. They weren't happy with the way I looked, or the fact that I stayed out every weekend; they also knew I was taking drugs.... And that was just the half of it.... I realised at the time that I was very mixed up but didn't know how to shed my demons.... I literally saw them and the devil and hell, when I was taking drugs, which opened a portal to the dark energies for me of which were sexual.

I feel very ashamed of myself when I look back now and wish I'd been stronger or sought help.

1969

Recap:

Fortunately for me, this was the year I met Sam Winchester and his friends. Now he really was my saviour.... When I first met Sam, I literally saw the light shining out of him, as he personified good-ness, kindness and virtue.... Even though he was a direct descendant of the Winchester repeating rifles founder, whose kin was responsible for taming the west with their rifles. Which meant they had bucket loads of blood on their hands.... But Sam hated guns and was opposed to our gun laws, he abhorred violence and didn't think our cops should be armed, as was the case in the U. K. New Zealand and Norway he said.... Sam was a kind and beautiful soul and we met and simply fell in love.

I met Sam through Priscilla Barr, from my psychology class. She and I got chatting after I'd presented a paper on 'promiscuity'.... I wrote that women who are sexually abused by a family member or friend in a position of trust, can in some cases lead them into prostitution. I did a lot of research on this, and interviewed five L.A. Hookers, who let me name them and quote them. They all use professional names anyway.... Needless to say, my paper raised a few eyebrows with my tutors, also because of its explicit content.

Priscilla asked me over to her house one night to meet her group of friends who were all at U.C.L.A. One of whom was Sam Winchester a Journalism student who was two years my junior as were all her group of friends.... Obviously, they had not heard about the wild Sophia West....

Strangely I clicked immediately with this group. They reminded me of the group of friends I would have had if I'd stayed at school, gained my high school diploma and attended university. And never gone to the U.K. and attended that fateful Rothschild party.... They were all bright, lovely fresh faced kids, who didn't take drugs, but who still liked to drink a bit and have fun.... So, Sam Winchester did tame the West, namely me, but without the use of one rifle, which was ironic.

Sam and his friends were all Christians but open-minded fortunately. This was tested on our first major spring break when we all decided to go away together in Priscilla's boyfriend Alan's VW Kombie van.... Sam had arranged for us to stay in the 'Winchester mystery house' over Easter. They all thought it would be a hoot, as it was supposed to be very haunted.... I did not warn them about my psychic abilities, but they were soon to find out.

Many believe that psychic energy is sexual energy, the Indians called it prana. I had been studying this recently and immersing myself in some of its practises. So much so that my sexual appetite had diminished with meditation, prayer, connecting with my guides and letting spirit back into my life.... That plus God of course which is what I did with this group of beautiful young people.

Sam never complained about what I taught him in the sack, and he was a quick learner after being practically a virgin when we met. I trained him how to pleasure a woman which I'm sure would hold him in good stead in the future.

Sam's great- great Uncle, was William Wirt Winchester, and his eccentric widow Sarah Winchester had taken thirty-six years to build the quirky mansion in San Jose, California where we all stayed. She had no surviving children so she'd used her immense fortune to build this huge rambling house.... It had staircases that went nowhere and never- ending rooms; well, there were a hundred and sixty.

So convinced was Sarah that she was haunted by the ghosts of hundreds of people who had been killed by Winchester rifles that she had builders working seven days a week, day and night, hammering and sawing to supposedly drown out any paranormal activity.... She also never slept in the same bedroom consecutively, of which there were forty.... The Winchester house, was originally built on four levels and had floating foundations which is how it had survived a major earthquake in 1906.... It was indeed a fascinating place.

Sam had arranged for us to stay at the mansion the entire Easter break, even though it was open to the public for certain hours, two of those days. The rest of the time we were free to enjoy the house and the surrounding area.... The caretakers lived off- site, so we four couples were alone there for five whole nights.... They thought we were all quite mad.

Sam was the name- sake of an earlier ancestor Samuel Croft Winchester who was involved in the Salem witch trials of 1693. Although, apparently, he was fair and tried to save as many as he could. Even so, nineteen were hanged after being tortured to confess and one died under torture. How barbaric this could have been me, Poppa or Oma if we'd lived back then.

On the first night Priscilla and Allan picked the wrong bedroom on the most haunted floor, the third, as he was pushed out of bed, and she had her hair pulled.... They were so freaked- out and came and slept on our bedroom floor so the next day we found them a room near us.

From the moment we walked into the mansion, I felt a strong negative female presence that did not want us there, except for Sam of course, as he was kin.... Over the stay I saw the spirit of Sarah Winchester several times dressed in her widow weeds wagging her finger at me or pointing to the exits. There were plenty of other spirits present as well that she had invited in. Some had huge gapping wounds or the backs of their heads blown off, it was quite macabre. I saw no red Indians, even though Winchester rifles would have killed thousands.... This was because they are a very spiritual people who are helped to the after- life by their ancestors. They tend not to stay earth- bound unless guarding their sacred territory, unlike the other spirits there.

On the second night we decided to play the Ouija board and the glass went flying around spelling out messages for us all, stating our names even.... It was saying 'get out' and 'leave or else' which freaked everyone out except for me of course....

So, I decided to show my friends what I could do as we sat in a circle the following night and asked the spirit of Sarah to join us which she apparently did, as she possessed me.... I don't know what transpired but the others said that my voice and body language changed and I answered their many questions as to how, when, and why she had built the house, in a strong Connecticut accent. I told Sam things only he knew about the family that he had never disclosed to me or anyone else in the room.... He was absolutely stunned, he told me afterwards.

Of course, everyone was amazed but even more freaked-out after that and no one would go anywhere alone anymore not even to use one of the fifteen bathrooms.

We spend hours exploring the house together and ran coloured string so we wouldn't get lost just as the caretakers had suggested. We often found it had been mysteriously broken.... I was good at finding us a way out though, especially as I had Sarah Winchester pointing to the exits. I recall we lived on eggs, baked beans, coffee, tinned fruit and beer for that long weekend and with being so scared there was a lot of nervous farting going on, which made us all laugh. Needless to say we stopped on the way home and gorged ourselves on burgers, fries and cokes.

We talked about it for weeks afterwards and although no one saw what I did they sensed spirts with cold patches of air and saw dark shapes.... I wished I'd been able to conjure up images for them like Poppa could, even so, I was impressed that I had obviously channelled Sarah Winchester, as were my friends, of course.

1969

September 10th

To learn more about myself, or my gifts rather, which so far, I had spent most of my life trying to ignore. I decided to spend my second summer break from university at 'Lily Dale' in New York State, or 'Silly Dale' or 'Spooksville' as it is sometimes called. I felt I could really reconnect with my Poppa if I went, as I was told that Clarence R. Smyth was still talked about and held in high esteem there. And photographs of him still adored public places such assembly halls, where he'd done demonstrations of clairvoyance.

Poppa had enjoyed spending time at Lily Dale with like- minded people Oma said, as it's always had the largest congregation of Spiritualist residents in the world apparently. Nowadays it is not like it was in its hey- day, which was before Poppa's time even, in the early 1900s, when it had a formal ballroom, a ferris-wheel and a bowling alley. And a lot of the pretty cottages were built then on the 126 acres of Spiritualist owned land next to the beautiful Lake Cassadaga. No individual can own a section but only lease it, plus to build or buy a house you must be a practising spiritualist.

In Poppa's day, he, Edgar Cayce and Jack Berry were the most famous psychics in America. Berry lived permanently in Lily Dale on Second Avenue and it is said that the famous busty blonde actress Mae West used to come and visit him there when she wanted advice on her career. Poppa had told me he met Mae West once whilst working as a stage designer in New York and said she was a very sexy woman who'd had him quite tongue tied.... She was in no way related to my late husband's family then who are all quite prudish.

As it happened, I suggested to Oma that we should take a break from the hot Californian Summer as she finds the heat draining. She suggested that we visit Poppa's cottage which she still owned at Lily Dale, in N.Y. state. Her agent had written to her that it was in desperate need of attention and could no longer be leased.

Now I don't recall Oma or Poppa ever talking about Lily Dale or a cottage which is strange as I already knew this is where we should go. Why? Because I had just had writing on my bedroom wall telling me to, which had me confused as to what it meant until Oma mentioned the place.... Oma said she had never visited Lily Dale much as she found the psychic energy there overpowering and had trouble sleeping. Not so for Poppa, it had the opposite effect on him apparently and re-energised him.

Of course, it was much closer proximity wise when they had lived in New York. For us from Los Angeles it was a cross -country flight to New York then a seven- hour drive, so we would have to hire a car. But we decided to go anyway, and I planned to enrol in as many classes as I could fit in during our stay.

So far, I had managed to compartmentalise my life well and I did open- up my psychic box on occasion. Although I saw the most spirits when I was drifting off to sleep and my guard was down. Some were strangers and were lost and searching for someone, others were deceased relatives of mine or of people I knew wanting me to pass on messages to their loved ones.... So, I decided once and for all that I should immerse myself in all this psychic stuff and see what I could really pull out of the bag.

I always had a lot of spirits with me as a child and could levitate and move objects with their help. But I had worked very hard over the years to shut them out, one by one, on a daily basis so most had moved on to other more willing mediums. That is except for my most devoted guides being Gretel who was German, and Doris who was English; both were related to me they told me clairaudiently. Oma told me that she remembered an Aunt Gretel on her mother's side, a spinster.

Poppa had told me the renowned author Sir Arthur Conan Doyle, whom he knew, thought this was how the famous magician Harry Houdini had worked, with the aid of spirit. Houdini however denied this emphatically and went even further as he became a great debunker of mediums.... He even wrote a book about it naming these so called frauds. My Poppa's name was mentioned, but he got off quite lightly he said compared to most. Sir Arthur Conan Doyle and Harry Houdini eventually fell out over their conflicting beliefs, Poppa said.

I found out that Houdini had visited Lily Dale more than once, which had most people locking their doors and refusing to read for him, because of this.... Even though Houdini had heard his dead mother's voice once when she had told him which way to swim after he'd fallen through ice and was trapped underneath. This had saved his life at that time, but he was still surprisingly a sceptic.

To work at Lily Dale as a medium over the busy summer season, you must pass a test. This involves doing a private reading for three of the board members, then a demonstration of clairvoyance for the entire board. Oma said it was political and often gifted mediums did not pass the test as it was a bit of a closed circle. Even so, there are usually up to thirty-six mediums working the summer season in Lily Dale. This is when the place swells by the thousands, with psychic tourists. The Lily Dale board had been sending Oma letters for a few years now requesting that she sell Poppa's cottage to another medium, but as she was still practising in California as a respected Tarot-card reader she didn't feel she had to. Oma only leased it over the summer as accommodation was scarce then, for the rest of the year it stood empty.... Mind you Oma is not really a practising spiritualist, she calls herself a 'New Ager' and embraces other esoteric ideas now, as well as Spiritualism. I had a brilliant idea to help my Oma out. I asked four of my student friends to come and earn some money.... I knew Tim and Frankie were handy with tools and Darla and Kimmy, their girlfriends were good at painting and gardening they'd said.... I was pleased when they all jumped at the chance, even though it meant a long cross- country drive. They said it would be an adventure and brought tents to pitch on our site; I think they wanted some privacy.

I helped where I could with the painting, but I was busy doing workshops as most were held during the day. When they were at night, I would work during the day.... Oma and Ruby were wonderful, they did all the shopping, cleaning- up and cooked us all delicious meals.

Jono went every day to the summer camp so that he could be with other children. They did swimming, canoeing and played lots of competitive games which he adored. The big kids really took Jono under their wing and he made a lot of new friends.

Sam Winchester, my boyfriend, came to visit for two weeks. He didn't need to do paid work coming from a wealthy family, nor did Priscilla and Alan. These were all the group of friends I had made through Sam who I went to the Winchester haunted house with last Easter. Priscilla and Alan were so freaked- out by what they had experienced there, that they would never have come to Lily Dale anyway. But the others were interested in 'spooky' things now, and had psychic readings in their free time.

We all worked hard. Well, everyone else did more than me and in six weeks the place was ready to be leased again with the agent. Oma was most happy to pay my friends as they had done a great job of painting the inside and the outside of this quaint two- story cottage. It had nice proportions and generous verandas, but the ornamentation was way too fussy like most of cottages in Lily Dale. So the boys removed some of the timber filigree from the front of the building before they painted it. I decided it should be painted white inside and out, with the outside having green trims. I then got the floor- boards sanded and re-varnished by a local tradesman, and had olive green carpet fitted in the four bedrooms. I also bought new rugs for the living areas.... The boys managed to install new bathroom fittings and kitchen appliances; they really were a handy pair.

Oma and I went shopping in Buffalo, which is an hour away by car. We scored some real bargains, as the cottage also needed new sofas, mattresses, bedding and curtains. Oma and I sewed the new curtains.... I recall this as such a happy time. I think because I felt it was my home as Oma let me make all the decisions and at age twenty-three I had never had my own home.

Sam was happy and did a lot of yard work whilst he was there, cutting down old trees and chopping them up for firewood and then doing the heavy spade work in the garden for the girls. He was a country boy from Connecticut after all, albeit one who didn't like guns or hunting.

I felt re- charged with all the psychic energy around me. Plus having Oma, Ruby, Jono, Sam and the companionship of my friends, I decided that Lily Dale was a happy place for me to visit.... I wasn't sure though, if Oma still wanted to keep the cottage. She had loved Poppa so much and it must have been hard for her to listen the locals talking about him constantly, him and Edgar Cayce. To them there is no death, or sadness around it. Loved ones have just stepped into another dimension.... When I finally got around to asking Oma, she said she would keep the cottage, but only if I could convince the board that we were both spiritualists and that I was the next generation of a practising mediums.... I said I would try but I wasn't prepared to do 'the test' that first summer.

I found out that Lily Dale had banned 'physical mediumship' in the 1940s in public places because of my Poppa, as most of the other so-called physical mediums were debunked as frauds. But Poppa was the real deal.... He could levitate, play musical instruments, move objects and make spirit faces and hands appear with the aid of spirits of course. He could also conjure up images where a psychic footprint had been left, this usually involved something traumatic but not always.

Lily Dale was literally inundated with spirit people, from the early settlers who wandered the streets to the red Indian braves who guarded the lake edge carrying tomahawks. I found the city of York in England very haunted also when I visited there, as are many parts of London of course. In York I psychically saw a group of Roman soldiers marching up the street at chest height, because that is where the road would have been back then.

Most historic places are haunted world-wide let's face it. I met some of my Rothschild Jewish ancestors at the wailing wall in Jerusalem the one time I visited. They even told me who they were.

No one in Lily Dale has ever been able to do what my Poppa could, conjure up psychic images or footprints. Although Poppa mainly went to Lily Dale to re-charge and often kept a low profile when there Oma said, just as I wanted to do, I'd decided. I wanted to meditate next to that beautiful lake and just 'be', but that would have to wait until my next visit.

I did really well in all my classes and workshops,' and it was pretty obvious to others in the group that I was already a gifted medium, which had everyone abuzz, that I was the new 'find'.... Most people were nice and said I had obviously inherited my grandfather's gifts and they expected great things from me.... Some were mean and tried to catch me out, but no one is 100% accurate, 70% is excellent which I achieved. I was very good at psychometry, which is when you do a reading from the vibrations off something metal worn on the person, like jewellery or eyeglasses.... I told one lady that her husband, whose watch I held, was only truly happy when he was riding his beloved horses. The rest of the time he was moody and difficult, she said this was true. Another lady gave me a wedding ring and I described her maternal grandmother Emily's, dining room. I said she was her happiest when cooking for family and friends which her granddaughter said was correct; plus, other information about her abusive father which I won't record.

We all had the most wonderful summer despite the hard work and Jono had a huge fuss made of him. So many mediums said he was 'special' and had an important job to do in this life. Saul came through one medium and told me that I had to be very careful who I got close to, and Jono in the future.... He said dark energies would seek us out, but added that he approved of my friends at the moment. I agreed with this. Another medium could see Jono entering politics one day, as he was a natural leader, she said, who will almost hypnotise people with his words.... I've noticed this about Jono that he has a way of getting other children to do what he wants and with very little persuasion, plus, he has Poppa's charisma. This has me thinking about Grosspappi Rothschild's prediction for him and is the reason I must keep Jono away from any future Rothschild influence.

Oma never reads the Tarot cards for me, she told me I have my own abilities and do not need her guidance in this way. She did tell me though that I didn't really need to do any workshops, all I had to do was work with myself.... Most Lily Dale mediums told me this, which caused a bit of envy from the other attendees. Even so, I enjoyed all the workshops, but I must admit I already knew intuitively everything they taught .... But it has been the start of some good friendships for me, although mainly with the locals.

Whilst I was there, I had a weekly chakra balancing. I was told my base chakra was too open and I needed to keep it in balance (to curb my promiscuity). This was no surprise to me. To be honest I felt happier and more balanced at Lily Dale, than in L.A.

That summer I decided Sam would make a good husband, and step-father. He was kind, decent and very patient with Jono, if possibly a bit young yet at only twenty- one.... But although I loved Sam and felt that I could live with him as he was so easy to be around, he didn't make me feel that I simply couldn't live without him.... He was a head choice rather than a heart choice. I knew that as I didn't want to be hurt badly again, like when I lost Saul. I never wanted to feel that pain of loss again, as I truly loved Saul and didn't appreciate how much until he was gone.... Sam said he understood and that it didn't matter, but I knew it did. It wasn't fair on him, he deserved a woman who loved him completely and I always held back. But I was faithful to Sam which was a tall order for me plus he did settle me down.

Before we went back to L.A., Sam and I visited New York City. My parents had recently moved back there to live for Dad's work and so Alexander could attend an American university. Sam and I chose not to stay with them though, but we did go there two nights for dinner.

We so enjoyed the stimulation of this major intellectual city with its great theatre, museums, architecture and art galleries.... Sam knew New York fairly- well, being from Connecticut north of there as his family used to travel down a lot he said. He had just been home the two- weeks prior to coming to us at Lily Dale....Why Sam chose to study in L.A. instead of New York, he never really said, perhaps he had wanted to get away from his family connections as well.

Of course, Oma, Ruby and Jono came to New York too and they did stay with my parent's....

Alex told us the first night we were there for dinner that he had applied to the Harvard Business School, which is four hours away by train, so he would have to live on campus, plus, NYU (New York University) .... So far, he had been accepted into NYU where surprisingly his tuition was free. Of course he is studying Commerce and Law to follow our father into the family banking business.... I was disappointed that he still acts like a spoilt brat.... I can't relate much to Alexander, never have done, not like I can with Philip. But Sam managed to engage him in conversation. He told me to cut Alex some slack. Perhaps I am a bit hard on him. Alex is very tall now, way too skinny and dark like father, he looks like a Rothschild.... Philip and I are fair and favour our mom and Oma more in looks.

Dad told us that New York was beginning to experience some financial issues which was starting to affect the Rothschild & Co. investment bank. That is why he needs to be here, he said.... I felt this was only the start of things to come and none of it was good.... So, I told him this.... And he actually listened for once. Then he spoiled it by saying that he couldn't understand why we all chose to waste our summer renovating an old cottage that should probably just be pulled down.... I decided that dad would never understand a lot of things about me, but Mom was really trying to connect with me now and of course they both adored Jono. They were impressed also I could tell that I appeared to have landed myself a Winchester....

Mom was in the throes of renovating the apartment which was the same one I had lived in as a child. It had never been sold. It was Art Deco in style and therefore quite opulent; nothing like the quaint cottage we had just left in Lily Dale, which I preferred.

Of course, there is the le Gout Rothschild style which is a detailed and elaborate style of interior decoration and living. It was established by the wealthy late 18th Century European Rothschilds which was then copied and still now is by the wealthy of N.Y. city, Newport and Rhode Island, such as the Vanderbilts and the Rockefellers even. But nowadays it is less opulent. Indeed, the Rothschild's French Chateaus still have those heavy textile fabrics such as damask, brocade and velvet, plus gilding, with parquet flooring, antique wood panelling, Louis XIV - XVI furnishings and suits of armour. But it is not my taste at all....

And a relative by marriage, Pauline de Rothschild, was on the best dressed list hall of fame for that year 1969, the only woman along with the likes of Douglas Fairbanks junior, Cary Grant and the Queen's husband

Prince Philip.... Mom liked to tell us these stories. I must admit that Pauline de Rothschild was quite an impressive lady though with a colourful past who did have amazing style and presence and whom I met on more than one occasion at Rothschild functions.

Alexander was just the same, after telling us about himself, he sat glumly observing us all. Surprisingly he was very patient with Jono though Oma told me later and taught him the rudiments of chess whilst they were staying.

Jono is only three and a half but because he is bright and tall for his age, people think he is older. Sam and I took him to the zoo and roller-skating which was such fun. I noticed that wherever we went people took his photo and never asked if they could.... One lady said she could see a light shining from him and another said he stood out amongst the children, and it wasn't just his blond hair.... These comments got me thinking that Jono may indeed be special.

On the flight home Sam said he was surprised as he hadn't realised that I was a member of THE wealthy Rothschild family. But then why should he, as I had never told him and even said my maiden name was Smyth, for some reason.

1970

Recap:

In the fall of 1970, I decided to move to New York to live.... Oma would never leave the Los Angeles climate now or James and Patty whom she adores; they are still at school being so much younger. Not that Uncle William and Aunt Selma would ever think of leaving California either, they love the laid back lifestyle, as does Philip, who is in his last year at U.C.L.A....He is mixed flatting now so is no longer living on campus, by mixed I mean males and females, which has our mom concerned.

Philip loves L.A. he is still studying to be an audio engineer and has already made contacts within the thriving music industry there. The last thing he wanted was a boring office job like banking, he said.... I'm concerned that he may be experimenting with drugs as he is quite moody and doesn't spend much time with the family now.... Oma said to leave him be, he is a young man just trying to find his place in the world. Although she agreed he was probably smoking marijuana, but hoped it wasn't anything stronger.... Not that I can talk, with my past.

I knew back then that I had a weakness for cocaine, so I just had to stay away from it and anyone associated with it which unfortunately included Philip's music scene. He had understood though.

Our cousins in Switzerland certainly don't have boring office jobs nor would they be experimenting with recreational drugs, being athletes. Christian is a champion speed skater who represented Switzerland at the last winter Olympics no less and his sister Isobel is a single figure skater, but she missed selection at the national trials; Uncle William is most proud of their accomplishments. Indeed he was a successful baseball player in his day and even played for the Brooklyn Bears. Both my cousins are also studying Sports Management at Zurich University, which was something new. Uncle William said that they need careers to fall back on one day. They are my Smyth cousins not the wealthy Rothschild- side. Who knows what those six silly creatures are doing, looking for husbands I'll bet. Two are engaged already, so I suppose these family weddings will be coming up soon.... Marlena, my favourite Rothschild-side cousin, is studying Art History at Zurich University and is in no hurry to marry she wrote me. She is the only one I correspond with.

Anyway, after I graduated university, I decided I needed a major change as my relationship with Sam had sadly run its course.... One day he suddenly appeared nervous around me, then he became quite aloof and finally secretive, so I suspected he was seeing someone else.... Then he broke it off.... Sam was very emotional and crying, he said it would never work, which was strange as the month prior he had introduced me to his family and seemed very serious about us, like he was getting ready to propose.... But then he changed. It wasn't his parent's influence I'm sure, as I got on well with them both, plus his younger brother and two sisters.... Needless- to- say I was heartbroken. I also felt at the time that Sam wasn't being honest with me and for once my intuition was letting me down as I was hurt and felt he simply didn't love me anymore.

Of course, with losing Sam I lost our group of friends who were originally his friends, as they took his side.... I was pretty- gutted. And what made it even worse was that no one could really tell me why I'd been dumped.... I had wondered if someone at university had told them about my wild past, but then, they were not judgemental people.... I've only just been able to write this down as I've been so upset.... I really loved Sam and was beginning to think that he was the perfect man for me.

1971

January 16th

Jono is a bright inquisitive child, so when we got to New York I enrolled him in 'The Dalton School'. This is a private school founded in 1919 by Helen Pankhurst, as a children's university school. I liked the fact that the children were taught to think there, and it was not just rote learning.... I also let my dad pay for the tuition fees, as he can afford it.

Jono did six months at pre-school and then at five started in first grade. He could already read a bit by then and add up numbers in his head. Plus, he had learnt how to play chess, beating us all now except for Alexander, of course. Jono could also swim thanks to his time spent at camp in Lily Dale, not that he would be swimming much in New York.

My dad respected my decision to not send Jono to a Jewish school, even though he had been baptised into the Jewish religion and circumcised at three days old. That was one decision his late father Saul had made for him.... Again I don't know where I fit in any more religion-wise, I'm certainly not a practising Jewess or really a Christian Spiritualist. I think I am like Oma a New Ager, only now agnostic, as when I lost Sam and our Christian friends, I seemed to lose God as well.

June 12th

I am twenty-five years old with a degree in social welfare starting my first full time job helping the job- less and home-less of New York City.... No doubt my psychic abilities will come in handy here. I had to wait for a fulltime position with (HRA) The Human Resources Administration to come up and had been working there as a volunteer.... How fortunate that a paid position became available so soon right here in

Manhattan.... My dad said that no-one would ever take me seriously in that industry if they knew I was a Rothschild. To which I replied that it was fortunate then that my name was 'West'.

New York is surprisingly not too an expensive city to live, but I decided to stay with my parents as they had a cook and a maid. Plus, I needed Mom's help look to after Jono.... I had not lived with my parents fulltime since I was aged twelve, of course my mom was delighted.

I recall that I did not want to live on my own with Jono as I felt nervous and vulnerable. This was because of the underlying threat that the Illuminati posed to me on a subconscious level, back then. I also felt that I was being monitored somehow, even though I notice I don't mention this much.

Of course, I missed my Oma terribly. She flew over for Jono's birthday in May, but it is not the same, although we speak often on the phone. I also missed Sam so much it hurt, plus our group of friends as we used to hang- out so much together....

Saul's parents were naturally upset too, when I relocated, but told me that they understood. I promised them I would fly home for each winter break. I can't say for Christmas, as they don't celebrate it. But they do celebrate Hanukkah, the Jewish festival of lights for eight days around that time, which is nice for Jono....They have never admonished me for not raising Jono in their Jewish faith, still I hate to hurt them as they are good people. But I just had to get away from Los Angeles for a while, after the loss of Saul and then Sam.

Of course, I never told Saul's parents that he was not Jonathon's father and because physically he was so like me no-one ever questioned it.... Saul's two brothers found out the truth years later, after their parents had both passed but accepted it well. To them Jonathon was their nephew and they loved him and were very proud of him no matter what they said and have always remained close.

Jono and I spent that first long school summer holiday at Lily Dale to escape the city. He joined the same kids at camp he'd befriended from the two previous years, and I worked as a medium. I hung my shingle out and did one-on-one readings in the front parlour. I used psychometry, as everyone usually has something metal that they wear and leave their vibrations on. I found that accurate information came easily to me this way.

My employers couldn't pay me much as a trainee social worker, so they were happy for me to have the summer school holidays off with Jono, they said. This was amazing as I had just started in my new job and was still learning the ropes.

Oma and Ruby came over to join us for the first three weeks and I did 'the test' which I passed with such flying colours that they could not refuse me. Then Oma gifted me the cottage legally.... I was now officially a property owner, which felt good.

I found most of the people in Lily Dale surprisingly down to earth and genuine, there were a few eccentrics of course, but they were pretty harmless. I also found real friendship there. Some work- shop attendees were the ones with the big egos, who thought they were the next 'new age guru'.... In saying that, there were psychic tourists who were looking to worship a spiritual guru, to hang on their every word and put on a pedestal. This was less healthy I thought, as they were also looking for someone to make all their decisions for them, who they could then blame for getting it wrong taking no responsibility for their own actions.... Some of the Psychics brought into this ego trip, but not me or any of my friends.

I could have owned a home earlier, both my father and my paternal grandfather had offered to buy me an apartment in Los Angeles, then New York, but I didn't want to be beholden to them. I see now that I had stubborn foolish pride, but admittedly as I have said, I didn't want to live on my own.

1972

August 30th

I am now twenty-six years old. Oma, Ruby and Philip flew over for my birthday and then Oma and Ruby came back and spent three weeks at Lily Dale with us again in July. I was only allowed four weeks off this summer now, being a fully- fledged social worker.

This year has been fairly uneventful, so far. I have dated a lot of men, most of whom I have slept with, but none I want to remember especially, except for that dishy actor Harrison Ford. Another actor Elliot Gould is an interesting man but eight years older than me; both are Jewish of course.

I am enjoying my work, but still feel a bit lost within myself.... My employers have insisted I now do all the fundraising speeches to the business leaders, plus the rich and famous at our charity events so I have somehow become their poster girl.... This is how I get to meet these well known actors. I've had to get a fashion house to loan me beautiful evening dresses for these occasions, I can't afford them on my salary. Fortunately, I am still a model size 4....I am often photographed and appear in the newspapers regularly and so far, no one has mentioned I'm a Rothschild.... Mom and Dad are delighted of course, confident now that a wealthy man will soon 'rescue me' from my lonely life of widowhood....

Jonathon is a bright student and gifted in maths. He also has the Smyth male charm and is popular at school. He is always chosen as a team leader and to play the lead in the junior productions being a confident speaker.... He is showing strong leadership skills, at quite a young age. As I notice the other kids just let him make all the decisions.... Saul would have been most proud.

September 15th

I've decided that I need to get my act together and stop sleeping with men that often I don't even like, as I will also be getting a bit of reputation. So, I went to see a Therapist, a Dr Turner, about my need to be promiscuous and he suggested hypnotherapy.... I agreed, so he put me under with deep mind and body relaxation, and then he regressed me.... I immediately went back to that fateful night at that Rothschild party. I got so distressed recalling it and was hyperventilating so Dr Turner brought me back. He said this was a good start and scheduled me for another appointment, but I never went.... With what I recalled though I was becoming more and more convinced that Laurent de Rothschild was Jono's biological father.... And I was feeling angry at him.... Then out of the blue he called in to see me at work.... It was most uncanny.

Laurent looked so dashing and out of place when he turned up at my work, in his white button- down shirt, grey trousers, brogues and well-cut navy blazer. He told me he was in town for business. He then insisted on taking me out to dinner in front of my work colleagues which left me no choice but to accept.... I said I needed to go home and change but he said I was fine the way I was. In contrast to him I was wearing a stock work blouse with slacks, no makeup and had my hair in a pony- tail.... I thought I would have felt angry seeing him.... but I didn't.... Quite the opposite in fact.

Over dinner in a little Italian bistro I knew, I told Laurent I was having therapy.... He seemed surprised by this.... So I decided to bite the bullet and tell him that I believed he was Jono's biological father.... To which he swore on his life, he wasn't, but said he could tell me no more at present. And although Laurent was charming and attentive that evening, he was not flirtatious. He only kissed me good night like a brother would, when we said goodbye. But he did say though that he would keep in touch.... This had me confused as to why he felt an obligation to, if he was not Jono's biological father.... I was also wondering why he had chosen now to come and see me, after all these years.

October 4th

Last night Laurent turned up again at my work and again insisted on taking me out to dinner. But I must have known this time. I had that morning decided to dress in a simple but well-cut navy-blue dress and put on makeup.... I even had a string of pearls in my handbag.

We went to a champagne bar first and then a restaurant he had booked, French of course. Laurent must have been confident that I would say yes.... And like last time he escorted me home, only this time he insisted on coming in to speak to my parents, whom he said he had met a few times in both Zurich and Paris....

Of course, Mom and Dad were delighted to see Laurent again and quizzed me after he had left, hopeful I suppose that he was a suitor.... But I had to dash their hopes. Although Laurent as usual looked very handsome in his beautifully cut French suit, and everyone just stared at us when we walked into the restaurant together.

I don't know why Laurent came to see me again so soon, but then he does have many New York based clients, he said.... Over dinner Laurent asked me if I was still seeing a therapist. I told him I was not.... He was a hard one to read, but again it was like having dinner with an older slightly distant brother. There was none of the chemistry that had been there between us years ago.... This time when he left my parents' place, he did not say he would keep in touch, I'd noticed.... But he did say he was disappointed not to have met Jono who was of course asleep in bed at that hour.

December 2nd

New York is experiencing some difficult times; in fact it is getting to be a terrible place to live. Most U.S. cities are experiencing some form of urban decay, but New York is troubled with an economic collapse, which has led to rising crime.... Middle class New Yorkers are leaving the city for the suburbs in droves, which is also draining the city of much needed tax- payers. There are also mass energy shortages, sanitation strikes and widespread police corruption.... And I know intuitively that things are only going to get worse; this is only the beginning. As a million local manufacturing jobs have also gone, and the city now has well over a million welfare recipients .... This math is never going to add up.

Dad said he is worried that New York City is getting itself into more and more debt, with no real means to re-pay, the now approximant $750 million debt.... And the lay-offs and closures that the new Mayor has implemented so far, have not solved the fiscal problem but only exacerbated other problems.... We are even busier at work and now under a lot of pressure to help all the struggling families to keep a roof over their head and food on the table.

All this has not prevented the opening of the downtown World Trade Centre though, as conceived by David Rockefeller. It has now displaced the Empire State building as the world's tallest building with its impressive twin towers. These are right in the hub of the financial centre in a city experiencing a major fiscal crisis.... How ironic.... Someone should knock them down.

1973

January 6th

We spent a wonderful ten days in Los Angeles, it was so nice to be warm. Saul's parents and brothers made such a fuss of Jono, and I was so happy to spend time with Oma and Philip again. Philip seemed more attentive and relaxed this time. I'm hoping he is no longer taking drugs....

Jono enjoyed participating in the festival of lights with his paternal grandparents, he also had a traditional Christmas with us.... So, this year I was asked a lot of questions about his dad, the West's, their faith and ours; I answered as best as I could.

March 10th

My Mom understandably wants to leave New York, but Dad says he must stay and ride it out. This fiscal crisis is affecting the Rothschild & co investment bank, which he is the chairman of. I'm proud of my Dad I've decided that he hasn't simply cut his losses, bailed out and gone back to Zurich as his father suggested he do.... But instead feels he should stay and help the city if he can, being one of a select committee who are 'in the know'.

I was also naturally suspicious too that my father, like his father was part of the Illuminati. If New York had gone bankrupt who would have benefited? The dollar would have devalued with the largest city in a country with the biggest economy in the world going down. Then gold prices would have gone up significantly....and who would have benefited from this? The Rothschild banks for one with all their gold, plus they set the gold prices daily in England for the world then.... Go figure.

But New York is simply living beyond its means and cannot repay the debt. I kept thinking of my late Poppa, he would have been appalled at the decline of New York, he always loved it, almost as much as his beloved London he'd said.... Maybe New York's first Jewish mayor Abraham Beame, will be able to pull something out of the hat yet; I do hope so.

Mom worries constantly about Dad or Alexander being mugged. For some reason she doesn't seem so concerned about me, possibly because of my intuition. I did witness a man being mugged by two men in central park recently, so I ran over shouting, and fortunately they ran off.... It was a bit of a foolish thing to do.... The victim said he was alright then asked me "where are the two men who were with you?" I said, "what two men?" which had me thinking that I had some manifestation of spirit protecting me, as I have been eyed up and followed more than once walking home, but have always been left alone for some reason.

May 21st

Last night we all went out for Mom and Dad's 28th wedding anniversary to 'Lutece' a beautiful- French restaurant in Lower Manhattan. The menu is entirely in French which we all enjoyed speaking again and we were trying to out- do each other, but Dad was by far the most fluent.... My parents still carry-on like a couple of newly-weds though, which can be a bit embarrassing.... It was wonderful as Philip had just flown in from L.A. it was a lovely surprise, and he is staying until after my birthday. Even Alexander was chatty for once, probably due to the French champagne .... This was one of the most pleasant evenings I have ever spent with my family.

Philip is so happy in L.A and loves being part of the 'happening scene' there he says. Talking to him made me realise that I still miss a lot of things about L.A. It is a young free and sprawling city and I like that you can drive yourself everywhere and don't need to rely on public transport .... As I get taxis everywhere I can't walk or train to in New York, but it gets expensive. But L.A. simply doesn't have the strong publishing or intellectual community that New York has, I feel, or the culture, even if it has taken over the music scene, according to Philip. But it does have the beautiful climate the beaches of course, plus the exciting movie industry.

Even so, I find New York a stimulating place to live and never think of it as dangerous really when I am out and about, as I love to go to the theatre and art galleries and often go on my own. I have my guardian angels to protect me, apparently, plus my intuition.... But there are still too many junkies, homeless people, and beggars around, which should not happen in a first world country like the U.S. Perhaps I am recognised as one of 'the good guys' from my place of work, which may also offer me some protection....

I notice I never mention 'the invisible men' then, as Poppa used to call them, or the Illuminati. I think that by not mentioning them, I was trying to convince myself that my life and that of my son's was not being monitored, but they were. I often saw men in dark suits, usually working in pairs watching us. And sometimes strangers said odd things to me, I think to unsettle me and have me living on edge.... Many mediums had told me over the years that I have an important role in this life, through my children.... Others have said that I was part of a powerful Cartel, one which I could never escape.... Both, of these statements were in fact true.

July 7th

My employers have finally found out, not by me, that I am a Rothschild and that my father is the president of the Rothschild and co. investment bank. And that we reside in a palatial six-bedroom five-bathroom apartment in Manhattan, with spacious reception rooms, staff-quarters and views over Central Park.... So, they have decided that from now-on, my role shall be to use my family connections to organise all the major charity and fundraising events.... which at first, I wasn't very happy about.... Mind you, I have already been their poster girl for about two years now anyway.

I had wondered who had let the cat out of the bag, as I was a very private person. Then it dawned on me that it must have been Laurent, when he visited me again recently, at my work. As he told Suzy the receptionist that he was a Rothschild relation, which was not untrue. But he would not have disclosed the details of my living arrangements, I'm sure. That has come indirectly from one of my parents' staff I feel....

I have decided though that if this is to become my new career then I am glad I had spent the last two years working at the coalface so to speak, seeing what issues face the poor, the homeless,and the junkies.... But what really makes my blood boil, is the wealthy fat cats who live off drug money.... All the misery drugs cause and the lives they destroy.... Plus, the corrupt banks who launder this money. As of course, some who benefit from this trade have prominent family names. *This conviction of mine to expose these people was nearly my undoing as you shall later read.*

August 10th

When I was working as a social worker, I used my psychic intuition to focus help on those who could be saved.... Everyone said I had an uncanny knack of knowing who would succeed given half a chance, but it was more than that. Still, I found that work more frustrating than rewarding and felt my new job may possibly suit me better, because despite everything, I can't fight against who or what I am.... A white girl born into a wealthy family who has always had the love, support and opportunities a lot of people could only dream of even if I have not always accepted them.... And like my brother Philip has always said with my up-bringing and my tall blonde model- like looks at the end of the day I was still a bit of a princess; he is so wise.

But at least I wanted to work. I doubt my Rothschild female cousins sought employment after they finished school or university.... Their only mission was to find themselves suitable husbands, except for Marlena that is. And yes, some have succeeded, but I am not joining my parents next month in Zurich for my Cousin Catherine's wedding.... Her father is a wealthy banker, and she is marrying a wealthy banker; no surprises there. I went to my cousin Helena's wedding last year, that was enough.... And I remember I was oddly stared at then ignored by a man who I thought was Andre de Rothschild. I wasn't certain though as there were many young Rothschild men present and many do share the family resemblance.

August 22nd

I have just seen the movie 'The Godfather' and although it is about an Italian cartel and not the Illuminati.... it's still a confronting movie. It reminds me of the danger I could be in if I stepped out of line.... My Poppa was threatened then he had two attempts on his life that he luckily survived. I was fundraising at a charity dinner recently when a man unknown to me yelled out after I had made my closing speech "why don't you just dip into your family coffers?". And he was rude and aggressive, plus inebriated of course; but it was most embarrassing.

Since I have been in New York I have been dating. These are usually fairly wealthy and well connected men, who already seemed to know that I'm a Rothschild. But I've noticed though that it is all about them and their careers with their big egos. Most do not appreciate a strong woman like me who has a mind of her own and who also likes to control things in bed. So, no-one has lasted very long. And this past year I have hardly slept with anyone, so I am improving.

I have dated Comedian Billy Crystal a few times and although he is charming and amusing, he is a couple of years younger and a couple of inches shorter than me, both of which are noticeable. He is by far the pick of the bunch though, plus

Jewish of course.... At least I don't go around getting drunk and picking up men in bars anymore, I haven't done that for years. But at the moment, I am single and celibate, the latter of which is very difficult for me.... The therapy has helped. *I fail to mention that both Harrison Ford and Billy Crystal were scared off dating me, by heavies. They told me this when I caught up with them at separate functions and both wondered if I had mafia connections or at least over-protective brothers. Billy told me he couldn't take the risk of having his face rearranged, as he was ugly enough.*

September 1st

At short notice, and finally after a six-year engagement, I received an invite to Veronica and Victor's wedding in the U.K. .... Veronica said that Victor was finally ready to marry and have children which was just as well as she was tired of waiting, she wrote me. Victor seemingly had been waiting for his father to die so that he would become Lord Coddington and inherit the estate, but his father was still hale and hearty apparently.

The wedding was to be held in the Anglican Church near Victor's home in Buckinghamshire. And I was surprisingly one of a select group of ten friends who had been asked to join them in France, staying at a beautiful chateau for their honeymoon. How very modern, how could I possibly refuse.... This seemed worlds away now from my chosen life.

Mom and Dad were delighted when I told them and said I should go and have a holiday.... My employers were not so pleased, but they reluctantly agreed to let me have two weeks off. I had to work through Thanksgiving and Christmas, organising meals for the home-less, after I returned though but I always found this most rewarding anyway.

At the wedding it was immediately obvious to me why Veronica and Victor were so keen to have me join their honeymoon party.... They had been coerced, by one Laurent de Rothschild, who's acquaintance Veronica had rekindled a few years ago, she said. Also at the wedding, was model and actress Chrissy Shrimpton, sister of Jean, who grew up on the estate next to Victor and who was now a close friend of Veronica's. Chrissy had split with Mick Jagger years ago.... And these were the only people I knew there, plus Victor's parents and his younger sisters Amanda and Felicity. I had never met Veronica's parents before, I found them a strange pair.

The wedding was sumptuous and the five days I spent at the chateau were wonderful. But the highlight of my holiday was going with Laurent to the surrealist ball, of our distant cousin Marie Helene de Rothschild.... This was held on October 12th at the Chateau de Ferriers, and I was mixing with the who's who of French society.... The famous artist Salvadore Dali was there. Plus, the beautiful actresses Marisa Berenson, who had on a large birdcage hat and Audrey Hepburn who I spoke to about the charming Cecil Beaton whom she then enthused over for the next half an hour. Laurent and I went with papier-mache' headdress props fixed onto our bowler hats and black suits- like Rene Magritte's paintings. It was enormous fun, as everyone thought me a man at first being so tall.

Our hostess disturbingly wore a horned deer's head with pearl tears with a beautiful long evening dress. I'm not sure about our host, what he was going as.... It was all most bizarre.... There were dismembered dolls bodies, skulls and mannequins dressing the ballroom, and black fur lined dinner plates in the dining hall.... I had never seen anything like it.

Laurent was far more attentive to me that night than he had been on our dinner dates in New York or at Veronica and Victor's wedding and the five-day honeymoon.... But I was far less attracted to him now than I was as a girl of nineteen I'd decided.... Even so, when he got me alone in a dark corner, as it had been such a long time since I had been kissed passionately by a man and Laurent was such a good kisser I responded.... He was a hard one to read though, as when he came to see me those three times in New York he had treated me as he would a sister with merely a goodnight peck on the cheek.

I decided to quiz Laurent again about that fateful party nearly eight years ago when I had conceived Jono.... But he kept to the same story.... That he and David Astor had charmed me all evening until I had passed out on a sofa and was carried to bed. He said he had no idea who the man claiming to be Charles Rothschild was....as he didn't recall anyone like that being present. I was being fobbed off again, only this time he did not offer to reveal the truth to me one-day.... I had hoped that he may have had his guard down from drinking French champagne as it tends to loosen the tongue, but he didn't.

Laurent was curious about Jono though and asked me several questions about him, so I produced a small photo that I always carry with me in my wallet.... He said he looked like me and I said that was just as well under the circumstances which he did not comment on. I then told him how bright and popular Jono was which made him smile.

At about ten o'clock after some mingling Laurent asked me if I had ever tired cocaine.... I said I had.... So, with a naughty twinkle in his eye he grabbed my hand, and we went down a long corridor which led to the drug room.... On tables were lines of cocaine.... I knew I shouldn't go anywhere near cocaine, but I wanted information out of him and thought maybe this might be a way to get it.... What foolish thinking.

Laurent expertly snorted one line and suggested I do the same, which I did. Then we both did another line.... He then asked me if I felt like being pleasured, which I said I did, because I knew instinctively that it was not going to be by him.... In fact, I was beginning to have my suspicions about Laurent, the way he dressed and how some men looked at him....that, he may be homosexual. And I'd excited him more tonight I'd decided, because I was dressed as a man. This came with such clarity.... Why, had I not realised this before.... It was the Rothschilds that made him pursue me.

My knees suddenly went weak and my breathing rapid as I knew I was soon going to have very heightened sexual arousal.... Just as I had done years before in the Rothschild mansion and at the drug fuelled sex romps I had organised in my student days.... The trouble with me was that my- problem lay too close to the surface, and I found it impossible to deny.

After the drug room Laurent and I walked into an antechamber where we both undressed and put on robes and eye masks.... We then entered an enclosed balcony with a huge bubbling Jacuzzi already filled with several people who all watched as I disrobed and descended into the tub.... A man of about forty sidled over to me and started to fondle my breasts. Then Laurent came over and kissed me deeply, before moving on to someone else. Another younger man started to kiss and fondle me and I was soon aroused and started to moan.... So, I was led out, towelled down and taken to the next room. I was laid on a bed and one man went down on me, and another gave me his cock to suck, which I did.... Again, the plateau for sexual arousal was very long and I felt like I was in a state of ecstasy for what seemed like ages.

I was conscious that there were other people around me, but I didn't care.... I was then lifted up and leant against a wall where I held onto straps. I was grabbed by the buttocks and penetrated again and again, first by one man until he deflated then by another until I had multiple screaming orgasms which I knew had drawn a small audience....Laurent however was no-where in sight, that much I knew; but I didn't care as no- one else knew me there.

When I awoke the next morning naked in my bed at the Rothschild Chateau, there sleeping besides me fully clothed was Laurent.... He kissed me on the forehead and told me that I was wonderful last night and had taken a pleasurable trip. But I knew it wasn't a drug induced dream, I knew I'd had sex.... But not with him.... Laurent didn't know that part of me which had organised cocaine fuelled orgies as a student, but they were nothing as grand as this.

Laurent and I then showered, dressed and breakfasted. We thanked our hosts and he then drove me to the airport. On the two-hour journey we talked about the wedding, the honeymoon, the Rothschild party and the guests present, but not once about what had happened after we had left the drug room.... He promised to keep in touch.... Again, I wondered why?

December 30th

When I got back to New York I threw myself into my work. And I successfully organised the feeding of thousands of homeless people for Thanksgiving then Christmas.... After which I decided that I was rather good at organising events, dressing up venues, arranging entertainment and not just the glamorous ones.... Of course, these were nowhere near as extravagant as the one thrown by my distant relatives, the French de Rothschild's, that I had just attended. But I still enjoyed getting my hair done and dressing up in beautiful, hired evening gowns. All to convince wealthy New Yorkers to part with their money for a good cause.... I got a buzz out of organising these events and with every successful night I usually found an attractive and willing young waiter to have sex with afterwards.... I never chose a benefactor although I had plenty of offers.

Billy Crystal often worked as a warm-up act at these events, that is how we met, so we hooked up again for a couple of dates.... I loved his Yiddish humour, so like my Poppa's.... No one ever believed that I was one of the social workers at these events and not one of the socialites. Billy took me to a fabulous New Year's Eve party, but I managed to resist the drug room this time, he was not into that anyway.... I was always well behaved around Billy; he was not exposed to my wonton ways.

Surprising a lot of people were not aware of the precarious financial position the city of New York was getting into at-this-time. Well, if they were they were not saying.... I remember this was my last date with Billy, as it was soon after he was warned-off dating me.

1974

January 23rd

As it was the start of a new year and a new year's resolution, I decided to see another therapist. A female this time, and I told her about my sexual fantasies and why I thought I was having them. I described to her what had happened to me that fateful night when I was nineteen, although I never revealed whose house I was in.... I said a part of me was still unsure if it was real or not, because of what I had induced, even though, I did have the physical evidence the next day to suggest it was.... I did not mention to her that this had probably resulted in a child.

The Therapist suggested that I may be a bit of a sexual Walter Mitty. In that my exciting sex life is a fantasy in my head and not real, and that my physical discomfort came from self-abuse. As I had admitted to her that I did I own a vibrator.... In other words, she did not believe me. She also told me that it was not unhealthy to have sexual fantasies. But what I really needed was a happy stable relationship where I felt loved and respected and had regular sex, then I would be fine. Plus, of course I had to stay clear of all drugs.... What else could she say really but it was nice to talk to someone about my problem.

April 13th

My life now seems a world away from Lily Dale, so I have decided to let my cottage out over the summer months with an agent. Jono said he was sad we weren't going this year, but Oma rang to say that she and Ruby would come to visit us all in New York instead for three weeks.... I am still living with my parents, but in the staff quarters now, as none of their staff live with them anymore they come daily instead.... This is better for

Jono and me as we have our own entrance and usually eat our meals on our own now as I have finally learnt how to cook.

(This is a recap of the second half of 1974....as compiled from scribbled journal entries)

After a year in my new position, I was head hunted and offered a job with the Rockefeller Foundation, doing similar work.... managing events and organising fundraisers.... The Rockefeller Foundation has a mixed reputation though. I remember my Poppa mentioning in his journals that this foundation had supported 'The Kaiser Wilhelm Institute of Anthropology, human heredity and eugenics', who conducted eugenics for the third Reich and funded Nazi racial studies.... It was also responsible for giving 800 pregnant woman radioactive iron, without their knowledge, which led to the deaths of three children, amongst other things.... Of course, this was all well in the past.... So, I said I would give their offer some serious thought.... Then something happened to me at the age of not quite twenty- eight, which changed the course of my life again.... I reconnected my acquaintance with the Rothschilds.... Or more importantly the de Rothschilds, during the shiva week of mourning, after the funeral of my Grosspapi in Zurich.

The whole family went over as my grandfather had died suddenly at home of a massive heart attack, which was quite unexpected as he was supposedly a fit and healthy man. Of course, this was an awful shock for my dad.... And as is the Jewish custom, he had to be buried as soon as possible. I had never been close to my paternal grandparents, but I decided to go out of respect for my dad. I also decided to leave Jono at home, so Oma and Ruby flew over from L.A. immediately to be with him.... I felt Jono was too young to attend, plus I did not want him upset or confused as I was not raising him strictly in the Jewish faith.... We did however join my parents for Passover, Hanukkah if we were with Saul's parents and Lent.

Grosspapi's funeral was enormous and very dour. Everyone was wearing black and the men all wore their yarmulkes.... I did not wear black as I had none in my wardrobe, but I did wear a navy dress that covered my knees and shoulders to be respectful, plus a torn black ribbon as did the rest of the family.... I still felt detached from it all like I was merely an observer.

The rabbi who officiated read the eulogy then my dad got up and spoke as did my two brothers. The family then went into Shiva.... Seven days of mourning. During this time, we had a lot of visitors who brought food and delivered kind messages about my grandfather. We were all staying in the Rothschild mansion, even my two aunts, who had homes close-by. Sadly, Dad's younger brother Edmund had died in Israel under suspicious circumstances, not long after my husband Saul in 1967. I never really knew him, only Dad had gone to his funeral.

My six female cousins only visited but they all seemed interested to meet me again. Most said how disappointed they were that I had not brought Jono, as four of them now had children. But Jono was the eldest great grandchild, and this was mentioned in my dad's eulogy.

It was strange doing all the Jewish rituals again and it made me sad as I recalled Saul's funeral. His funeral had to be delayed as they had to do a post- mortem on him, being the pilot, to ensure that he didn't have any substances in his system. I remember this had upset Saul's parents greatly at the time; of course, none were found.

To my surprise on the third day Laurent and his younger brother Andre de Rothschild came to the mansion to pay their respects.... And Andre actually spoke to me this time.... Thankfully they also rescued me from the house and took me out for a meal.... I never told my parents this of course.

I had not been close to my Grosspapi and found it difficult sitting listening to people talk about him like he was an angel sent to us from heaven. Plus, I was missing showering, as immediate family were only allowed a cold sponge bath each day, as is the Jewish custom.

Laurent told me I was not immediate family, being only a granddaughter. So, I gratefully went to his hotel room had a warm shower, washed my hair and changed into the more colourful clothes I had sneaked out with me.... I had found it so difficult making small talk with all the Rothschild relatives as I didn't know any of them really, having lived in the U.S. for many years.

Laurent was his usual charming self. We talked about Veronica and Victor's wedding and about the splendid de Rothschild party, but not about the 'trip' I had taken which I know was real and quite wicked.... Nor did we talk about that fateful Rothschild party back in 1965.... But we did recall those wonderful few days we had all spent together with Veronica on the French Riviera a few months before that party nine years ago, when I was a young and care-free London model.

I'd never forgotten those heady days nor the heavy petting that Laurent and I engaged in and how it had made me feel then, being so young and naïve, as I had never been kissed like that.... I think Laurent was very skilled also at pleasing woman with all his charm and flattery. But that is where it ended. Of course, I still wasn't sure if I'd ever had sex with him because of the drugs and masks worn at both of the parties we had attended together, but I thought not.

A lot had happened to me since we first met, I decided then.... But Laurent was still the same supposed playboy, who still worked for the Rothschild parent company 'Paris Orleans' on the luxury yacht side of the business; only now he was thirty-two years old.... I had been curious as to why our paths kept crossing even though I had refused some of his visits over the years when he had phoned unexpectedly to say he was in town, be it L.A. or New York.... That is why he probably just turned up unannounced at my work those three times, then got himself invited to Veronica and Victor's wedding.... But why?

I had always been suspicious as to why a wealthy, handsome, popular French supposed playboy and future baron would been interested in me anyway.... Especially as I now suspected that he was gay, or at least bisexual.... As he could have any woman or man for that matter that he desired.... I really couldn't work Laurent out and what's-more I'd decided, I was sick of trying....

Now Andre his younger brother was a different story altogether. When we first met all those years ago he was only eighteen and very quiet and shy.... Not now though.... Andre was now aged twenty- seven and a respected architect who was confident and very passionate about building preservation and urban design, I soon found out. He was also, I'd decided, the most attractive and interesting man, I'd been in the company of for a very, very long time.... And his body language showed that he was attracted to me also and not just paying me lip service....as Laurent did.

Even though we met during Grosspapi's Shiva.... I felt weak at the knees and tongue tied, when I met Andre de Rothschild again.... Laurent must have noticed our immediate attraction to each other.... I think for me it was love at first sight.... Andre later admitted that he'd had a crush on me since we had first met as teenagers.And was disappointed he said, that I chose his brother over him that week in Cannes, plus Laurent had told him then, that we'd slept together.... which was not true.

Andre then heard I had married and had a child less than a year later, so he thought me a lost cause.... He was later informed, by Laurent, that I had been tragically widowed and was attending university in L.A....But, he said he could think of no-good reason to contact me, out of the blue, without me thinking it odd.... What a pity, as it didn't stop his brother from contacting me over the years after such brief encounters, even if we did kiss passionately on a couple of them.

After Shiva ended, I decided to stay in Zurich for another week.... Andre also stayed and we barely left each-others side.... Laurent departed. He could see how lit up I was around Andre, as I couldn't hide my attraction for him, and as usual I could not read how he, Laurent, felt about this.... I also think all the emotional energy around the funeral had intensified my feelings for Andre somehow. As any emotion heightens my sexuality, and I needed a lover.... And Andre was impressed with the passionate lover I became, he said, as after Laurent left, we hardly left the bedroom.

These de Rothschild brothers have certainly unsettled me over the years, what is this connection between us? I can't help but wonder now, that I was always destined to be with one of them.

Grosspapi had made a provision for Jono in his Will, a trust fund for his future education. I had no choice but to accept it graciously.... When I was staying with Grossmami and my family in the Rothschild mansion, I decided that she was alright.... She is much loved by her two daughters, six granddaughters and their children, and will be quite content, I felt, with her controlling husband gone.... At seventy-four she was still an attractive woman, with good bone structure and posture and tall like me, although I tended to favour my Oma and Mom more in looks and colouring. My parents had now inherited the Zurich mansion, so Grossmami agreed to move into their much smaller but still grand, lake-side villa, as it was nearer to both her daughters. It would suit her better she said.... But not my Mom I felt.

My Rothschild relatives could not believe the work I did, they said, or that I owned a modest summer cottage that I'd even helped to renovate.... I wondered then why I had turned my back on a more privileged lifestyle and decided that I now had to work out what was best for Jono and his future also.... Especially as after only two and a half weeks I decided that I was madly in love....

I had never fallen for anyone so quickly or so passionately and he was a de Rothschild.... It was uncanny especially as the

Rothschild's are encouraged to marry within the extended family.... But I also decided, that I was so infatuated with Andre that I wasn't thinking straight.... It was like he had be-witched me and I did not like this feeling of not being in control. So, when he asked me to relocate to Paris to be with him, I'd refused and said that I needed more time.... I couldn't just run off to Paris anyway, even if I'd wanted to and not just because of Jono.

I rang my Oma a few times. She was staying on in New York with Jono until I got home. My parents and Alexander had only just arrived home after staying a week on the French Riviera. Dad told Oma that he had no choice but to stay another two years in New York. Or at least until he had improved the bank's situation and my brother had attained his degrees.... Of course,h Alex is ear-marked to take over from our dad one day at the bank.

Philip will never get into the banking business his chosen career path is a bit of a disappointment to our parents.... But then he did turn up at the funeral, was a respectful grandson, spoke some well received words which charmed everyone just as he has always done. I think he was a bit high on marijuana at the time, but I didn't say anything.... The day after he caught the train to Paris to attend a rock concert and no one said a word.... How does he do it?

Oma told me that my mom was not keen on giving her beautiful lake side villa to Grossmami and moving back into the cold Rothschild mansion, where she'd been so unhappy as a new bride. The villa was leased out anyway, whilst they were living in New York.... My dad said to give Grossmami some time, and then he would discuss selling the mansion with her. This had Alexander storming off to his bedroom according to Oma, as he'd assumed one day it would be his as he knew Philip and I didn't care for the place.

I also knew Alexander was bitter that despite the Rothschild money he had not been accepted into Harvard business school in Boston, straight away and had to waste a year at NYU, he had told Oma. I think his English writing skills had let him down, as he could speak English very well but wrote far better in German.... Philip said it was a shame he'd got in at all, as he would become an even more arrogant prig at Harvard.

Mom said she was relieved as she had worried about Alex living in New York. Now she would worry about him arriving at the train station here for his mid-semester breaks after the four-hour journey from Boston.... Mom just liked to worry, I decided, especially about Alexander.... Unlike Philip, Alex has always had trouble making friends, but at Harvard he made some in a few weeks he said, good for him, they were probably also Jewish.... I wish him well in life even though we don't understand each other.... My Oma loves all her grand-children and never judges or says a bad word about anyone so I've never told her how I feel about Alexander.

August 31st

Despite the huge attraction Andre and I feel for each other, he will not consider living in the U.S. and I will not consider living in Paris, at-the-moment, so he flies over to see me as much as he can. We are passionate lovers and each time he leaves, I find it so difficult to say good-bye. But I don't feel in-control when I am with Andre which is a feeling I am not used to, especially in bed, as he is very intense and dominant and likes me to be submissive.... He also likes to seduce me and not have me instigate sex, which is difficult when we are so mad for each other.

December 30th

Even though I was busily involved with my charity fundraising work, I missed Andre so much when he was not here.... especially sexually.... and because of this, I am not proud to say.... I started an affair with an older man, a Lawyer I knew through work.... He was newly divorced with two teenage daughters and therefore not ready for another relationship, as-yet.... Just uncomplicated sex.

Tom Collins, yes as in the cocktail, had been flirting with me outrageously and asking me out for weeks....and he was crazy and sexy with a wicked sense of humour and up for anything. This was a dangerous combination for me, especially as he also adores a woman who dominates in bed.... So one night we went out for a drink, and I had one too many and of course that's where we ended up. And because he turned out to be such a fantastic lover I couldn't leave it at one night, plus he pursued me constantly saying those magic words 'no strings attached'....

I am not proud of myself, as I knew I loved Andre madly, but I could not cope with the feeling of not being in-control, when I was with him.... Also, I could not with him being absent so much.... Then disaster struck....as three months later I knew I was pregnant, and that Andre was not the father.... as I had spent every morning for three weeks vomiting.... So much for my spirit guides including Poppa, my psychic Oma and my own intuition.... Again.

There are gaps here in my journal. But I was just as fated to be the mother of the psychically gifted Elizabeth, (Beth) Collins. Like her Paternal Grandmother Beth could end up the most powerful woman in the Illuminati, but I may never know, as sadly we are mostly estranged and have been for decades. Occasionally she will phone me out of the blue, but she never really tells me anything about herself.

1974 recap....

New York in 1974 was a fairly dangerous place to live. Alexander had now graduated and was working with our father at the Rothschild and co bank.... I never really understood why my parents chose to stay on in New York, perhaps my father enjoyed the challenge, as the situation then was looking pretty- hopeless for New York. Even President Ford was refusing to help bail out America's largest city and financial hub.... It was ironic really, that it could not repay its huge six billion dollar debts. And because of this there were massive lay offs of utility workers, police, fireman, health workers and teachers, as the city could no longer afford to pay them. New York was now being called 'the smelly stupid city'.

And these were the people who gave their pension funds to save the city from sinking in debt. If it had not been for the teacher's pension fund, New York would have gone bankrupt, ironically it did not save all their jobs.... What may one ask, were all the wealthy New Yorkers doing at the time, to help their city?

Parts of New York like Queens, now looked as bad as television images of Beirut, as junkies accidently or landlords intentionally burnt down once beautiful apartment blocks, they could no longer afford to sustain.... My dad and I went to a Charity dinner, and Tom was there also in his capacity as a Lawyer and Property Developer....I was now showing with my pregnancy, and this is when I decided to introduce my dad to the father of my unborn child.... My dad was polite, as was Tom, but they were both mad at me, I could tell, for putting them in an awkward situation.... I don't know why I was such a bitch.... My parents had just assumed that I was pregnant to Andre and hoped we would work things out like they did, their first year of marriage. They saw that I was to upset to talk about it, and as Jono and I were safe still living in their staff quarters, they knew me well enough to wait until I felt like talking.

But Tom was furious I had hurt his pride.... He told my dad that he had every respect for him and his daughter and asked then for his permission to marry me.... Which my dad flustered.... granted.

1975

April 5th I have just heard that my beloved Andre has married a distant cousin, Celine de Rothschild who is six years his junior.... He got engaged only four months after hearing I was pregnant and that he was not the father.... They married in the Ritz ballroom in Paris two months later, Laurent told me, as he still comes to New York on business occasionally and we went out for a drink.

I was so gutted than my knee jerk reaction was to marry Tom Collins my lover, and father of my baby daughter Elizabeth, as he had asked me to several times....

Tom is fifteen years older than me and a bit of a father figure in some ways, as he is funny like my late Poppa and so protective, which I never really had with my own father.... When I announced to Tom that I was pregnant he was genuinely shocked, as he told me the first night we went out, that he'd recently had a vasectomy....so something went wrong there.... I knew it was Tom's though, as due to Andre's work commitments at that time, I hadn't seen him for over a month.... I was not on the pill either as after so many years I felt that my body needed a break; plus, Andre and I always used protection....Tom and I, however, did not.... And as with Jono I knew immediately after I'd conceived.

I was angry though and said to Tom that I was going to put the father down as 'unknown' on the birth certificate.... as I didn't need his help, nor did I ever want him to stop me from moving away in the future.... I could have bluffed and told Andre it was his.... but I knew that I could never do that to anyone again.... And I would never have considered a termination, even though I told Tom that is what I would do if he didn't agree to my conditions....so he agreed.... Why should I marry him now? We are still involved as I feel comfortable around Tom, he is like wearing an old pair of slippers that I'm reluctant to throw away.... Even though I know I should. And he is kind to me and Jono and thoughtful.... although I don't like his family, well his mother mainly and his younger brother Robert. But I'm not sure I love Tom enough to marry him, well not in the way I loved Saul, Sam, and Andre.... What a mess I've made once again!

But Tom does have a way of turning me on with his interesting mind and humour. And he has arranged so many interesting rendezvous for us, at different high-class hotels, clubs and parties, suggesting what I wear or not wear. Then we role-play and have a night of wild uninhibited sex.... So, I won't need any other lovers with Tom as he appeases the naughty side of me.... But I instinctively know that in his capacity as a Lawyer and Property Developer Tom has a light side and a dark side.... Plus, I also suspect of course that he is Illuminati with a surname like Collins but I've never told him this.... *Tom told me once that every woman should have at least one dangerous man in their life and he was certainly mine.*

Therefore, I do not see Tom as husband material as I don't respect him enough. I know he's done things that are not ethical by what he intimates and the people he mixes with. I always got what I wanted for my clients when Tom was pursuing me and afterwards, he saw to that.... Plus, we don't have the same principles, values or even vote for the same party, as he is a Republican for heaven's sake.... I am talking myself in and out of this.

Tom is good with Jono though. He now has three daughters and enjoys having a son to take to ball games he said. And when we went to Lily Dale, Tom taught Jono how to fish.... He also takes an interest in Jono's education and attends his school events if I can't. So, Tom is already like his father.

July 8th

Despite my conflicting emotions and my opinion of his mother, who I thought was a witch we got *(I didn't know then how close my assumption actually was)* married by a celebrant on June 1st 1975, in The Loeb Boathouse in central park, the reception was held there also. 70 people attended being immediate family, and people we worked with who knew us both.... Tom insisted I wear a white floor-length tulle lace wedding dress, with a veil. As I would have chosen something simpler. But it was a beautiful wedding and reception. And Tom made quite an emotional speech. I know that my family were surprised at my choice of a husband though but were too polite to say. Even Oma.

Like me Tom is a non-practising Jew.... His ex-wife Barbra, I met when she picked up his two teen- aged daughters after the reception. She is lovely, and Tom and Barbra are still very amicable. The Collin's are also a wealthy family. Barbra asked me what I knew of the family, and I said not much and I was happy to keep it that way.... She said that was wise and I should keep my children away from them also.... *At the time I thought this may have just been bitter ex-wife talk, but I was wrong. Barbra was always a friend to me and told me then that as long as I accepted Tom would never be faithful and I made sure I handled my own financial affairs, then my journey with Tom would be an enjoyable one.*

Tom also owned a beautiful Manhattan apartment overlooking central park, which we moved into after the wedding. We had decided to defer our honeymoon due to work commitments. We then employed a housekeeper/nanny called Reba, to help with Elizabeth.

I've decided that I must have the dominant genes, as both my children despite having different fathers, look like me with their fair hair, blue eyes and tall for their ages, well Elizabeth is a long baby.... Tom on the other hand is my height with thick dark hair, brown eyes, broad in the shoulders and with a stocky build.... He was not my usual type, as Saul, Sam, and Andre were all well over six feet tall, fair and slim in build.

Unlike Jono I had a difficult pregnancy and birth with Elizabeth, she was reluctant to be born and after a twenty-four-hour labour, I finally had to have a caesarean- section. This put me at odds with Elizabeth, as I also found her a fretful, clingy baby and was happy to hand her over to her Nanny and go off to work.... I thought of my own mom and our relationship, which got off to a rocky start and I didn't want the same for us.... As I was also conscious that my one real chance at happiness had been ruined by my falling pregnant with Elizabeth and hoped I wouldn't blame her for this.

Reading this back I appear to be a selfish madam, I am pleased that I matured after this. Note: I have with his permission included a couple of diary entries of my Cousin Piers who's existence I didn't know of at the time. Or any of the family for many years. Coincidently Piers also kept a diary.

Piers

1962

December 11th

For some reason I was awakened last night and I saw a man in his sixties standing at the end of my bed.... It was a vision, clear like a big cinema screen only fuzzy around the edges. The sky was so blue and there were palm trees, and the man was wearing a short sleeved checked shirt. At first, I thought it was my father aged in his sixties, as he looked so familiar. Then it dawned on me who it was.... So, he did know about us after all, I decided then.... He just smiled at me then faded, but I felt at peace somehow.

At breakfast I told my father of my vision. He said that he had the same visitation. I asked him what it meant and he said Clarence had probably passed over and he was letting us know that he will always be watching over us....

I am nineteen years old and in January I will be an undergraduate student at Cambridge studying History.... But ultimately, I would like to follow my parents into working for British Intelligence.

My parents Peter and Norma Huxley both work for the British secret service or MI6. They met whilst working on an assignment together during the war, when my father was twenty-three and my mother twenty-six. I was born a year later on September 16th 1943, in a partially bombed-out hospital in central London.... As they sare both career agents, I don't think they planned on falling in love or having me, and they made sure there were no more after me as I am an only child. Despite not being planned, I have always felt much loved by both parents.

From an infant I spent a lot of time with my paternal grandmother and two aunts, as my parents are often away with their work. Therefore, my aunts' children younger cousins Charles and George Fairley and Alice, Heather and Simon Grayson are more like siblings to me.

At eleven I was packed off to a boarding school in Kent where I stayed for the next seven years. I only came home to London for the holidays even though it was only an hour away by train.... My Gran had sent my father to the same school. She had always talked about her old friend, the well-known clairvoyant, Clarence R. Smyth and I found out that he had also gone to the same school.

My father's mother was born Dulcie Hester Dingleby and the Dingleby's were wealthy importers and exporters. At seventeen she married her childhood friend, Gordon Peter Huxley who lived in the next street. Sadly, he had come back from the First World War a bit disfigured and partially blinded by mustard gas, which had also affected his lungs.... And Gran admitted to us that she had married him out of pity but fortunately grew to love him very much.

I didn't have many years with my grandad, but I remember he was a kind and patient man. He had a studio at home where he sculpted in clay and many of his figures and heads were later cast into bronze.... He was very talented despite his disabilities and had many commissions.

Gran always worked in her family's business and she and her younger brother Albert eventually took over when their father retired. But she was the one with the good head for figures.

My father said he had a happy childhood despite his parents' commitment to their work.... I think this was where he gets it from as his work has always comes first.... Father said they'd had a lovely Nanny until his youngest sister Catherine turned six and a housekeeper Mrs Bryant. And their house was always filled with warmth and much laughter he'd said.

Gran and her family had spent the duration of the First World War in a prisoner of war camp on the outskirts of

Berlin.... My great-grandad Digby Dingleby had owned a house and huge warehouse then in Berlin as well as London.... He was foolish though as he should have got the family out of Germany before the war started, he had been warned. But he didn't want to leave his property behind. So, the family endured four years of hardship, as they were interned as enemies of the state.... Although they survived my great-grandma Maud never regained her health and died in her late forties. My Great grandad always mourned her, and he never remarried.

My Grandad Huxley was a gentle man quite short in stature with sandy blond hair and blue eyes. My Gran was also petite and fair as are my two aunts Anne and Catherine, my father's younger sisters.

Father always knew he was different to the rest of his family. For a start he looked nothing like any of them, being always tall for his age with dark hair, brown eyes and a slightly prominent nose. He was also not like them in nature being out-going and charismatic, aggressive in sport and passionate about his opinions. He told me he couldn't be more different to his parents, although his Grandad Dingleby was aggressive in business apparently.

Father's teachers used to argue about what career path he should take as he was always one of their more promising students. Like me he attended Devonshire House School in London and then Kent College, as a border. He later went to Cambridge to study History but was called up to do his duty during WWII.

From a young age my father was clairvoyant as am I. We both see spirit and have visions. Father says that his abilities have been invaluable to him during his career, and he trusts his own intuition above anything else.... I'm pleased my father understands my gift as no one else in the family really does.... Mother being an analytical person believes Father and I have over-active frontal lobes, or something. But she does trust his intuition she says, as it has saved them several times when they find themselves to be in a dangerous or tricky situation. As they often go on assignments together, ironically posing as a married couple.

I don't really know much about my parents' work, but I know they travel to Eastern Europe a lot. Father is fluent in German, Italian and has passable Russian, my mother is fluent in French, German, Russian and speaks some Czech. Mother studied languages at Cambridge then she was also enlisted in 1940, and spent the war involved in dangerous information gathering, of which she has never said much about.... But she insists she wasn't a 'spy'.

My Mother was born Elanora Marie Rothschild. She is the youngest sister of the third Baron Victor Rothschild, whom after the war ended, she followed into working for MI5. With her fluency in a few languages, she was soon transferred to MI6 where she changed her name to Huxley, after she finally agreed to marry my father, two years after I was born. This means I was technically born a bastard. My Mother said I am not a bastard my father was, for not marrying her sooner. But Father told me that she had been the one who was reluctant to enter-into matrimony.

My Mother is a direct descendant of the Rothschild founding father Ashmel Mayer Rothschild who in 1778 sent his five sons to start banking dynasties in different cities, being London, Vienna, Naples, Frankfurt and Paris.... We descend from the third son Nathan Mayer Rothschild who was sent to London.

Sophia

1975

September 18th

I've been offered a position with the Rockefeller Foundation again. They won't seem to take 'no' for an answer.... Poppa wrote in his journal that The Rockefeller Foundation provides large amounts of money to universities, seminaries and other religious organisations.... Their goal, is to control education and religion with their foundation, which is funded by their major companies: The Chase Manhattan bank, Standard oil, Texas instruments, General Electric, Eastman Kodak and Boeing Delta, et cetera.... They were also involved in the creation of the F.B.I. apparently.

Poppa believed that the Rockefellers are part of the Illuminati, and his notebooks are even more defamatory about this than his journals were, as he names some of the other families involved.... I think he didn't want all his family to have this information, as it could be dangerous for them.... So I'm the lucky one, or unlucky, depending on the way you look at it being in possession of his note-books.

At times I still feel watched, but I have become more confident married to Tom. Now when I see those men in dark suits and sunglasses, I quickly walk over to one of them.... They soon dissipate into the crowd, as it is usually a public place.... I have never told Tom about them, nor have I ever discussed the Illuminati with him or asked if he is a member. He would never admit to it anyway.

October 16th

It's crunch time! My Dad and I went to the Waldorf Astoria hotel last night, with 1700 other guests to attend the Alfred

E. Smith memorial foundation benefit dinner.... And top of the agenda was the urgent bail out of New York City.... All the top dignitaries were there.... Then Mayor Breame dropped a bombshell by saying that President Ford was not going to bail out New York City by buying the city's bonds, as he had hoped.... Mayor Breame has already stopped free university, laid off scores of service workers, teachers and police and frozen the wages of the rest. He had also hiked up subway fees and closed several hospitals.... But this was still not enough! What else can he do if The U.S. Government won't help.... "Desperate times call for drastic measures" he said.

I can't believe what has happened to America's largest city so I have to ask these questions again. Where are all the wealthy New Yorker's? What have they been doing? Who allowed this to happen? And why?

Tom gave me his invite as he thought it was better that I attended with my dad than him. I'm glad he did.... Everyone present was in shock as no one could see a way to stop New York from going bankrupt.

I don't think my dad knows quite what to make of Tom he looks at him nervously, as if he said something wrong Tom might take him outside and beat him to a pulp.... Tom does look a bit like a wrestler but I like that about him, he makes me feel safe.

October 17th

What a difference a day make's as 24hrs later....

The teacher's pension fund has saved the day by submitting a check to cover the fall out of debt. They may have saved the city but not necessarily their own jobs.... The immediate crisis may be over but there is still a lot of work to be done yet.

1977

August 17th

It came over the radio this morning that Elvis is dead.... Jono is at school, so I am home alone with Beth.... I started to cry and couldn't stop. Poor Beth has been crying too. They have been playing Elvis's music all day and I have been crying for him, Tom, Saul and me.... I think I was just overdue for a damn good cry....

Now Beth is having her nap I have decided to sit and reflect on my life. As over the past seventeen months I have been too occupied just coping on a daily- basis.... Now these trials now have me asking some of life's big questions.... I know we are in this incarnation to learn, but what are my life's lessons then? What important signs have I missed, if any, along the way? Have I done well, messed-up or had no choice? Plus, what is my so-called destiny even? My head is in a total spin as I simply do not know what is best now for me and my children.

I have been seeing a therapist, but can I even trust her? A Dr Wendy Klum. She probably thinks I'm suffering from paranoia, because I have been honest with her about what I think, see and feel. She has seen me levitate off the couch though so that is something as I have told her about my psychic abilities.... I have also told her about my sexual promiscuity that resurfaces when I have any emotional upsets....as does my vulnerability to mischievous spirits, or even dark entities.... And although Dr Klum has sat and listened patiently to me, she has said very little. I have refused her suggestion of medication though, as I feel that I need to have my wits about me.... I sense the children and I are in danger; although I'm not exactly sure from whom.... but I have my suspicions.

At-the-moment I am still living in Tom's Manhattan apartment with the children and Juanita my new housekeeper.... As three months ago Tom was murdered.... The police said it was suicide.... Supposedly he had shot himself.... But that is not what happened as Tom told me more than once that what he was doing was extremely dangerous and that his days were probably numbered.

Oma is now seventy-seven years old, and I don't want to worry her. I have told her I am okay and seeing a therapist as two months ago Mom, Dad and Alexander moved back to Zurich to live.... Not good timing for me.... So, I am feeling quite alone in New York and vulnerable.

My two closest friends Linda and Karen, have been supporting me, as has Tom's ex-wife Barbra, my neighbours the Goldsteins, plus some of my work colleagues.... Oma, Mom and Philip all phone me at least three times a week, usually during the dinner hour, as I find that the worst time of day.

Mom had been busting to leave New York for ages, but the twenty-five-hour power blackouts in July and the rioting and looting that ensued had really finished her off.... As 40% of off-duty police officers did not even respond to the call for back-up. This was because of the way they've been treated over the past few years, with massive lay-offs and wage freezes.... I don't blame them.

I'm not surprised Alexander did not want to stay here either as he can't stand any dis-harmony I've noticed. Plus, he was keen to take up a position with the Rothschild and co. bank in Zurich with our father he'd said.... Alex has always felt more Swiss than American. At least he and I talk more now. He told me he had made some good friends here who he would miss, which is a rare thing for Alex. That is something he and I do have in common as we both have only a few close friends, unlike Philip, who seems to know half of L.A. already.... Philip keeps telling me to come back there to live, which is something I am now considering.

It's not just me, a lot of New Yorkers, have been living through some stressful unsettling times.... Although not everyone has had a murdered spouse to contend with.... But generally, the American people are not happy.... They are still angry about the Vietnam War and the cost of so many young lives and have lost even more faith in the government with the recent Watergate scandal. Because was Nixon 'just the one who got caught'? And everyone has been reeling from the 'Washington Post' bombshell that basically exposed four past presidents as ignoring all the reports starting with the McNamara report, whose findings were.... That the U.S. could never win the war in Vietnam.... Then each successive President passed this issue on like a hot potato as none wanted to be the one who lost face for America by losing the war.... This is 70% of the reason why the war continued, to avoid loss of face. How despicable! All that senseless loss of life 58,000 American soldiers alone, plus millions of innocent Vietnamese.... I blame stupid, arrogant men in the government and the military. It's time we had a female president.... seriously.

At my work we are seeing far too many young physically and mentally damaged war veterans, who had fought an inglorious war and who now can't hold down a job or stay in a relationship. We are trying to house as many as we can, but the government is simply not helping enough.

Plus New York has recently also been terrorized by the 'Son of Sam' serial killer, David Berkowitz. I am sad six people had to die. I gave the police a profile of him and nearly got his name right, but I was then hauled into the police station and interrogated myself.... Mediums are often treated with scorn, even though we are listened to far more than is publicised.

I also knew my husband was going to die.... But I simply didn't want to believe that I could be so unfortunate as to lose two husbands in under ten years.... My poor Tom, I am still coming to terms with it.... I am trying to get his case reopened for further investigation, but powerful people at the top are preventing it, I feel.... Tom didn't deserve to die like that, alone and in fear. It's despicable.

Other members of my family have also suffered recent losses. My cousin Christian was tragically killed in an avalanche, whilst skiing in Switzerland last October, he was only twenty-seven. The family were devastated as he leaves behind a wife and infant twin sons.... Uncle William was inconsolable as was my brother Philip. He and Christian were close growing up.... Oma said it should have been her as she is old, and Christian had his whole life ahead of him.... My Cousin Isobel coped well as did my Aunt Katrine, Christian's mother, being both strong women.

Mom's cousin Marigold whom I met at Poppa's funeral lost her younger son Neville in the Vietnam War back in 1969, he was a pilot. Her older son Anthony did a few dangerous missions. He was one of the pilots who airlifted the last soldiers out of Saigon on April 30th 1975 but at least he survived. The war was finally over by then as troops had been pulling out since 1973.... *In 1962 I predicted that both Marigold's boys would wear military uniforms one day and their lives would be in danger.*

Our new President, Jimmy Carter, a peanut farmer from Georgia is at least an improvement on Gerald Ford. It is no thanks to him than New York survived its fiscal crisis. But then Ford wasn't really elected, he only became president because of Nixon's downfall.

Even though New York is in a better financial position, it is a fairly dangerous city to live. There is too much crime as homelessness is on the increase, not decrease, as we have been led to believe. Families with one low wage earner are ending up on the streets, being no longer able to pay the now higher rents and because of this the homeless shelters are full to capacity every night. New York supposedly has a legal obligation to provide shelter for these people, so our workload has increased dramatically. This means I am no longer fundraising. I had gone back to working in housing placements a while ago, even before Tom died.... *Sadly, this housing crisis got even worse in the 1980s.*

I can't blame New York for the death of my husband though, as he was in Greensboro, North Carolina, when it happened.... Poor Jono losing another father at aged ten and Elizabeth who we call Beth is just two.... Tom's two beautiful daughters from his first marriage, Chrystal and Kimi, are also naturally grieving for their father, as is Barbra his ex-wife.... Tom and Barbra had remained close and she has been very kind to me.... We have been supporting each other as I think Barbra was still in love with Tom but could not cope with his infidelities.

Painful as it is to recall, these are the events that led to Tom's, tragic death.... Fourteen months before he died Tom simply saw the light and became a born-again Christian, literally overnight.... This led him to go on a self-imposed quest to expose the Illuminati as a cabal of wealthy and powerful families, even naming them.... including his own.... He called them Secret Society Satan worshippers, who already mostly rule the world through banking and other core businesses, the military, and all levels of government. And whose aim it is, to get rid of Christianity and replace it with a 'One World Order'.

Tom tried to tell this to as many people as he could targeting religious groups all over America and many did listen.... He also quit his job and went through most of our savings during this period travelling around the U.S. spreading the word, so to speak.... And he had some pretty damning evidence to support this in the form of written material, signed witness statements, photographs and tape recordings of key Illuminati members....

His life ended with a single bullet shot to his temple, in a modest motel room in Greensboro, North Carolina where he was found with the gun still in his hand.... It was stated at the inquest that Tom had a brain tumour and that was the reason why he had committed suicide, his doctor said. This also explained his recent obsessive and erratic behaviour. X-rays were then produced by his doctor to confirm this.... What a load of crap! Barbra doesn't believe it either.... I have been shown these x-rays. But I do not believe they are his, or that he had a brain tumour, or that he died by his own hand.... His doctor must have been paid a handsome sum.

Tom told me that what he was doing was like signing his own death warrant. But said he needed to do it to protect me and Jono whom he loved like his own son, plus his three beautiful daughters.... My husband was not delusional, he had just turned from dark to light and this made him a loose cannon, one who simply had to be gotten rid of .... And where was all the damning evidence against the Illuminati that he always carried with him as he had trusted no one else with it? None was found in his room apparently, only his clothes and toiletries were returned to me. Although I am not really surprised.

Tom's family, although visibly upset at his funeral, were part of it, I felt. His behaviour threatened their highly held positions in 'the Order', especially that of his mother Eve and brother Robert.

Tom told me about a month before he died, that he never planned to love me and Jono as much as he did, and that if anything happened to him, I had to be very careful who I trusted in the future. He also told me to stay away from his family and to not let our daughter Beth anywhere near his mother especially.... Then he shocked me by saying that this was because she was the chief Collins witch....'The Grand Dame'.... Why did I not sense this?

Whilst we were at Tom's funeral our apartment was broken into and ransacked. The police said this was not uncommon when funeral notices are put in the paper, but I knew it was not the case. They did not get the copy of Tom's notebook though, naming the Illuminati families, major and minor, the roles they play in 'the Order' and the companies and institutions they control.... I had that in a safe place.... This was the one thing Tom had left me.... Of course, the burglars had to take cash and jewellery to make it appear convincing.... *I later gave Tom's notebook to Andrew Y, a key member of the 'White hats'.*

The 'Grand Dame' selects children from the elite Illuminati families, who are to be trained to take over important roles one day, within 'the Order'. Tom said U.S. Presidents are 'selected' not 'elected' plus their key staff. Those who do not play by their rules are gotten rid of, as in the case of both the Kennedy brothers and Senator McCall, who was killed with my first husband Saul; to name a few. Alarmingly Tom also told me that one of the children chosen was Jono, as he admitted to me that he had taken him to a meeting without my knowledge, and this was when he saw the light. Tom said he had an epiphany and instantly regretted taking Jono there.

The 'White hats' say that 'the Order' sacrifices a kidnapped child, for every child selected.... But Poppa told me they do sacrifice kids, young goats, not young children. As he witnessed one of their initiation ceremonies, where he was also given heroin and nearly died. Oma told me that they also tried to initiate Poppa into a sex and drug orgy, but he'd refused.... Good for him, I wish I had been that strong, but I never told my Oma that.

I must say that I had a difficult time believing any of this at the time. But Tom had taken Jono to a grand secret meeting, because Jono had told me about it.... He said he wasn't scared, but a lot of the other twelve children there were. As everyone wore long hooded robes and had half masks over their eyes except for the children. And nobody spoke, except for the main man with a full head mask with antlers, and 'The Grand Dame'. She had sat on an ebony and gold crescent throne in the centre of a huge room with red carpet surrounded by four circles deep of people. The smallest circle around her had thirteen Illuminati members called 'Olympians', one from each of the elite families; this was according to Tom.

Jono told me that he knew there were men and woman present, because some of the robed people were smaller. He also knew that the Grand Dame was Tom's mother he said, because when she briefly spoke to him; he had recognised her voice.

Looking back, why wasn't I really concerned when Jono told me this, as it was not long after that Tom began his so called, touring.... I now realise that I did have my head in the sand.

I hadn't seen much of Tom during his final weeks. He was away mostly and when he was home he was frantic at times yelling at me that I had to know the truth in case he was killed. He accused me of skirting around the issue and of not wanting to face it, for years. He kept telling me that I had to listen as I needed to learn how to protect our children.... I had never, ever seen, my funny, sexy rock of a husband like this before. It frightened and distressed me no-end, so much so, that I was quite relieved when he went off touring again.

I was still working fulltime then as someone had to pay the bills. Thank heavens I had the support of Juanita our live-in housekeeper she was an absolute brick and looked after us all. Mom and Dad were concerned about us with Tom not working so Dad paid Juanita's wages, which I was grateful for at the time. But I could not tell them the truth then about Tom's absences.

There was an inquest into Tom's death of course. It was recorded as a suicide, open and shut case, even though he had left no note. Fortunately, Tom's insurance company still paid out and he had provided well for me and his children, including Jono.

I was far too distressed to be reached by Tom in spirit myself, so when Oma left two weeks after the funeral I drove to Lily Dale with the kids and had three weeks there. I also wanted to be some-where his family could not contact me easily.... It was Robert mainly who I was trying to avoid, as he had always given me the creeps. I suspect he fancies me, from the way he leers at me, plus the lewd comments he made to Tom when I was in earshot.... Tom told me he was a jerk and to ignore him.

My circle of medium friends at Lily Dale all agreed that Tom had been murdered and that he had been warned but had ignored those warnings.... And now those same dark powerful forces were encircling me and the children, they said. They also suggested that we should move permanently to Lily Dale, where we would be protected under a beacon of white light and healed....

I thanked them but said this was not possible at-the-moment.... I knew I could never threaten the peaceful existence of Lily Dale, with its pretty pastel houses and air of spiritual positivity. But I felt none-the-less, that it would always be a safe-haven for me to retreat to occasionally. Funnily enough the F.B.I. never came to Lily Dale to recruit mediums, and I never felt 'watched' there. It was like a psychic Shangri-La.

Of course, whilst I was staying at Lily Dale, my old problem resurfaced. So, one weekend I left the children with Juanita and booked into a motel in Buffalo, an hour away and went in search of some partying and sex. Both of which I found in a late-night bar as I ended up with a long-haul truck driver whose name escapes me, but who did manage to go the distance with me in an all-weekend sex romp. I drove back to Lily Dale on the Monday morning feeling ashamed, dirty, hardly able to walk and promising myself that I would seek therapy.... Juanita was not stupid she knew what I had been up to, but wisely said nothing.

When Tom died, Mom and Dad were all set to go back to Zurich to live. I insisted they still go as they had offered to stay on with me after the funeral. I told them that was not necessary as Oma and Ruby would be staying on for two weeks afterwards, plus I had Juanita. I think Mom especially was relieved, as she was over living in New York by then. For me though, it was unfortunate timing. Oma agreed with me that Tom's death was suspicious, and that I had probably never been off the Illuminati radar either. I was beginning to realise that, as in the past, if I strayed from their path of influence, like my association with Sam Winchester and his friends and other friends I have been close to, like Lori and Sandy from school.... Then suddenly I was dropped like a hot potato by those people and for no apparent reason really.

My friend Veronica who I have managed to keep in touch with over the years, has an association with Laurent de Rothschild, he approached her apparently.... I believe that he was the one who was supposed to rescue me after I was impregnated, to get me into the Illuminati circle, not Saul West. But then, were the West's meant to be our neighbours or not? It was confusing, as they were living there before Poppa and Oma bought the house next door, so how was that arranged I wonder. Also Saul's mother was a Bonfman, from the Canadian Illuminati cabal, which was also suspicious....

This was all pointed out to me by Tom, just before he died.

I remember Oma telling me that they had a very helpful and insistent Jewish real estate agent, who she was grateful for at the time with an unwell husband and a feisty twelve-year old in tow, namely me.... I must say I find it impossible to believe that Saul or his parents were part of any plan. It is all so confusing.... Have our lives always been manipulated I wonder.... And am I even thinking rationally now or getting a bit paranoid myself with all that has happened.

Tom warned me though, that I would never get away from them, or beat them, just before he'd died.... He also told me it would be safer for me to join them, but I was to never, ever to trust any of them.... 'Them' of course, being the powerful, all-seeing Illuminati....

But I know that sometimes unforeseeable things in history have thwarted their plans. Poppa told me this. Indeed, a lot probably hasn't gone to plan, because of the power of the masses or man's inventiveness, or even the forces of nature I feel.... But maybe Tom was right, that's what I need to do to survive, play along with them.... This is what happened to the heiress Patty Hearst after she was kidnapped, she felt safer joining her captors. She should never have been sent to prison, as she was still a victim taken against her will, Stockholm syndrome or not.

Poppa had a quirk of seeing key Illuminati family members as reptilian, especially when they got angry, well the men anyway. I had no such warning system in place, unfortunately. But I do have my intuition and I know instinctively that not all the U.S. Presidents have been or will be Illuminati, or at least I hope not....

After Tom's funeral Oma told me about the 'White hats' who are a group of people opposing the Illuminati. This group was actually started by my Poppa, in New York, in 1928. They used to meet under the guise of being New York Theosophical Society members. For obvious reasons they were also a secret society.... Oma told me that after Poppa died, she had lost contact with practically everyone except for a Martin X, who still lives here in New York. So, I have decided that I will get in touch with him soon.... I am so proud of my late Poppa for starting this group.

Note: This was my only entry for 1977

1978

February 2nd

My employers have given me another two weeks off work. They are concerned as I am not coping well, so the children and I have come to visit Oma in Los Angeles.... Oma thinks we should move back here permanently to be near the family and I agree that this would be the best course of action. This also gets me away from the Collins family, especially Robert, who is interfering under the pretence of being concerned about me and the children. But he is trying to control us.... At least his horrible mother has been strangely absent from our lives though, probably due to her guilt.

Whilst I am here, I have decided to read Poppa's journal again and his notebooks and letters, as Oma has had them stored for me.... I need to find out why I have now lost two beloved husbands and I feel they may hold the key, or at least reinforce the information in Tom's notebook.

February 7th

What a surprise, Sam Winchester came to see me at Oma's as he had read about Tom's suicide in the New York Post he said. Sam now works for the L.A. Inquirer, but stated that he had come to visit me as an old friend not as a reporter.... But then he did ask me straight out if I thought Tom had killed himself.... I decided to trust him and said "no". Sam then disclosed to me about what had happened to him all those years ago, when he had broken-up with me.... He had been warned-off he said and was sorry that he hadn't been braver at the time. Our friends were also threatened apparently, but not with death like he was.... Sam was told that he would be shot with a Winchester rifle, and it would be blamed on someone with a grudge against the Winchester family.... None of this came as a surprise.

Sam had changed his surname by deed pol now, to his wife's family name Alderman, which had upset his family he said. He also said that he was happily married with two young daughters.... I told him I was glad to hear that, and I meant it.

I told Sam that he had made the right decision all those years ago. As two men I have loved are now dead and I was glad he at least had survived his association with me.... Sam asked me why this had happened and even offered to find out what he could for me, but I told him to leave it, as it was too dangerous.... We promised to keep in touch as he was leaving but I knew we wouldn't. Even so it was good to see him again, and to have my earlier suspicions confirmed.

February 15th

When I got back to New York I decided to resign from my job, lease-out the apartment and relocate back to L.A. for a while.... My employers said they had expected as much and thought I was making the right decision. They then threw a huge leaving party for me which was so special as many of my clients came to wish us well.

Jono was not happy with the idea at first, as he loved his school and friends he said. He also said that if we must relocate, then from now-on he will be called Jonathon, as Jono is for a little kid.... Of course, we all respected his wishes.... Jonathon has a knack of getting his own way anyhow. Other kids have always followed him around and let him make all the decisions I've noticed and of course Beth dotes on him.

March 3rd

Before we left for L.A., I'd decided I wanted to find out more about the Illuminati, so I rang Malcolm X and we met at a local café. Firstly, he said he was delighted that I had made contact as of course he knew who I was and was sorry to hear I had lost my husband so tragically.... I said two husbands which raised an eyebrow....

I thought that Malcolm X was far too old, stooped and white- haired for this sort of intrigue, but I decided to trust him anyway.... So, I told him what Tom had been doing, why I thought he was killed and who I felt was responsible.... I also explained my theories on Saul's death, but I did not tell him about my son or his supposed future roll.

Malcolm X just sat and listened. He was quiet for so long afterwards that I wondered if he'd heard one word I'd said.... When he finally spoke, he said he was sorry I'd had to endure so much tragedy in my young life. He then suggested that the best thing I could do now is to get myself into a key position where I would be asked to join the elite Illuminati circle, if possible, with my family connections.... I could then report back to the 'White hats'.... He realised this was no mean feat. In the meantime, he said he would do everything he could, to find out who was responsible for the deaths of my two husbands.

I thanked Malcolm X but said I had to thwart that plan because I was moving back to L.A. to live. But he was not deterred and gave me a key member's name and phone number to contact in L.A. He told me I was in a unique position to be of maximum use to the 'White hats', but I had to be extremely careful.... He said I was basically to trust no one and to contact only him or this Andrew Y, in L.A.... I told him that I would try to do what I could.

Later that night I phoned my brother-in law Robert.

Robert, I knew has always fancied me. So, I told him that I had been to two 'Brotherhood' masked parties....one in England and one in France and was therefore keen to go to one here. I said I was feeling sad and unloved and felt this would help me enormously. I also said that I wanted him to know I was still loyal to 'them' despite Tom's behaviour......Robert I could tell was surprised, so I told him a bit about the parties I'd attended, and he sounded even more surprised and said he hadn't realised I'd been initiated so.... I could also tell that he was keen for me to attend, and fortunately there was one coming up soon, in two-weeks-time he said.... I deliberately did not mention 'the Order'.

April 4th

Robert did not know that we were all packed up and ready to leave New York when he arrived to collect me the evening of the party, as I didn't invite him in. Juanita was there of course, minding the children.... Robert was wearing a black dinner suit and me a short, fitted silver evening dress with matching coat. It was a cool evening and I noticed Robert looking at my legs as I got into his car.

We arrived a short time later at the Lower Manhattan Freemasons building. No surprises there. After entering the building and past a doorman, who just nodded at Robert, we went through two dimly lit foyers and two heavy wooden doors, until we arrived at a huge circular room with red carpet and several red doors.... I decided that this must have been where Tom had brought Jono. We went through one of the red doors to a lobby where a masked woman told me to strip down to my bra and panties and to robe and mask up, which I did behind a red curtain. Robert did the same.... I insisted on keeping hold of my evening bag though to the protests of the attendant.

Robert then grabbed my hand and led me into the drug room where we both did a line of cocaine and were each given a flute of champagne. We then did another line before going through yet another red door, where we parted ways.... As he went to be pleasured by women, and me by men. I was feeling quite high by then, but decided I was going to enjoy the sex and put on quite a show. Stripped to my bra, panties and high heels, I knew I still looked great for a thirty-one-year-old mother of two. And others thought so too, as I turned a few heads when I entered and de-robed and I nervously took my time to hang up my robe and evening bag.... Then I circled the room. Everywhere woman were being pleasured, some were cuffed or bound some were splayed out on or over sofas; there was lots of oral sex being enjoyed. Some of the women were pleasuring other woman, so I joined in.... A few people, I decided, never left this room, happy to be satisfied here, and then to watch, or the other way around. Everyone involved, males and females wore eye masks and were aged under fifty I would say, with good bodies I was pleased to note.

After what seemed like and age of pleasuring and being-pleasured I went through another door to the fucking room. It was animal like in there with every conceivable position in play and even more cocaine and champagne if required. I circled the room getting even more highly aroused. I strutted around confidently selecting one stud and then another, and there was a lot of apparatus around designed for different intercourse positions.... I had multiple screaming orgasms which drew quite an audience, some I knew with envy.... This sort of exhibition sex is incredible and heightened with long arousal and orgasm stages especially after cocaine. Unfortunately, there is also nothing like it once you have experienced it, so it tends to be a bit addictive.

I never saw Robert again that evening, as I knew he would consider it bad manners to fuck his brother's widow in this place anyhow. Vulnerable and alone in my own home, yes, he would have enjoyed that the bastard. I swore then to never see him again.

When I was satiated, a voice who I recognised whispered in my ear "let's get you out of here". So, I got up completely naked except for my high heels, and went next door and grabbed my evening bag: my underwear I was not concerned about. I made sure I grabbed my coat on the way out though which I managed to pull on just in time as I was pushed out an exit door into an awaiting taxi by a man I knew to be, Laurent de Rothschild....

Inside the cab we took off our masks and fortunately Laurent had grabbed my dress. But neither of us spoke .... We soon arrived at his hotel and as it was late there were not too many people around which was good, even so we pulled our collars up on our coats put our heads down and quickly entered the private elevator to his suite.

Once inside, Laurent ordered some food, poured me a glass of champagne and ran me a hot bath. He hadn't spoken a word to me, but then he said, "that was quite a show you put on tonight".

I just answered, "did you fuck me?" To which he answered "no".

I then asked if he had ever fucked me and he said "no" and I said "not ever, at any Rothschild party?" And he said "no, not ever".

To which I answered, "well who the hell is Jonathon's father then?" to which he replied that he wasn't really- sure.... And for some reason, I believed him.

Laurent bathed me, fed me and then put me to bed and said that he was sorry things had turned out this way for me. I told him that I wanted to join 'the Order' and he said that I already belonged. I told him I wanted to serve them, and he said I had already done what was required of me, but for my own safety I should never attend any more of those orgies.... He then hugged me, and we slept.

When I woke Laurent was gone but he had left me a note telling me to take care. I then checked my evening bag and the small camera I had concealed in there. Of course, no one had checked me or my bag because I arrived with Robert.... I had to use ISO 400 film with no flash, but I managed to get off six hopefully good shots, by facing my bag with its built-in camera and timer at the activities.

Robert tried to call me three days in a row before we left New York but each time Juanita said I was unavailable.... I felt sad though, as I knew Tom had probably attended those orgies even after we were married. Barbra his ex-wife probably knew about them too.... But at least I knew I'd not dreamt them, they did exist, only this time I had been in control.... Of course, I also now knew that Laurent was part of the Illuminati.... as was Tom.... I wondered about Andre, he must be involved somehow too.... I also knew Laurent was right, I had to be careful as I had probably already served my purpose.

Even so, before I left New York I decided to give an in-depth interview with a tabloid reporter and I gave him four explicit photos from that orgy and foolishly a photocopy of Tom's notebook. The original notebook I gave to Malcolm X, who warned me that I was putting myself in danger handing this information over to a journalist, but I already knew this.... Of course, only a tabloid newspaper would print something like this, and the journalist was putting himself in more danger than I was.... The Journalist had no idea who I was, as I wore a black wig and dark glasses. I also spoke in broken English and kept slipping into German, but I did say however, that I was a Rothschild.

I did not mention then what was in Tom's notebook.... The most damning evidence was about corrupt banks owned by very wealthy elite Illuminati families, who were also involved in the drug trade and money laundering amongst other things. I gave this information to a journalist and to the 'White hats.'

April 12th

After a week at Lily Dale sadly getting it ready to re-lease and after leaving New York; Jonathon told me that he had finally accepted we were moving to L.A., but we were never moving again.... Beth said she wanted us to buy a pretty, white house with blue shutters, which of course we did, not far from Oma and Ruby in Santa Monica. It was a spacious, five-bedroom, Spanish styled bungalow.

Now Jonathon was not what I would call psychically gifted, but he had good intuition Oma said and because of the three 6s in his birthdate numerology, he had great creativity for problem solving. Plus, with his 1, 5, 9 arrow of determination he was a strong person and quite brave for a young boy, according to his numerology.

Beth had the arrow of hypersensitivity with 2, 5, 8 missing and lessons in this life of loss with 2 x 7s. She had already lost her father and wasn't a strong child emotionally, which made her a bit vulnerable, because she did have psychic abilities.... So, I decided to do for her what Poppa had done for me as a young child, which was to clear her every day of any spirits she had with her. This usually was when she was sitting watching the Muppets show on the television, which she adored.

I was proud of both my children, I decided, they were resilient and had been so helpful and well behaved since we had left New York. They both adored their Great Oma of course and funny Great Uncle William. Uncle Philip was also very good with the children.

1978

August 17th

We are now settled into our new bungalow.... But yesterday after I dropped Beth at Kindergarten it came over the car radio, that it was the first anniversary of Elvis's death, and his music was being played again all day.... So once again I started to cry and couldn't stop. When I got home as I was alone I just sat and bawled my eyes out again like last year.

That night Poppa came to visit me and told me clairaudiently not to be upset that I would find love again soon and from a surprising quarter. Someone I already knew, who was already an ally in a dangerous camp.... Why do dead people talk in riddles it is so infuriating. Surprisingly Poppa has never commented on my sexual appetites though.... But he did say I needed to open myself up to the universe and its wonders, and to focus my prana (sexual energy) into healing work. So maybe he did know.... Poppa also warned me to be careful and to watch for signs.

August 30th

I was at the supermarket carpark today loading groceries into my car boot when two men in dark suits approached me. The tall one told me aggressively that if I ever pulled a stunt like that again I will be as dead as that slab of meat I had just loaded into my car.... The other one then thrust a New York tabloid newspaper into my face and said that the journalist who wrote this, had just had an unfortunate accident.... He then said that only my family connections had saved me from a similar fate.... The tall one then told me menacingly that I had better stop meddling.... He also told me to be a good girl and to accept the terrific job that would soon be on offer....

I remember shaking so badly after they'd left trying to get my key in the ignition and on the drive home, I kept looking repeatedly over my shoulder.... Of course, they already knew where I lived .... I knew I'd been foolish. I also felt sick because someone else had probably been killed because of me.

I read the article but was very disappointed as it focused mainly on the sex orgy. It said wealthy, powerful and influential people attended these. And that they also engage in Satanism, even drinking human blood, which is obviously not what I said.... It did mention 'the Illuminati' it said for nearly two hundred years they have controlled the government, the military, the banks and most major businesses and manipulated world events to benefit themselves.... which was the only sensible thing it said, the rest sounded a bit whacky. No family names were mentioned or even intimated. The two photographs were also a bit grainy, and black lines were put over the eyes and genital areas of the men and women shown.... *I don't know if I was spared then because I was a Rothschild or a Collins.*

September 21st

Oma was concerned that I was depressed, after leading such a busy and stressful life. She thought I had hit a bit of a wall mentally, physically and emotionally as I seemed tired all the time and un–motivated .... So, she insisted that I look for another type of job.

Juanita had moved with us from New York and was much happier here in a warmer climate she said, plus she had a sister only a half hour away by car. But I needed a job to support us all anyway. Especially as the bungalow I bought had taken most of the money Tom had left me. We were only living on the rent from the Manhattan apartment which didn't stretch far enough with its rates, insurance and letting fees to pay. Fortunately, my dad was still paying Juanita's wages and our medical insurance.

Jonathon was attending the same school that I did when I first came to L.A. with my grand-parents, Santa Monica High school or SAMOHI. Like me he also found the kids very friendly more casual and less competitive compared to his school in New York, he said.... So, he was now top of the class in all his subjects. Jonathon loved living near the family again, especially Uncle Philip, who took him to music gigs at the weekends. My nineteen-year-old Cousin Jimmy, was also very good with him and taught him how to play golf. So, at twelve years old Jonathon had some cool, positive, male role-models....

Beth was happy going to morning kindergarten, being with Juanita, and visiting Great Oma who is still very sprightly for someone in their seventy-eighth year.

By October I'd landed myself a dream job with Macy's, as a buyer. I couldn't believe my luck as I got the position over thirty other applicants, especially as I'd been working in Social Services, not Fashion.... My new employers said they were impressed with my personal style, my fluency in other languages, plus the fact I had worked as a model in London, albeit briefly. They also said as I'd also organised large fundraising events, I clearly did not mind hard work.... Their one concern however was as a widow with two children, I may not be free to travel, but I assured them I had excellent family support, which I did.

November 1st

How exciting! My new job involves a lot of international travelling which will take me to London, Milan, Paris, where I can practise my French, and on occasion Barcelona, buying for every season. Thanks to Oma's companion Ruby, and my housekeeper Juanita, I can also speak Spanish. This came also came in handy when I was a social worker. Of course, I knew this job had been arranged for me somehow, to keep me busy and out of trouble. I also knew I could never escape them.... I would never be able to expose them either and remain living. *'Them' being the 'Brotherhood', 'the Order', 'The Illuminati'.*

December 4th

I am in seventh heaven with my new job though as it means I can keep in touch with my friends Linda and Karen in New York as I've been there also.... In London I saw my friends Veronica and Carol who are both married now with a child, Veronica has a son, Victor junior and Carol a daughter, Emilia. I've even managed to meet-up with my parents in Paris one weekend. So, I literally flying high with my new job, and everyone was helping Juanita with the children, when I am away.

My employers were right, I do have a good eye when it came to popular products as I buy high end fashion, accessories and some luxury household goods as well.... But life is a bit hectic.

December 20th

I am enjoying my new life so much that I wonder why I had struggled working in the area of social services for so long.... And for once I was on an excellent salary with bonuses. Mind you I will miss organising Christmas dinner for the Homeless this year. My New York co-workers say I am missed also. Apparently, one of the reasons that I had been so popular with my clients in social work was because I was attractive dressed stylishly and lit up every room I entered, everyone said.... Tom had tried to tell me this, that I was a stand- out beauty and not just because of my height. My co-workers said their clients were less disruptive when I was around. They called me 'The Ice Maiden', because I was so cool, classy, and generally people were calmer around me, for some reason. Plus, I had this aura of mystery they said, as no one could work me out, or quite pick my accent....

Strange, that I never admitted this to myself, at the time. But I do know many men were too intimidated by me to ask me out, I usually asked them, except for Tom Collins of course, which makes me sad.... I miss him so much.

I know I have always had my own style and worn plenty of colour compared to most, especially in winter. And I wear cool based rather than warm based colours, because of my skin tones.... I feel colour is important to our everyday well-being. Some days I can change three times before finding the right colour to wear, although I do have several different coloured silk scarves to brighten up any outfit and I rarely wear black.... Although both times I was widowed I wore black and other sombre colours for weeks afterwards, mostly because I just wanted to disappear.

I really enjoyed being Mrs Sophia West-Collins, International buyer.... Years later I would work out why I really got the job. Still, it was preferable then to being 'bumped off'.

Note: I have a big break here from writing in my journal, probably because I was so busy.

Recap:

In April 1979, a significant thing happened. I met Andre de Rothschild again.... I read that he was giving a lecture on urban architectural design, at Descartes University, when I was in Paris, so I decided to attend and approached him afterwards.... Andre was very surprised but delighted to see me he said, so we walked to the bar of my near-by hotel for a glass of wine.

I thought that Andre had aged and grown quite cynical in the five years since I had seen him.... He did not start to relax until we'd consumed our second glass of wine, so we ordered a third.

I recall a newspaper had been left in my room open at that page, advertising Andre's lecture. Was this planned, or was it fate? I'm still not sure.

Andre told me he hated America and all it stood for and said that France had been ruined by an invasion of technology and consumerism and he resented American commercial companies like IBM coming to France.... America was only respected for its power, he said, and not its contributions to world culture and standing. They were also to blame, he felt, for pushing France to one-side as a world power, with the emphasis now on money, speed, technology and efficiency. And because of this France was now a middle-ranking country, where they had once led the world and been superior in every way, be it cultural, political, intellectual or gastronomic and now even the latter was being threatened with the recent introduction of this dreadful American fast food.

Andre was really on a roll and quite angry about America it seemed. He then quoted President George Clemenceau who had led France through the First World War who said that "America went from barbarism to decadence without passing through civilisation" .... I just sat and mostly listened, wondering then, if I'd made the right choice coming to see him at all....

After two hours of talking, putting the world to right, and anti-Americanism. Andre suddenly grabbed my hand and kissed it, and said he was not happy and that he should have married me. He said it was his fault that I took another lover, as he should have relocated to be near me.... He then stated how sad our lives had both now become.... I never asked him about his wife and he never mentioned her.... But he did say that he was sorry to hear I'd been widowed again.

We moved to the restaurant adjoining the bar and ordered dinner. Then I threw caution to the wind and decided to trust Andre for some reason.... I told him what I suspected about the Illuminati, the families involved, and the reasons why I thought both my husbands had been murdered.... I even told him I felt his brother was supposed to be the one to bring me into 'the Order'.... I also revealed Grosspapi's prediction for me and my son, with the underlying threat to my Poppa and me, that we could not stop what was my destiny.... I had never, ever unloaded on anyone so honestly, as I did that night to Andre and it was a relief.

He listened, asked a few relevant questions, but never once scoffed or said I was delusional.... I still never told him what had happened to me the night I had conceived Jonathon, or the fact that his brother had been present.... That would have to keep a bit longer I felt.

After dinner we went up to my room where we made mad passionate love, then slept until nine o'clock the following morning. We both had somewhere we were meant to be that morning but both cancelled.... By lunchtime Andre told me he was divorcing his wife.... Neither of them was happy he said and as they had no children to worry about, why suffer any longer.... By dinnertime we were holding hands, gazing into each- other's eyes and planning our future together....

Things had always moved quickly with Andre and me.... Andre had even decided that he would relocate to L.A. where a lot of modern experimental architecture was happening, he said. He agreed that my children had experienced enough upheavals and should not be moved again.... He then got very emotional and told me that he wasn't worthy of me, but intended to spend the rest of his life making himself so now that he had another chance.... I was confused by some of his talk and wondered if there was something important Andre hadn't told me, or if he was just being French....

As usual, when I'm around Andre, I find it hard to keep my head, it's like he bewitches me. But I did agree that I would be safer married to him, snd he would be safe also as long, as he didn't go rogue.... I never asked him if he was part of the Illuminati and of course he never said, but he seemed to know an awful lot about them. Of course, he could be a member of the freemasons and not the elite Illuminati, that was also likely.... *This was wishful thinking on my part.*

The following morning, after another night of passionate lovemaking, I told Andre it would never work as he hated America and all it stood for.... But he told me when I left for the airport by taxi, that he would find a way for us to be together, forever.... Then he kissed me passionately goodbye.... I wondered on the ride to the airport why my life is always so full of drama because I knew intuitively that there was something important Andre hadn't told me, but I could tell he wanted to.

Oma was concerned when I got back to L.A. and told her about my meeting Andre again. Even though Poppa had come to me in spirit and told me something like this was going to happen.... My mom had just flown over to visit us all and was staying with Oma when I got back. Now she was delighted when I told her. She did not comment the fact that Andre was still married though, I'd noticed. Mom was also pleased that I had relocated to L.A. and was living near the family, now she could stop worrying about me, she said.... She also stated that I was much more suited to my new job than the type of work I had been doing in New York; neither of my parents really understood me.

Philip's choice of a partner mom did not approve of though, as he was involved with a talented singer who currently sang in nightclubs but was breaking into recording. Her name was Stephanie Nicks, but everyone calls her Stevie.... Stevie is blonde, petite and pretty and Philip adores her. I told Stevie that she would be famous one day and her friend Lindsay Buckingham, but not with their current band 'Fritz'.... I did not tell Philip that I felt Stevie and Lindsay were more than just work partners though.

June 12th

As always happens after I am bewitched by Andre de Rothschild, I come back down to earth. Now the practical side of me has taken over and I realise, sadly, that our relationship would never work. So, when Andre phoned me for my birthday after sending thirty-four red roses, one for each year, I told him that I now had some doubts.

But this time Andre wasn't taking no for an answer.... He was winding up his work contracts and had already left his wife, which so far was fairly amicable he said. And after six months they can get a divorce as she agreed that they were miserable.... 'Amore' is important to the French.... Andre then said he was going to relocate to L.A. and see what contracts he could secure .... He told me that he loved me and always had but this time I was to be patient.... What a darling man.

I wondered then if he had spoken to his brother about the rekindled us, as I was pretty sure Laurent wouldn't want his baby brother to marry such a wonton woman as me. So, for Andre's sake and mine I decided to meditate more and channel my sexual energy into healing. I joined a group that met once a week and attended when I could; we did Reiki (hands on healing). I also learnt to balance my chakras regularly.... I was not going to screw up another chance at happiness, I decided.

Like Poppa I had always worked at some level as a healer, mainly with my heart chakra and empathy, rather than hands-on. I just had to think of someone, and I had them in my space, so much so that I often took on other people's ailments and then had to send them to the ethers. I always cleared myself daily with meditation, no matter where I was. But unlike Poppa and his male ego, bless him, I rarely talked about it.... I just accepted that this was something I did daily.... helping people, like brushing my teeth.... I also gave people information or advice all the time, that I received clairaudiently and most people were very receptive to it. I also felt it was wrong to record this as it was other people's business.

Sophia
1979

March 3rd

I need to record some of the discoveries I have made recently as I have slowly been piecing together this puzzle that is my life.... As I also need to be able to properly advise my children one day.

After I moved back to L.A., I got so busy that I was distracted from the task of trying to work out who exactly, was behind the deaths of my two late husbands and why? Even though the reason for Tom's death was a bit more obvious.... I then got my new job and was away a lot plus I got involved with Andre again and was even more distracted with him flying to L.A. regularly.... Sometimes Andre and I do manage to have a weekend off in Paris together, if I can fit it in to my busy work schedule.

I now realise that this was probably planned by someone, as how else did I get such a plum job. As I know there were others more deserving than me, for my position.... Still, I am doing a good job and my employers seem happy with me.... But I was told that this was going to happen by the two 'Invisible men,' who'd accosted me in that supermarket car park.... They warned me then "to accept the job, behave myself, or else" ....

But it was my decision to go and hear Andre speak though I wasn't coerced.... Although, I did read about his lecture in a newsletter left in my room in the hotel where I always stay when I'm in Paris. And there was an Architects conference on, as many were staying in my hotel, so maybe it was fate or then again, maybe not....

Before this all happened, I had been reading through Poppa's journals again, but to be honest had gleaned more from his scribbled notebooks, especially the quotes he had recorded.... This one is from the late President John F. Kennedy, who talked about a conspiracy to control us all, by an elite and corrupt cartel:

"For we are opposed around the world by a monolithic and ruthless conspiracy that relies on covert means for expanding its share of influence. On infiltration instead of invasion, on subversion instead of elections, on intimidation instead of free choice, on guerrillas by night, instead of armies by day. It is a system which has conscripted vast human and material resources into the building of a tightly knit and highly efficient machine that combines military, diplomatic, intelligence, economic, scientific and political operations".

And there was a conspiracy to have Kennedy assassinated, it was not one gunman working alone. The C.I.A. operative David Sanchez Morales, said at a cocktail party in Bueno Aries in 1975 "That Kennedy got what was coming to him." Implying it was orchestrated as he blamed Kennedy's lack of Air support in the Bay of Pigs invasion in Cuba, for its failure, back in 1961.... And the C.I.A. and L.A. police department need to explain what they were doing in Dallas that fateful day when Kennedy was assassinated, as three C.I.A. men were present apparently dressed as tramps.... This was the secretive nature of the C.I.A. at the time and it had a reputation for high level assassinations in the 1960s; Lee Harvey Oswald was just a patsy. And he was not the only sacrificial lamb.... At least fifty people who had crucial information that conflicted with the lone gunman theory either died under suspicious circumstances or were silenced in other ways.... Morales also stated that there were unsuccessful plots to kill Fidel Castro.

Andrew Y and the 'white hats' believe that anti-communist, anti- Castro extremists in the C.I.A. planned the assassination of Kennedy.... The reason was to maintain tension with the Soviet Union and Cuba and to prevent a U.S. with-drawl from Vietnam, as they feared the spread of Communism. Also, the Illuminati cannot control any country economically, under communist rule.... Back then, 25% of the U.S. voters believed that a secretive group with a globalist agenda were conspiring to eventually rule the world with an authoritarian one world government. That is also why Kennedy was assassinated, because he didn't want to be part of it. Put simply, he did not play ball....

This is another quote from John F. Kennedy spoken only seven days before he died, that Tom had recorded in his notebook "There is a plot in this country to enslave every man woman and child. And before I leave this high and noble office, I intend to expose this plot".

And this on the 27th April 1961 in New York City, when Kennedy was again talking about secret societies but this time the F.B.I., as recorded by Poppa.

"The very word secrecy is repugnant in a free and open society. As we are as a people, inherently and historically opposed to secret societies, and secret proceedings".

Nowadays 60% of Americans believe there was a conspiracy to have J.F. Kennedy assassinated.

The Senator McCall who was killed with his secretary Nelson on the chartered plane my late husband Saul was flying had been investigating the Kennedy assassination. He was ready to expose the whole plot apparently, according to his wife.... And Mrs McCall was very selective who she says this to, as she lives in fear that she may be disposed of also.... As The F.B.I came and removed all her husband's files immediately after his death claiming that they were 'highly classified'. She said they weren't as most of his work was fairly, low-level.

I also believe, that this is why Saul was chosen to fly the plane, to get rid of two birds with one stone.... As Jonathon, even before his conception, was prophesised to be a future leader of the free world (a U.S. President possibly) the first of Jewish ancestry and the puppet of the Illuminati.... And Saul was obviously not one of those selected to influence him.

Fortunately, I have discovered and as history will tell, that even the best laid Illuminati plans, can go awry and I hope this one will too.... As I shall do everything within my power to try to prevent Jonathon from joining the Illuminati.... He is only thirteen, but he has read all of Poppa's diaries and believes every word that Poppa wrote plus what his Great Oma has told him also, which is fortunate. When he is older, I shall give him Poppa's journals and notebooks and my copy of Tom's notebook. I hope he can deal with it all.

And this Morales fellow, he and two other top C.I.A. operatives, George Joannides and Gordon Campbell, were also at the Ambassador Hotel in June 1968, the night before Robert Kennedy was gunned down.... Morales died of a heart attack in 1978 a few weeks before he was due to appear before a U.S. select committee on 'assassinations'; how convenient.

July 7th

The second time I met Andrew Y, I gave him Tom's notebook, this was not long after Tom died. He said it would be invaluable.... Since then, I had been either too busy or not in the right frame of mind to see him again but yesterday we met; I contacted him....

Andrew Y said he was delighted to see me again and commented that the information in Tom's notebook had confirmed their suspicions about many people.... He said he was still keen to get me into a key position for the 'White hats' as there was no one like me enlisted.... He then said I would easily get a position with the Edmond de Rothschild foundation here in the U.S., or the Rothschild foundation in Europe with my family name and social services background.

I felt then I had to disclose to Andrew Y that I was now involved with a distant cousin, Andre de Rothschild. Who I said was a renowned French Architect, but unfortunately not one who works for a Rothschild owned company. But I said his older brother Laurent did and I knew him well also.... I told him Laurent worked for Paris Orleans, the flagship company for the Rothschild banking group. Which does assets management, private banking, mixed farming, luxury hotels and yachts: the latter of which Laurent races and sells in Cannes.... And all these companies are connected to the Rothschild Foundation I said, so this may be possible if I asked for his help.... I also said that I could always ask my dad to pull a few strings for me, even though I had to admit to Andrew Y, that I had never accepted my dad's help before....

Of course, Andrew Y was excited by all this.... But I realised I was getting carried away and my ego was coming into play, as although I would love to be of more service to the 'White hats', I simply couldn't keep re-locating my children.... As the most probable location for me would be Paris, and my son would not be happy to move again, and my daughter was far too fragile.... So sadly, I had to admit this to Andrew Y....He said he understood that it was not easy for me being a single mother.

I now also had Andre to consider although he would be happy if we relocated to Paris. As the winding up of his work contracts and relocating to L.A. was taking him much longer than he had anticipated, due to his lengthy architectural projects.... I never told Andrew Y this, but I did say I would give it all some serious thought.... Poppa had it so much easier than me, being a man.

I think a part of me then was hoping that if I took Jonathon out of the U.S. it could change the course of his life and therefore keep him away from American politics and being a player in any sordid Illuminati game....

Andrew Y told me that now only nine key countries were without a central Rothschild bank, being Russia, China, Iceland,

Cuba, Syria, Iran, Venezuela, North Korea and Hungary. He also said that the City of London is controlled by the bank of England and that Nathan Mayer Rothschild, the first Baron Rothschild, crashed the English stock market in 1812 and then took control of the bank of England....That is how it came to be a private corporation owned by the Rothschild family.... Poppa had already told me this when he was alive.

Andrew Y then quoted the same Nathan, Mayer Rothschild....

"I care not what puppet is placed on the throne of England to rule the empire. The man who controls Britain's money supply, controls the British Empire and I control the British money supply."

I asked Andrew Y if he thought my father was part of the Illuminati, but he never answered me. I don't know whether he was impressed or disgusted that I was a Rothschild, and he may have even wondered if he could trust me at all, especially as we had discussed the fact that my Grosspapi was a member of the Illuminati.

In 1998 The Bank of England became an independent public organisation. In 2004 N. M. Rothschild & Sons withdrew from gold trading and price-fixing which a Rothschild had been doing for over two hundred years.... They still apparently have trillions invested in gold bullion.

Andrew Y said corrupt banks take a lot of the risk out of laundering illicit funds for corrupt people. And one, the Bank of Credit and Commerce International (BCCI) who of course are into shipping, insurance, commodities, real estate, plus charitable works, are corrupt. Fortunately, the authorities recently rejected their offer to purchase The Bank of America. *Although they did control it anyway, for many years....*

As the American dollar is the world's dominant currency and BCCI's activities are in 73 countries, BCCI internal operations are split. This is probably so their executives can move assets around to cover up their loses and cheat. Their behaviour ranges from questionable to positively criminal he said.... But are they Illuminati, this is unclear? I suggested not to Andrew Y, as they are a bank predominately owned by Arabs and not Jews. He agreed that this was a valid point. *The bank was eventually closed- down due to corruption in 1991 with a $10 million debt.*

Andrew Y said he felt the recent defeat of the black liberal movement which has been so prominent this decade with millions of black people rebelling against capitalism, was strategic. As there has been an emergence of educated middle class influential blacks, now that the past legal and social barriers have been lifted.... But although some have risen socially and economically instead of looking after their own people they are looking after themselves.... As the poor working class blacks are still oppressed so this has only divided the black people, he said.

I didn't agree with him about the defeat of the black liberal movement then, as it was still strong I felt. Look at what happened with the 1968 Olympics Games solidarity.... Indeed, Poppa predicted a future Afro-American president, who although popular would still not do much for his own people. This came true with our 44th President Obama, but then he was raised by a white mother and grand –parents. And things still have not improved enough, look at the 2020 'Black Lives Matter' riots.

Andrew Y believes that the power of the Illuminati won't end until capitalism ends and the only way to stop oppression and exploitation, is to attack the way that society is organised. As it is organised and manipulated by those controlling and elite few.... I told him that I agreed with this as this is why the Illuminati have always feared the spread of communism.

Even now the U.S. state department media establishment, the U.S. government and most large corporations are controlled by a central banking cartel. This includes the Rothschild's, the Warburg's and the Rockefeller's, to name a few, and this is no secret....

Andrew Y also said that these elite few have been manipulating wars and getting countries into debt with their banks, since the Napoleonic wars. And that they played both sides in the first and second world wars.... I told Andrew Y my Poppa wrote about this in his journals....

Andrew Y also believes they were responsible for the sinking of the Titanic and its shortage of lifeboats. This was because Benjamin Guggenheim, Isidor Straus and John Jacob Astor were on board. They were all very wealthy and influential men who were opposed to the creation of the Federal reserve bank and had stood in their way for world economic domination.... And they conveniently all went down with the ship....

He also said these elitist Illuminati had manipulated the assassination of the last Tsar of Russia by the Fascists, for the same reason.

I told Andrew Y that Poppa believed Astor was part of the Illuminati and not disposed of by them. But he would have agreed with him about the Tsar....

Then Andrew Y and I discussed a subject close to my heart as he stated that most U.S. cities have enough vacant buildings, to house all the homeless.... And the world produces three times more food than is required to feed everyone, but so much is wasted.... Just one example of this is if a truck load of watermelons or cabbages don't reach their price at market they are literally dumped, what a waste.... Plus, the lack of distribution of food and other essentials to those-in-need world-wide, is due to corruption or bad organisation.... As these elite few in positions of power encourage division and anarchy to control the world; they also manipulate poverty I believe, as does Andrew Y.

I told Andrew Y that I had read the book by Nesta Webster the English aristocrat who wrote 'Secret Societies and the Subversive Movements, the need for Fascism in Great Britain' back in the 1930s. She believed that the spread of communism and capitalism was encouraged to divide the world, and it was set up by the wealthy Jewish elite who controlled it.... She was a woman ahead of her time I feel.... Webster also believed the Illuminati was paid for by this secret group of Jewish (Zionist) bankers, and their quest for world domination. She said they would eventually appoint their own world leader who some may call the anti-Christ, as they were all anti-mainstream Christianity.

I must admit that even Christian fundamentalists believe in the coming of an anti-Christ.... A niggling part of me is concerned that this anticipated new world leader may be my son, but I did not tell Andrew Y this.

Andrew Y lost me a bit though with the Illuminati and satanic rituals. Although I agreed with a lot he said, I don't agree about that.... No doubt Satanist's do exist, and some are just sexual perverts and predators, but this is not a part of the Illuminati agenda for control, I believe. They do have rituals, but this doesn't include killing children, eating their body parts, making them into ritual candles or sexually violating them, that is too extreme.... Poppa also thought this way.

The orgy I attended with Robert is a way to reward those who do well in 'the Order' I believe nothing more and the Rothschild parties I attended were purely hedonistic, not ritualistic.

When I was driving home after my meeting with Andrew Y, I asked myself the difficult question. What was I supposed to do now with my knowledge of the Illuminati? Because I know people who reveal their secrets are murdered.... Perhaps I should be re-developing my psychic gifts to my full potential.... But then who do I trust with them? To be honest Tom was right I am scared and I have had my head in the sand for years.... I could use the excuse that it is because I am a single parent, but that is not entirely the case.... I am simply not as brave as my Poppa and Tom were.

Poppa comes to visit me occasionally (in spirit) and had already told me a lot of what Andrew Y said especially about the corrupt banks. He said it will get worse before it gets better, as bank CEO's will soon get paid even more obscene salaries. Far more than the Presidents and Prime Ministers of the countries they live in. Plus, greedy Bank executives will pay themselves enormous bonuses causing much suffering to their customers, and be responsible for more than one world recession.... And this will be first world countries, he said.... In the new Millennium, some will be brought to justice, but not enough.

Poppa said there will also be enormous scandals, involving the Catholic Church to do with children being sexually abused by priests and it being covered up for decades.... This had me wondering about Satanists again, as a lot of abuse victims in therapy under hypnotic regression say they were initiated with sexual rituals in the basements of churches. And some even mention witnessing the sacrificial murder of children.... I really don't want to think about that but perhaps I am being a bit naive.... The world really is too wicked a place.

After Poppa's last visit I decided that the future doesn't sound very good at all. But he said there will not be another world war as such, but many minor wars, some civil, plus a war on terrorism. He said Islam will rise-up and extremist Muslims will terrorise us infidels, but not for many years yet.

He said the Illuminati will engage in germ warfare to prevent the spread of communism as it needs capitalism to survive. And said China and its allies, and the U.S. and its allies, will come close to starting a nuclear war, not long after this.

I now realise this was the 2020 pandemic and the potential war over Chinas takeover of Taiwan.

1980

January 17th

I was suspicious after having had one meeting with Malcom X and three with Andrew Y as to why out of the blue the U.S. Military's department of psychic research were interested in me.... Was I being monitored somehow, or had they read my mind, as I had recently decided to reboot myself psychically anyway.... I know the U.S. has been in a psychic race with the U.S.S.R. and not just a space race, which the U.S. won anyway, by putting a man on the moon first in 1969. Although the 'White hats', believe it was faked, and they offer up a convincing case.

My Lily Dale friends said they know of many psychics who have been asked to participate in psychic research, but none from Lily Dale itself, as strangely no one from the department has ever visited there.... I have mentioned this before, it's like Lily Dale it is out of bounds.

I first received a telephone call and then two men dressed in military uniforms visited my home in L.A. and asked me 'as my patriotic duty' to submit to one to two weeks of voluntary psychic testing. The length of stay depended on how well I did, they said.... I admit I found it impossible to refuse....

My Oma was concerned though, as was I, as they said they had documented the impressive work of my famous grandfather Clarence R. Smyth and heard I had inherited his psychic abilities.... This had me suspicious as I had kept a pretty-low profile in psychic circles.... I had been working but only with those I encountered in my daily life plus my healing group and the 'White hats' under the radar, or so I thought.... And there were plenty of mediums seeking any publicity they could get and with high profiles, filling halls, doing psychic demonstrations all around the world, writing books and on television even.... So why chose me and why now? After what I had been thinking the past few weeks it was uncanny.... But like Poppa always said there are no coincidences.

My psychic abilities have, since the time I was a teenager, been sporadic. I can go for weeks with- out anything, then have a run of spirit visitors with messages for me, or others that I know.... Poppa visits me about four times a year, plus my guides, as I see them clairvoyantly and sometimes hear them clairaudiently. Although mostly I just sense what they are telling me. I also get signs such as writing on the wall or have visions I see in fleeting moments. These are often as clear as a colour television screen only fuzzy around the edges.... But mostly I just get on with my daily life.... This is what I wanted, just to be normal.

I was picked up late one afternoon in early February by car and flown with four others to a secret location. The flight took only an hour and none of us said much past introducing ourselves. When we arrived at an undisclosed military base, we were given supper, a comfortable room to sleep in with our own facilities and a television, but no telephone, so I decided on an early night.

The next day I wasn't sure whether to disappoint or impress. Or if that decision was even up to Me, being a medium, because someone from 'the other side' may have had a different agenda.... There were ten of us, four men and six women ranging in ages and ethnicity. And the first thing we were asked by our assessor was "what is our location?". Which we had to write down on a piece of paper and pass to him.... I wrote that we were approximately one hour's distance by car due west from Las Vegas. It just popped into my head. The papers were then read out and we were told I was the most accurate.

Next, we started off with the easy stuff, psychometry. Which is giving information relevant to the owner of something worn on their person and usually metal by reading their vibrations. So, we all put something on a tray away from the group which was then brought out and we each selected an item.... In turn we read for each other. This was also a good way for us to get to know the other participants....

I was spot on with my information for Tara, whose watch I had selected. She confirmed for me that she was a single junior schoolteacher from Illinois, who loved cats. She also confirmed she had been close to her deceased grandmother June, who I said I had with me in spirit. June told me she approved of Tara's new boyfriend, and said he was 'the one'. I Told Tara this which made her smile.

Gerry who read for me was very accurate. He said I had turned my back on a more privileged life, and that I was a widow with two children, a boy and a girl. He said there was a lot of sadness around me but much happier years were ahead.... I felt that he wanted to say more but decided against it.... Everyone in the group managed to read something accurate for the person whose item they had selected.... They were a gifted group.

The next day involved map reading to locate a downed aeroplane, the irony of which was not lost on me, having been involved in finding my late husband Saul's missing aeroplane, thirteen years ago. We were allowed to use pendulums, but this was difficult as no one had been killed in the crash so there was no trauma for us to tune into.... One person found it by luck more than anything.

The third day we spent finding a soldier supposedly lost in the forest by holding onto something he owned. I was the second one there, Greg another participant was just ahead of me. This was also difficult as the soldier was not distressed so my spirit guides did not appear to help me. But it was a fun exercise as the group were friendly and lively. I had an image of a man in uniform sitting under a distinctive tree eating a chocolate bar which is what he was doing when we found him.

By day five we were deciphering an unknown language. I thought this was extra-terrestrial so I sat and tuned-in to a sort of tablet I was given to hold when it was my turn. What was inscribed on the tablet was also copied onto a white board, but I got nothing from that.... The tablet I thought was surprisingly light.... I closed my eyes and found myself to be in a large cigar shaped spaceship. I was naked and had smooth skin and a large head with black almond shaped eyes and I was sending a report to my home planet, that I was injured and the sole survivor.... I felt distressed, not only had I failed to secure all the samples required, but we had crashed due to an interference of the magnetic ley lines we used for flying, and my three other crew members were dead.... I was also finding the inhabitants of this planet very hostile and quite frightening looking....

A lot of churches are built on these ley lines apparently, as priests used to select a sacred place to build.... It has also been documented that most UFO sightings are on these ley lines.

By day seven I'd had enough of being tested I decided as that last exercise had upset me. I was also ready to return home.... I needed to get back to my children and my job, even though the military said they had cleared it with Macys' head office....

I decided I had only cooperated the past week because we were in a ground level building with big windows and low security, so I felt safe. No 'invisible men' were there I felt, although they may have had access to the results. We were also fed well and given down-time to play pool, walk, or jog around a track.... I noticed we were always being filmed though.... At night we could watch T.V. in our rooms or movies in the theatre, so I caught up on some movies I had missed due to my busy life. I did not fraternise with the other mediums much even though they all said they had heard of my famous grandfather and asked me about him.... Still mostly I enjoyed the week, but then I was asked to stay for another, which I was not happy about.... I was allowed to phone home on Sunday night and although we were all sworn to secrecy, I told my Oma what we'd been doing.... She said that she and Poppa had done similar tests.... I was told so-far I had passed all the tests, but I already knew that....

The first day of the second week we were asked to channel, and I went first. There were only five of us now and I had no idea who came in or what I said, as the assessors would not let me see what they had recorded.... This annoyed me somewhat, so I decided that it was time for me to go home if they would not also co-operate with me.... I have always had a problem with authority.... The rest of the group said they had not understood one word I said as I spoke in German with a deep voice that was not my own.... One said, being dramatic, that they thought I'd channelled Hitler.

I told my assessors that I wanted to leave, but they asked me to do one final test the next day.

The final test involved making an object move and or levitating.... Poppa had come to me the night before and told me not to worry, these people were not a threat to me.... So, I decided to do as they asked and called upon my spirit friends who lifted the object, a glass paperweight, after which I levitated to the ceiling with their help and much to everyone's surprise.... As no one else could do what I did they were dismissed for the day.

I asked my main assessor again to see the film of me channelling but he refused, so with the help of spirit I flew papers around the room, flew open the door and walked back to my room to pack. I then tried to walk out of the complex but two soldiers stopped me.... They asked if I would please join the panel in the conference room in an hour, so my staged tantrum had worked.

When I walked into the conference room there were already five men seated at an oval table. Two were civilians, one being my main assessor, plus there were three high-ranking military personnel.... They all introduced themselves and were very polite....The Major General, thanked me for my co-operation then a screen was pulled down and the room dimmed so we could watch the film of me channelling....

For the next half an hour tears rolled down my face and they wouldn't stop, because coming through me was my dear Poppa.... I told them all this.... What Poppa said had been translated for them earlier and they were now reading that script. I don't know why I was so upset because Poppa had visited me many times, but somehow this was different.

This is what my Poppa said....

"When you die and pass over, everything you have accomplished, careers, power, wealth is stripped away.... How you have lived your life and treated others is what counts. How you loved and what you meant to others being the most important. This is your day of judgement and there are consequences for your past actions, as you are here to learn and to grow from these life lessons. If you have hurt others, you will feel their pain.... If you have not learnt your lessons in this life you will be back to do them again sometimes with the same souls, even if you do not remember each other.... This is called karma....so think again about your actions, and how they affect others."

Poppa then predicted what would happen in the future, a lot of which I had heard before, about how wars would be manipulated to control the world's most valuable commodity, oil, which would involve two future U.S. Presidents from the same family, protecting their own interests.... Then he stated there will be many acts of terrorism around the world, carried out by extremist Muslims. One being a major calamity on American soil early in the 21st century which will lead to tighter security and immigration procedures in the free-world.... But when the truth finally comes out decades later as to who was behind it and why, it will shock the nation to the core....

Of course, Poppa was talking about presidents Bush senior and junior and the 9/11 disaster.

I knew Poppa had said more but this was all they were going to show me.... They possibly thought what I had been shown was improbable, but the rest was more relevant to now.... After hearing what Poppa had said I told them that the U.S. may be in a psychic race with Russia, but I didn't want to be part of it.... The Major General stated that was fine, as although I was obviously gifted, they had many others who were more-so which meant, I would not be required to complete the week or called upon in the future....

I was relieved but a bit surprised, as I knew no one had done what I had and levitated.... But maybe I had rattled-their-cages too much with my channelling.... So, I got up and walked out. I then grabbed my belongings and was driven immediately to Las Vegas airport where I was given an airline ticket home....

Looking back this was probably their main objective of getting me there. Hoping my famous Grandfather would come through with his predictions for the future.

Whilst I was waiting for my flight I called Andre, as I was a bit upset, fortunately he was in L.A. for once.... During the flight I decided I had a lot to think about.... Then I got distracted again, as when I arrived home Andre was waiting for me, with roses, champagne, a candle lit dinner and no children, they were with Oma....And this time he wasn't taking no for an answer, he said.... So when he asked me once again to marry him.... I said 'yes'.

The way I behaved at the military base was not like me, I think I had my Poppa in my space as I was acting on ego.... I also realise now that Andre was a constant distraction for me back then as whenever I tried to concentrate on my quest for truth, he came into my mind.... I thought that by marrying him this may have resolved but it didn't, he always blocked me somehow.

June 10th

Happy Birthday to me! My wonderful new husband is taking me out for an intimate dinner tonight.

Andre and I married May 26th 1980 at the council office or mairie in Montmartre in Paris's 18th arrondissement. We saw no point in waiting so managed to organise our wedding in just eight weeks.... Andre's mother put on a mid-day wedding feast in her nearby villa for the thirty Rothschild family members and twenty-six friends who were present.... And because we had both been married before, me twice, everyone appreciated that we wanted something fairly-low-key.

I wore a long white muslin dress with an embroidered sleeveless bolero jacket. I had my hair down a floral wreath on my head and sandals on my feet.... Andre said I looked beautiful. He looked very handsome in cream linen pants and waistcoat with a billowing white muslin shirt, he also wore sandals.... My children were our attendants and Laurent and Philip our witnesses. Oma and Ruby flew in from the L.A. with Juanita our housekeeper, plus Uncle William, Aunt Selma and my cousins Patti and James. My parents, Alexander and his wife Marguerite, flew over from Zurich, as did my Cousin Isobel and husband Etienne....The biggest surprise though was Veronica and Victor and Carol and her husband Nigel from the U.K. I was so pleased they came. I told everyone to dress informally.

The day before the wedding we all just relaxed and mingled over a long lunch at the villa. The next day we had a short marriage service at the council office, then returned to the villa for some more even more sumptuous food than we'd had yesterday. Then we cut a profiterole wedding cake and danced in the beautifully lit outside courtyard until the wee hours. It was wonderful.... The day after the wedding we relaxed, swam in the Villa's heated pool, ate, drank and danced some more. On the fourth day, exhausted, we all went home.

It was a truly memorable wedding and I had never enjoyed the company of my family more. Philip made a wonderful speech that had us all laughing. Laurent also made a speech which was from the heart. I genuinely believe he is happy for us as are Mom, Dad and my beloved Oma of course.... Oma said, 'third time lucky', and got this saying correct for once.

I notice I didn't say much about Andre's family, as our wedding was held at his parents' Paris villa. The family's main home Villa Ephrussi de Rothschild, on the French Riviera was most stunning but Andre didn't want to be married there.... Andre and Laurent have no siblings, but there were a few de Rothschild cousins they were close to who attended; I found them all delightful. His mother the baroness was always charming to me, her husband the baron not so much. I never knew what he really thought of me.... He died six years after we married, and Laurent inherited the baronetcy.... I should have wondered then why his parents made such an enormous fuss of Jonathon ....

Of course, they knew, as did some of the other de Rothschild relations at the wedding I'm sure.... Fortunately, my family always got on very well with Andre's family.... they were kin after all.

Sophia

1981

September 3rd

This year has been wonderful....Firstly in March we moved into our amazing new home in the Hollywood Hills, that Andre designed and had built for us....Then on July 11th we celebrated the arrival of our beautiful twins Oliver and Martine....They arrived two weeks early but at least I had a normal delivery this time at the Cedars-Sinai Hospital, where I then stayed for three whole weeks. Andre has employed a Nanny for me now as I have been so exhausted from the constant breast feeding of two babies with different routines, as Juanita has had enough on her plate running our busy household.

I am finding it harder to recover from this birth at aged thirty-five, than I did with Jonathon a month shy of twenty and Beth at twenty-eight. I try to swim twice a day in our pool as it is a good way for me to tone-up and the weather is still so warm.... The twins are fair, chubby and adorable and I feel twice blessed....

Jonathon at fifteen is a bit annoyed with me for having more babies I feel, as he needs a quiet house to study he says. Thank heavens he is now living downstairs as we are upstairs. Jonathon is very independent and ambitious and aims to be top in all his subjects.... Juanita, has finally learnt to drive which is a big help as we are constantly driving him to meetings of the various clubs he belongs to. Most of which he is the captain of, like the chess club, the drama group and the debating team. In another year he will be able to drive himself which will be even better.

Andre spends a lot of time away unfortunately, as he has clients in Europe as well as all over the U.S. He is in demand for designing dramatic minimalist houses on difficult sites which involves some clever engineering.... Paul Jarvis is his architectural engineer and Andre says he is a genius.

Our stunning new home is being compared to the well-known Stahl House, with its sleek stream- lined structure, panoramic glass walls and open concept. It has already been nominated for a few prestigious architectural awards, both here and abroad.... The infinity pool with its glass edge is cantilevered and looks like it is floating above the city, it is so dramatic. Even the fireplace appears to float above the bear skin rug.... We both like minimalism and the house has lot of built-in furniture also designed by Andre, such as all the shelving and storage cabinets, and some of the seating. In the spacious living- area the stereo, television and drinks bar rise-up from a cabinet below with the push of a button. Only the dining suite and two Corbusier chairs are not built in, we even have a built- in tropical fish tank.... The house is splendid I am so proud of Andre. I was allowed to choose some objects de art but not too many but we were lucky enough to acquire a Joan Miro painting.... All our personal belongings are all hidden away behind sliding doors including our books. Our bedroom is minimalist, but the children's rooms are less so as they like a bit of colour and clutter. In the kitchen Andre wanted nothing on display so the everyday items like the coffee maker and toaster are behind sliding doors.... The only problem is we have to remember where everything is.

Jonathon loves it with his structured mind, but still Beth prefers our pretty Spanish bungalow and was sad when we sold it, she said.... Beth is a happier less nervous child now who can't do enough for the babies.... Jonathon has his own pad downstairs, with a bedroom, bathroom, kitchenette, sitting room and entrance, next to the triple garage and Andre's office. This should suit him for many years.... Tamara our Nanny and Juanita have their own spacious bedsit rooms with bathrooms and Beth and the twins have the other two bedrooms with a shared bathroom.... Tamara is only with us until the twins turn two then Beth can have her bigger bedroom.

Our bedroom is huge and has double doors that open out to the patio and pool area, we also have a huge walk-in wardrobe and a massive bathroom with a sunken bath.... Andre, has completely spoilt me.

I know Andre is a successful architect and we can afford a house like this, but I still don't know how much Andre's family are actually worth or mine for that matter. To be honest money has never interested me, but that is easy for me to say knowing it was always there if I really needed it. I have noticed though that none of the Rothschild's or de Rothschild's ever discusses business or money matters socially, it is considered the height of rudeness. This also comes from being very wealthy and assuming everyone you mix with socially is in a similar financial position.... Therefore business matters are discussed strictly during office hours and behind closed doors.

The 'White hats' members I have spoken to over the years have asked me how wealthy all the Rothschild's are combined.... I've to admit I don't really know, but I 'feel' around three trillion dollars.

Andre has never interfered with my decision to not send my children to private schools but insists Jonathon must go to a good university.... Of course he will anyway, as Jonathon is a top student so he will probably get a scholarship.

Andre works from home, but he is either very busy or away a lot, so I've had to join things to make a life for myself.... Well, that was before the twins arrived, as now I am busy.... I still run a weekly psychic circle where we do readings and give healing. It is so popular that we always fill our thirty client spots and it is by donation only.... Poppa usually comes through and gives me advice.

I haven't worked as such since Andre and I married, he insisted that I needed to put more time into my children, especially Beth and as usual he was right. Andre did offer to adopt my children legally but I decided against it, out of respect for both their late fathers. So Jonathon is a West and Beth is a Collins, which is a bit confusing for strangers as I am of course Mrs de Rothschild. My full moniker is Sophia, Elizabeth, Rothschild-West-Collins-de Rothschild, but of course I never use that.

Jonathon is adamant that he is keeping his late father's surname, even though he does like and respect Andre he says. They get on well thankfully as in many ways they are alike being both highly intelligent, ambitious, charming, and a touch arrogant.... Jonathon, still sees a lot of his Uncles Zeke and Rueben West, Saul's brothers, and their families, as they both live in L.A. Plus his Uncle Philip when he is in town.

I never did get the opportunity to do that key role for the 'White hats'.... I didn't even speak to Andrew Y for the two years after the twins were born, but got in touch with him after the family skeleton came out of the closet.... Because of my concern for Jonathon.

1982

April 15th

I thought it would never happen, but Philip has finally gotten hitched.... To a lighting designer named Mitzi Foy....They both work on music tours which means they go on the road together. Mitzi said it is far better for her to have a husband around, as there are always a lot of men but very few women. They have both toured with bands like Guns'n'roses, Arrowsmith and Def Leppard, to name a few.

Mitzi is six years younger than Philip and pretty and petite at 5'2", he is 6'2". They are well suited though and even look and dress alike. Both have long fair hair and wear the uniform jeans or black leather trousers with a limitless number of t-shirts, depicting different bands. They also have several black leather jackets each as they get a new one on every tour.

Philip said he was ready to settle down as he was sick of drinking, taking drugs and having casual sex.... I doubt that he and Mitzi will ever have children though, but they will have hearing loss.... As Poppa would say their bands are 'not my cup of tea' or that of my conservative brother Alexander.

Alexander has a two-year old son Alex junior and another on the way, a girl I feel. They still live in Zurich, in the largest apartment of my grand-parents old Zurich mansion which six years ago my parents had converted into six luxury apartments.... Grossmami Rothschild, now lives in the smallest apartment as Mom and Dad went back to live in their beautiful lakeside villa.

Philip and Mitzi's wedding was the last time we all got together. It was held in Orange County on their rural property in a huge red barn, complete with hay bales; they even had a catering truck. The obligatory rock band started playing after the service which was conducted by a celebrant. They had written their own vows which were quite beautiful and brought a tear to many eyes.... Alex was a witness as was Mitzi's sister Rachel and I was asked to do a reading. Of course, Philip made a hilarious speech.

I decided Philip definitely has a type, as the petite Mitzi in her tall white thigh high boots, white hot pants with matching coat- dress was very reminiscent of his former girlfriend Stevie Nicks. Philip wore black leather pants and waistcoat with a white collarless shirt.... Needless-to-say it was a memorable wedding, as there were many well know people from the music industry present. The two families got on well....Surprisingly Mitzi has rather conservative Jewish parents and siblings, of which there are three, an older sister and two younger brothers.

1983

April 19th

A bomb has just exploded in our household, well not literally, but enough to tear apart the delicate balance of our blended family.... But it was destined to happen one day.... I think I subconsciously, I had worked it out years ago, after I had found out that Andre's brother Laurent was actually gay. But I didn't want to face it.... Even so, it still came as a bit of a shock.

It started with Jonathon doing a project in his advanced science class, albeit a questionable one which did have me wondering at the time.... Why was he studying the new exciting area of DNA in this way. But for some reason I remember going along with it, giving him samples from everyone's hairbrush even. As Jonathon was told that by having a half-brother and half-sisters, we would be a good case study.... Why did I not sense the danger in this? I also wonder if any other skeletons came out of the closets of any of his classmates due to this exercise.

On the day of the results, I got a call from the school to say that Jonathon was in the sickbay and could I come immediately to collect him.... The school nurse didn't say much but she did say he'd had a major melt-down in class, which was unusual for him.

I could see Jonathon was pale and visibly upset when I arrived, but he didn't say anything to me then or when we were walking to the car.... When we sat in the car, he angrily thrust a piece of paper at me and said.... "DNA doesn't lie, but mothers do" ....So I read the paper.... I recall that my hands were shaking and Jonathon could see that I was shocked and baffled.... The hurt and anger would come later.... As the analysis clearly stated that Jonathon had one half-sibling Beth, and two full siblings.... Oliver and Martine.... Which obviously meant, that Andre was his biological father.... But how.... I was stunned.

I don't remember driving home that day, I must have been on auto-pilot and Jonathon could see I was in shock and wisely said nothing.... When we arrived home, I told him that I needed to speak to Andre alone and would talk to him soon.... And thankfully Andre was home for once and in his office.

A lot of things were suddenly starting to dawn on me.... I could now see what Andre had meant before we married, when he said he wasn't worthy of me and needed to make it up to me which he intended to spend the rest of his life doing.... Plus, other things obviously, like his similarity to the non-existent Charles Rothschild, that I met that fateful night.... Of course, my mind was in a whirl and I could not hold back the tears as I was feeling very betrayed....

Andre could see when I walked in that something serious had occurred and was relieved when I said no one was dead or injured.... But, as soon as I said a DNA project at Jonathon's school, he knew immediately what was coming next....

Andre came over, sat me down on the sofa and took both of my hands in his....He said he was so very sorry that Jonathon and I had to find out this way and he should have told me years ago that this was a probability.... But he simply didn't know how.... And this is the reason Laurent had been keeping an eye on me all these years because he'd felt too ashamed to.... And yes, Laurent was going to offer to marry me if Saul hadn't, because he was still too young and immature himself, he said.... Of course, a marriage to Laurent would have ended in divorce, as he is gay and never 'came out' until after their father died.

Andre kept repeating how sorry he was. He said he was so young and totally dictated to by the Rothschild cabal.... Then said he and Laurent were told from young boys that one of them had a destiny to fulfil, as the father of a future leader of the free world. And that the mother had already been selected from another branch of the Rothschild family.... As was confirmed by the Grande Dame at the time, not Tom's mother.... Andre said he could not believe it was him, until

Laurent confessed a year before they met me that he was gay, and he had been concealing it, to not upset their father.

Andre then admitted that when he first met me at those two parties he found me so beautiful but he was so shy then. He knew there was no-way he could possibly seduce me in time to fulfil the prophecy as he could barely even speak to me.... He was only eighteen when he impregnated me that fateful night and a virgin, he said (so he never had sex with Vanessa). Andre also confessed that he had dyed his hair and moustache black, and was high on cocaine at the time, posing as the English, Charles Rothschild, so he was therefore unrecognisable to me. Although I do remember commenting to Laurent, on Charles's similarity to his brother Andre, that evening.... And yes, they had slipped me something.... But he swore there were only him and Laurent in the room at the time.

Laurent, he said, has not then, or ever had sexual intercourse with me, or any woman in fact, despite being such a charmer as, he can't, Andre said. Apparently Laurent only went to those heterosexual orgies to try and 'cure' himself and was only ever an observer. But of course, he couldn't.... Andre then admitted to me that he has never touched cocaine since.

After confessing all this, Andre broke down and sobbed. He said there were so many times he had wanted to tell me and couldn't bear it if I hated him now, or Jonathon.... He knew I had suffered because of that night and it has caused him and Laurent so much guilt .... Especially Laurent he said as it was his idea, as he had seen first-hand what it had done to me.... Andre then admitted that he had deserved to lose me to Tom.... And he and Laurent were hopeful, he said, that I would finally be happy and were so upset for me when they heard that Tom had died also....

At that point, I recall, I didn't really know what I felt, anger, relief, as I was still stunned. But I did feel once again that my whole world had been turned upside down....

Andre and I just sat there for a while holding each other. I said that the most important thing for us now was to put on a united front for Jonathon.... I suggested we tell him we first met at a party in England when we were both young and silly and we got drunk and had a one-night-stand, and that we both never knew, until now, that Saul was not his father.... which was not entirely untrue.

Jonathon sat and listened to our confession but he said nothing. Then he barely spoke to us for weeks.... He did go and see Oma, but I had already pre-warned her disclosing the full true story, which she was pretty upset about, understandably....

I pleaded with Jonathon not to tell any of the Wests, I said it would kill Saul's parents and thankfully he agreed.... He only had that one afternoon off school, and fortunately no one said anything to him as they all had exams to concentrate on, then it was term break.... But I was so angry about this invasion of our privacy that I complained to the school principal, and he agreed it was a breach of ethics and reprimanded the teacher.... But his job was done I'm sure, as this information was probably passed on for a fat-fee to the Illuminati. And not surprisingly that teacher resigned and never came back after the term break.

This information did come to light during Jonathon's political campaign, but blessedly Saul's parents were both deceased by then.... Of course Jonathon denied it and it never really caused too much of a stir as Saul's name was on his birth certificate as his legal father.... Jonathon said he did not care to inherit the de Rothschild baronetcy anyway, so when Laurent dies, it will pass to Andre if he is still alive, then to our son Oliver.

What caused me even more distress then was I was told that my late husband Saul had a part to play in all of this.... By disclosing to the Illuminati my menses cycle, in exchange for flying promotions. Andre admitted this to me and sadly I believed him. He also admitted that the Rothschild's had got me my buyer's position at Macy's, but I already knew that. I think Andre decided I needed to know everything, so we could finally move on from it all....

May 26th

The only good thing that came out of this for Jonathon is that soon after we bought him his first car. He was now seventeen and had done very well in his term exams despite this enormous upset.... And although he is still respectful towards me, he has become more distanced. And Andre he mostly ignores.... That is after telling him he would never recognise him as his real father, which I know hurt Andre very much.

It took a few years but Jonathon and Andre did grow to have a mutual respect and affection for each other again...This was my last journal entry for that year as we all spent the rest of it healing.

Jonathon and I both had counselling.

1984

March 23rd

I didn't know at the time if it was going to be a blessing or a curse when Jonathan and I were summons to Zurich for the reading of a caveat of the will, of Grosspapi Rothschild.... Although he had actually died several years earlier, this caveat was only to be read after Grossmami had passed also, which she just had.... Jonathon wasn't going to attend, until my dad insisted, because as the executor of the will, Dad knew about this as-yet, undisclosed caveat.... My Grossmami's passing was very timely it seems, as Jonathan will be eighteen in May, and he was going to be informed of an inheritance anyway, which was already generous, when he turns twenty-one, in three years- time.

We arrived in Zurich and were treated cordially by the rest of the family at the funeral. That soon changed however after the full wills of both my paternal grandparents were read out the next day by Kruger, the family's solicitor.... Present at the reading were my father, Alexander, my two aunts, plus their six daughters and four of the fifteen-great grandchildren, aged sixteen years or older of which Jonathon was the eldest.... And to the shock and dismay of the rest of the family no one was really mentioned, except for Jonathon.

Of course, my father had already inherited the Rothschild Mansion and his two sisters, my aunts, valuable stocks, furniture and jewellery; but that seems to have been forgotten.... Plus, the fact that both my aunts, having married into wealthy banking families, were already very wealthy women.... After Kruger read the two wills, which were relatively simple, you could have heard a pin drop in the room. Alexander especially was seething.... As all of the investments that were left in trust until after Grossmami's passing, went solely to Jonathon Clarence West.... So Jonathon was now a multi- millionaire.... My Grossmami's apartment belonged to my father, so that now went to Philip as Alexander had already taken possession of the largest apartment in the former Rothschild mansion. Grossmami did state though that her remaining furniture, artwork and jewellery were to be divided amongst her seven grandaughters, of which I was one.... but I decided on one keep-sake only.

Alexander however did inherit her luxury BMW and driver until he retired. But the remaining bulk of the family fortune, as listed as various stocks, shares and other investments, was to pass solely to Jonathon now, not at aged twenty-one.... I looked over to my dad, but I could not tell how he felt about this....

After the reading and over coffee, my cousins were all bemoaning how unfair it was that they were left out of receiving any investments, until I said that I was too, plus my siblings. But they did not see it that way.... Jonathon wisely went for a walk to let the others cool off. I couldn't read what he was thinking either but when he came back an hour later, he said to me he didn't think he would now be eligible for a university scholarship, to which we both laughed.

My Dad said he had known since 1976 about the caveat to his fathers will, but couldn't say anything.... All he said was that he hoped Jonathon would continue to keep his head on straight.

I know my Dad syphoned off some funds and investments to secure his and Alexander's fortunes, that is probably why Grosspapi had the other inheritance put aside for Jonathon to receive at age twenty-one. As Grosspapi knew his own son.... I don't blame my dad though.

September 2nd

Fortunately, over the past year, Jonathon and Andre's relationship has improved somewhat. He still favours the company of his two uncles, successful L.A. stockbrokers, 'Best out West', so he chose them to manage his new stocks and shares portfolio, which I know upset my dad and Alexander.... Jonathon is so young at eighteen, but I think he made a sound decision as he knows and trusts his uncles.

Jonathon's uncles taught him how to invest well and how to play the stock market which is the reason he was able to increase his substantial fortune, even more. He snubbed his Rothschild-side family in this way which they resented, although he is close friends with French financier Benjamin de Rothschild, whom in later years he may also have taken advice from....

So, by the early age of twenty-five, knowing he was financially set up for life and with degrees in Political Science and Law from Yale, Jonathon was able to set his sights upon a career in politics. So yes, obviously the Rothschild money did benefit him enormously.... Which he and I hate to admit.

Piers

1990

My father and I were surprised to encounter Sophia Rothschild again after all these years. And what was even more surprising, is that she is now married to the baron Laurent de Rothschild's younger brother Andre....

We know Andre is a talented and respected architect....We also know that he the biological father of Sophia's rather clever and charismatic son, Jonathon Clarence West.... Who has been selected, by, the Grande Dame herself, Madame Collins and Sophia's former mother-in- law.... To be a future U.S. president, no less. Not an aide or an advisor like past Illuminati members, but the top job.

And supposedly Sophia's daughter Elizabeth, is similarly gifted to that of her grandmother the Grande Dame and has been ear-marked, to succeed her one day.... What a select pair of siblings.... Sophia must be so proud.... With Sophia's genes and her position in the bloodline I should have married the woman myself, even if we are first cousins.... Although Sophia doesn't seem to know we are cousins. Even though she has repeatedly said how like her late Poppa, my father Peter and I are, when she met us all those years ago.... Plus, she also heard then of his association with my late grandmother Dulcie.... So personally, I think she has been a bit thick not to have worked it out. Or possibly she didn't want to face it, as it would have upset her beloved Oma too much.

My father and I are active freemasons, and we are also part of 'the Order' as we will call it and so is my mother. Father joined after he met her, as of course, key people already knew who he was and who his biological father was? One Clarence R. Smyth, the famous clairvoyant, physical medium and founder of the 'White hats'.... So therefore, anti the Illuminati.... He was also a talented stage designer, a water-colourist and a bit of a wit, apparently.

My Grandma Dulcie was a very good businesswoman, and a pragmatist. Hence my father got the balanced genes.... Unlike me, who got two fearless, rebellious and idealistic parents, even though one was also psychic, father, of course.

Anyway back to the unfortunate Sophia, as Andre is her third husband..... When we first met Sophia she was a sweet, pretty, nineteen-year-old model living in London who had an American pilot for a boyfriend, one Saul West.... So, I didn't get a look in anyway..... We were then informed that she and Saul had married hurriedly and returned to Los Angeles U.S., where a few months later she had given birth to her son Jonathon.

Less than two years later we heard Saul had been tragically killed in a plane crash.... Seemingly, he was dispensable as he was piloting the aircraft carrying the way-ward Senator McCall and his secretary and their plane was sabotaged, by 'the Order', of which Saul was also a member. He was the 'fall guy', as the crash was blamed on pilot error.... After Saul was killed his father made sure his two younger brothers never joined 'the Order' even though they were invited to.... The Wests were not a chosen family but their mother had an affiliation, as she was a Bonfman, from the Canadian branch of the Illuminati.

Sophia's second husband Tom was also a member of 'the Order' as he was the oldest son of the occult Collins family of New York.... His Mother is the current Grande Dame. And Tom was selected to be the father of Elizabeth or Beth as she is called, Sophia's daughter, which meant he had to leave his marriage to do so.... Tom eventually went rogue for some reason and tried to expose the truth about 'the Order', so he too was eliminated, although the official verdict was suicide of course.

Now we all think the poor woman has been through enough and we hope her third husband will behave himself as must she. But Sophia is no longer the naive girl we first met.... She is still tall, slim and strikingly attractive, but she now has a confident bearing.... And when she looks at you with those penetrating blue eyes she has one feels quite compelled to be truthful.... Because you know that she will deduce when you are not.... Sophia must have got her children to behave with that icy look. Plus, she still has that air of mystery about her.... I must say she terrified me. I had wanted to ask her out all those years ago, but she made me too nervous.

Sophia's youngest brother Alexander is high up in 'the Order' as are her current husband's family. So, this must give her some protection now, surely.... Her other brother Philip has completely bowed out of everything Rothschild and is apparently free. I'm not sure how he achieved it, probably due to the fact he is childless. I do envy him, as I'm sure does Sophia, whom has been constantly monitored.

Anyway, when Sophia and I met again after all those years, we chatted amicably. Sadly, I Know Andre and his brother Laurent, more than I do Sophia. She appears though to have no knowledge of what my parents used to do, or what I do, as our family profession is 'spying'.... Although she could know more than she is letting on.... Our job has been to gather intelligence over the years, to help keep the power of balance and the economy flowing, for the British government, whilst also looking after the interests of the Rothschild family. Of which we are part of. In fact, if I write down anything more about this, I shall have to kill myself.

Sophia

1990

March 10th

Jonathon has just finished his degrees at Yale in Law and Political Science. And I know he is part of the 'skull and bones' fraternity which has me somewhat concerned because of their elitist links....

Julia Bundy, his lovely fiancée, has also completed the same degrees at Yale, and both are being capped on May 30th.... What a year it is for them both, as at aged twenty-four they are also getting married at the end of the year.

Jonathon was voted by his peers as the one most likely to become the President of the United States.... Julia was voted the one most likely to become a campaigner for human rights.... They are a dynamic pair. Both are Democrats from wealthy investment broker families who know each other. They should consider themselves a political and financial match made in heaven if they weren't both agnostic, although Julia's parents are both Protestants. They are currently planning their wedding which involves a marriage celebrant in a fancy hotel, somewhere.... I will have to wait for an invite as although I am the mother of the groom, I am not privy to any more information, at this stage.

April 16th

Andre and I went to England for my great Aunt Edith's funeral, she was ninety-four. Her sister Violet is the only one of that generation who is still alive now in the U.K. and my Oma here of course. It was a nice funeral. Edith has such loving family; it was so good to catch-up with all the relations at her wake.... Carol was there alone it was lovely to see her we had so much to talk to about. Great Aunt Violet is doing well at eighty-four. She gave such a wonderful funny speech and held the floor after-wards, all whilst managing to look immaculate and sip a glass of sherry or two.

After three days in Tunbridge Wells Andre insisted that we visited some of the Rothschilds as well which I wasn't all that wild about. But he had already accepted an invite to a family party, at yet another Kensington address in London. How did they even know we were here? And who should we meet again, but the Huxley's.... Peter and wife Elanora, (nee Rothschild) and their son Piers with his charming wife Diana, who I had never met.

Peter and Elanora are both retired they said, and I already knew Piers now worked for MI6.... Of course, when I entered the party, I recognised them immediately.... Because again I was struck at Peter and Piers resemblance to my late Poppa.... They all appeared pleased to see us and were as well informed as ever about our family. Peter asked how my Oma was, as they had recently lost their beloved Dulcie, at aged eighty-eight, he said.... They also knew about Jonathon's achievements as did everyone I spoke to at the party. And everyone seemed to know somehow that he had his sights set on a political career.... I wondered how or even why they all knew?

When I am at any Rothschild party, I ask to be shown by my guides who are Illuminati, as not all Rothschild's are, of course. But I am never shown. I wish I had Poppa's quirk of seeing them as reptilian, but then he only saw this when they were angry.

Sophia
1995

May 18th

Oma has just died....She made it to ninety-five and died peacefully in her sleep at home with us.... Her passing has made me reflect and on my life again....

I can't believe I haven't written in my journal for so many years, but then I have been busy raising our twins.... I wasn't going to make the same mistake twice, as I am still mostly estranged from Beth, and Jonathon and I are a bit distanced.

My family now are my main priority.... I support Andre in any way I can. I entertain his clients and travel with him sometimes, to record the stages of his projects as I am now a keen photographer. I'm still very involved with the twins schooling, interests and sports, being their main taxi service. I will be pleased when they can drive themselves everywhere in two years- time.

I was also there for my beloved Oma, as five years ago she came to live with us. She moved into Jonathon's old downstairs pad, after her younger companion Ruby, who she reversed roles with and nursed, had died.... Oma then went downhill herself.... But she had been quite content living with us and listening to her beloved music, she said, which gave her some solace.... Now she and Poppa can be together again.... The funeral was lovely. Jonathon did a wonderful eulogy and spoke part of it in German, Oma would have liked that. She had outlived all her siblings, and most of her friends so she was ready to go.... Poppa was there for her she said, I felt him too.

Of course, my parents, Alexander and his family, my Cousin Isobel and her family, all came over for the funeral. Uncle William did the eulogy mentioning some of her funny sayings which made us laugh. I shared some special memories, and Philip showed a video he had compiled with photos of Oma over the years, to recorded music of her playing the violin.... It was wonderful Oma would have loved it and been most proud of her family.

To everyone's surprise, Beth turned up for the funeral.... Her hair has gone dark, and she is quite plump, but otherwise she looked the same.... It was the first time Beth had been back in L. A. since she left with her Uncle Robert at aged sixteen; she was now nearly twenty-one.... I didn't know she was coming, Jonathon had contacted her. I knew he would try. Surprisingly she was also staying with him as he had purchased her air tickets and arranged a car to collect her from the airport.

I went over and gave her a hug, but she didn't hug me back.... She did however make an effort to talk to the family afterwards, at the wake, but revealed very little about herself.... I was more upset about seeing Beth than Oma's passing, I decided.... Oma was now at peace which is more than could be said for Beth....I couldn't understand why she had chosen this path in life, surely not just to get back at me. As I could feel she was struggling, on so many levels.

The day after the funeral even though I was exhausted Beth and I went shopping. She phoned me to ask if I would take her which I was so pleased about. We shopped all day and I spent over a thousand dollars on new clothes and shoes for her. We even got her hair styled. She looked pretty. Beth told me there was a man she liked named Brad and thanked me for my help.... I then offered to send her funds, as I had always done over the years, but as usual she refused. She said the Collins took care of her financially. That is all she said about them....The day we spent together was nice, it was almost normal.... I felt so sad after she left, and cried all the next week for Beth, and my Oma, Andre couldn't comfort me.... When-ever I thought of my daughter I kept getting 'sacrificial lamb'. Why had she imposed this life on herself, I couldn't help but wonder.

May 23rd

Jonathon is a Representative, as soon as he turns thirty he will be sworn in as a State Senator of California....He also has ambitions to run for the Presidency one day but says that timing is crucial. We are so proud of him....

I don't think Jonathon is involved with the Illuminati, but then I can't really be sure....I have also wondered if he is in regular contact with his sister although he says not. But Beth did appear more relaxed around him than anyone else at the funeral. And Jonathon certainly doesn't tell me every-thing.

I'm still in contact with Barbra, Tom's ex-wife, we phone each other every few months. She has always told me what she can, as Beth is quite close to her daughters Chrystal and Kimi. So at least Beth has had the love and support of some family there. As I can't see her grandmother Eve nor her Uncle Robert, being kind or loving towards her.... Although Beth did tell me in one of our rare phone conversations, that Robert's wife Susanne was kind.

Barbra told me that Beth works in the Collins property rental office that her late father began and she has a boyfriend called Brad, although it was fairly- new.... Beth only told me she was working for her uncle, nothing more. She also told me she was sharing a large apartment with four others in Lower Manhattan, but did not offer the address.... I did get a phone number though.

After Beth's visit, I decided to bite the bullet, so I phoned Barbra and asked her if she thought Beth was involved with 'the Order,' I called it.... She said yes, probably, but I noticed she was was quick to tell me that she was not involved herself, nor her daughters.... And although Barbra and I are fairly close I still don't know if I can trust her by mentioning the word Illuminati. But she herself has spoken of 'the Order' and their part in Tom's murder. To me they are one in the same.... But I tread carefully with Barbra as she is a too valuable a link for me, to Beth.

Sophia

2000

January 13th

It is the dawn of a new century and a new millennium. To think my Oma and Poppa were born a century ago, as the first of January would have been Poppa's 100th birthday.... His younger sister Violet is now in a nursing home in Oxford, England and is still of sound mind at aged ninety-four. I phone her fairly, regularly but I should go over and visit as she enjoys talking about Poppa.

Jonathon is running for Governor of California. If he succeeds, he will be the youngest Governor ever, at thirty-five, but then he was a young senator as he got sworn in at just thirty.... Jonathon certainly, chose the perfect wife in Julia, she is a real asset to him. Plus, he has two great kids in Benjamin and Samantha. I'm sure will never be an embarrassment to their father, unlike his mother, if I finish writing my memoirs and decide to publish. But I won't, I can't.... They are a record only for the family, like Poppa's diaries and journals were.

Strangely my husband Andre has encouraged me to write down my story, even though it shows a side to him and his family that must be kept hidden.... Perhaps he thinks it's good therapy for me, which it has been, as it has helped put everything into perspective.

I've just read in the Guardian newspaper that British politician Denis Healey, who has been involved with the Bilderberg group for decades, has been quoted as saying recently.... "That to say we are striving for a one-world government is exaggerated, but not wholly unfair, as those of us in Bilderberg felt that we could not go on forever fighting one another for nothing, killing people and rendering millions homeless.... So, we felt that a single community through-out the world would be a good thing." .... Needless-to-say, the Bilderberg group is part of the Illuminati.

And this is the 60th anniversary of the Bilderberg group, world power brokers, who apparently meet to express their opinions away from the public eye. It is made up of bankers, CEOs, politicians and other leading figures, such as the U.S. banker David Rockefeller. There are 120 members, 80 are Europeans and 40 are from the U.S....And the U.S. Republican Party is controlled by these secret Kingmakers, plus the European Union, and they possess a mountain of smugness. Henry Kissinger is also, a Bilderberg Member.

Bilderberg and 'Skull and Bones' are the same of course and the 'Skull and Bones' fraternity secret society selected at junior year Yale are the power elite. Although they were founded in 1832, there are no records available after 1982...? Those of interest though are Prescott Bush, class of 1916, father of George H. W. our 41st president, who is also on the list class of 1948. As is his son George W. who is now a senator, class of 1968. Before him there was Senator John Kerry, class of 1966, and McGeorge Bundy, class of 1940, who was an advisor to Kennedy...? And way back the 27th President, William H. Taft, class of 1878. Plus named were numerous advisors to all the presidents over the past nearly two centuries....

And now my son, as he was one of the fifteen selected his year 1988. But of course, there is no official record of this.... I mention McGeorge Bundy, as he was kin of my daughter-in-law, Julia.

Poppa also listed Bundy as a prominent Illuminati family.

According to my late husband, Tom Collins, his mother the Illuminati Grande Dame, also selected George H. W. and George W. Bush to be future presidents of the United States, from elite Illuminati families.... Seriously though, I hope George junior doesn't get elected as he doesn't seem that bright.

We need also look at 'The Council of Foreign Relations' Chairman of the board, David Rockefeller. Plus, it's seventy-four founding members, who are also part of the United Nations.... 'The trilateral Commission' is another one, of which Jimmy Carter joined in 1972 then was quickly groomed to become the next president of the United States....As these people work quietly behind the scenes. They have the power and the money.... If the 1980 assassination attempt of Ronald Reagan had been successful it would have put George H. W. Bush in the white house earlier, as he was Vice- President then.... I'm pleased it didn't.

So many of these secret societies like 'The Council of Foreign Relations', 'The Bilderberg Group', 'The Trilateral Commission', their members meet to discuss matters which quickly become policy.... Why don't the majority of people, realise this?

February 9th

I want to reflect upon my family and how they have developed into adults. As I can see their differing childhoods have influenced them....

Despite Jonathon's rocky start to life, by losing the man he believed to be his father as an infant, then his devoted stepfather Tom Collins at aged ten, he has obviously fared well. As all this made him grow-up to be very independent, especially emotionally. Fortunately, he is also a strong person and highly intelligent.... He handled his mother well whilst growing up mainly by telling me what I wanted to hear, even more-so as a teenager.... A sign of a true politician.

By Jonathon being so independent meant that he never really needed me or my approval. So as he moved into his twenties he became quite aloof, especially after he married.... I am pleased that he appears to be a good husband and father, despite not having had the continuity of one father himself, growing up.... Although he always had good male role models on both sides of the family, ours and the Wests. As he has always gravitated towards male company, finding the females in the family annoying, he said, except for his Great Oma that is.

Jonathon was close as a teenager to his Uncle Philip, my brother and to my much younger cousin Jimmy or James as he now likes to be called. They managed to bring out the fun side of Jonathon as he has always been fairly, serious.... Plus, he had his Uncles Zeke and Rueben West, with whom from a young boy, he always discussed politics and business with.

Jonathon never strived to make us all proud of him, he simply focused on his own goals from a surprisingly early age.... Which were to do well, and to make the most of the opportunities given him to try to make a positive difference in this world.... his words. And fortunately, he met his wife Julia young, when they were both sophomores at Yale, so he never had a wild past.... unlike his mother.

Julia is also a graduate in Political Science from Yale and an idealist.... Her loving but more conservative parents Mark and Jennifer Bundy, are successful investment brokers who made their fortune investing in real estate. They provided a solid foundation for Julia and her two siblings to build on (no pun intended) .... More actually than I ever provided for Jonathon, to be honest. Although it wasn't my fault that two men who were fathers to him were killed, or should I say murdered....

After Andre and I married our family life did stabilise, much to the relief of my parents and Oma. That is when my relationship with my parents improved dramatically, as they think highly of Andre and we all now enjoy each-others company.

The only person Jonathon ever tears ups when talking about, is his beloved Great Oma, they had a special bond, he was always patient with her.

Jonathon is agnostic so he neither believes in nor denies the existence of God.... He still respects all religions, he says, but states that is his opinion religion should have no place in politics.... He believes we are all born free and should make our own choices, religion should not be forced upon any child.... Therefore, he does not associate with being Jewish, or a Rothschild, but respects that he carries his late father's name West and that Judaism was his heritage and mine.

Julia's family are Protestants, but Jonathon and Julia had a non-religious wedding. They were married by a celebrant in a large reception room at the Four Seasons Hotel in Los Angeles, in 1990, both were twenty-four.... And because of their shared non-beliefs, they have sent their two children, eight-year-old Benjamin and six-year-old Samantha, to a private non-religious school in Los Angeles near their palatial Hermosa Beach home.

Oddly enough, and despite not trying to associate with any branch of the Rothschild family, Jonathon is close to Benjamin de Rothschild, the son of Andre's cousin Pierre. They 'hit it off' as teenaged boys when they spent time together sailing with my husband's relatives on the French Riviera, those few wonderful summers. Jonathon even named his son is after him.

Andre and I have spent a lot of time in Europe, Jonathon far less, he can understand French and German better than he can speak it. But thanks to our home help over the years, like me, he is fluent in Spanish. Jonathon is also an excellent golfer for someone who hardy gets time to play and has an eight handicap. Andre also enjoys golf as does my Cousin James who is also on a low handicap.... I have never really seen the point of hitting a little white ball all over grassy hills with a stick, but I'm pleased the men in our family enjoy doing this together.

If someone were to ask me if I have a close relationship with my son I would have to say no. I am loved and respected but tolerated a bit I feel. But then Jonathon is a man's man, and I am a woman.

My daughter Beth is another story entirely and for me, so far, not one with a happy ending.... Beth lost her beloved father Tom Collins also as an infant, but insisted she had some memory of him. She was always a sensitive and clingy child, the opposite of Jonathon, as she was dependent on me. At sixteen, fed-up because I could not give her what she wanted as she had to share me, first with Andre, then the twins, she defected to the Collins camp.... Despite all my warnings and those of her half-sister Kimi, Barbra's daughter.

Without my knowledge Beth had been in contact with her grandmother Eve Collins and they had planned a date for her Uncle Robert to fly from New York to collect her.... This was on October 17th 1990, a month after she had turned sixteen.... Robert, apparently met her after school and they flew back to New York together.... Beth had with her only a few keepsakes.... I was home that day but sensed something was wrong .... By five o'clock when Beth was not home, concerned, I called her friends Connie and Suzy who she usually walks home from school with, both said she was not at their last class, Science....By 5:30 pm, after calling her only other friend Marty, then around the family, I was starting to get worried, as no one had seen her.

At 6 pm I received a phone call from the Collins Lawyer, Jarvis....He said that Beth had flown to New York with her Uncle Robert, at her suggestion.... He then threatened me by saying if I tried to get her back, the Collins family would be forced to prove I was an unfit mother, being a former cocaine user and high class call girl.... Jarvis then faxed me through some compromising photos of me at that orgy I had attended years ago with Robert.... Sadly, I knew then.... that I could never win against these people.

My Lawyer told me that because Beth was sixteen and had gone of her own free will there was not much legally I could do at the moment.... And a week after she left, I received a letter from Beth telling me exactly that. She also said it was time she got to know her Collins family and fulfilled her own destiny....

I heard via Barbra, Tom's ex -wife, that once there, unlike me, Beth abandoned herself to her psychic abilities.... We always knew she was a medium and channel from a young age, so much so, that we were never sure at times who we were actually, with or if we knew the real Beth at all.... It makes me sad to admit this, but as her mother I know failed her.

I have only seen Beth six times in the past ten years, all in New York, although she did fly over for her Great Oma's funeral in 1995, but only stayed for three days.... Over the years, Beth would phone me sometimes from Chrystal or Kimi's, her Collins half-sisters. They were both married then with young children and Beth would stay with them. But she would still tell me very little of her life.

I knew Beth had lived with her Uncle Robert and his wife Susanne, until she finished high school. They had three young sons who Beth would babysit. She said Susanne was nice but never mentioned Robert, or his mother Eve....I did have their phone number but if I ever called to speak to Beth, I always got Susanne who said she was unavailable. Sometimes Susanne would tell me that Beth was happy and what she had been doing, I think just to be kind.... I wrote weekly to Beth, but rarely got a reply.... It was heart breaking.

After Beth left school, she went to work in a Collins rental office, one her late father had started. Then soon after she moved into some sort of mixed flatting arrangement. Of course, I was sad she never went to university.... I didn't even know her school grades, but I suspect they were a good average like me.

Jonathon who is over eight years older than Beth, always just found her strange and annoying and mostly ignored her when they were growing up. But as I have said, he always gravitated towards male companionship.... He was not unkind and would look out for her like most big brothers do when we were engaged in some physical activity, like swimming, sailing or ice skating. But he never went out of his way to interact with her much at other times.

Nowadays Beth looks like her paternal grandmother, as she is of average height, plump and her hair has gone dark.... It is not unusual for mediums to be plump, especially the women apparently as the work can affect their pituitary gland. What really has me concerned though, is that I have been told by Carl Z that Beth has been selected to take over as the Grande Dame for the Illuminati one day, when her paternal grandmother Eve Collins steps down.... This I know as I am still in contact with the 'White hats.

Sadly, Beth and I are still mostly estranged, but occasionally she will phone me out of the blue from Lower Manhattan where she now resides with her husband of two years Brad, and their flatmates still. They have no children as-yet.... I met him once before they married, when I was visiting New York with Andre and found him a most unusual young man.... Sadly, none of our -side of the family was asked to their wedding, which was apparently fairly, low-key.... Barbra told me via her daughter Kimi who'd attended.

When-ever I try to phone Beth, I usually get a different person on the phone each time, who says she is unavailable.... I don't even have an address for her; this makes me very sad. I could have done so much for her.... Beth is now twenty-six, hopefully we have time yet to reconcile, perhaps when she herself becomes a mother herself. To my knowledge Beth has had no contact with anyone else in our family, but is still close to Kimi and Chrystal. Their mother Barbra who I am still in contact with, has always been honest with me and says there is not much I can do.... She passes on what information she can to me about Beth which I am grateful for and recently sent me a photo of her taken on her last birthday.

Barbra told me that Tom was instructed to pursue me and get me pregnant. He lied to me about having had a vasectomy.... The Collins family knew I was vulnerable, but they knew the single Robert would not appeal to me. Barbra also said Tom really did love me and hated himself for how he duped me, also for what he'd done to her and the girls, for the sake of 'the Order'....Why was I not surprised to hear this!... I believe Barbra, as it was not said with malice.

Now my children with Andre, our twins Oliver and Martine de Rothschild, have fared the best I feel. Born when I was aged thirty-five and Andre was thirty-four, we were more mature and settled as parents by then and we have had a strong and happy union. One which, so far, Andre has managed to survive, thank heavens, unlike my first two unfortunate husbands.... Our annus horribilis was 1983, the year of Jonathon's DNA test, but we managed to work through that thankfully.

Like their Architect father, the twins are artistic, and at aged nineteen both are in their first year of university. Mind you, they could have inherited some creative talents from the Smyth side also.

Oliver is studying at the Southern California Institute of Architecture and hopes to work with his father one day. Martine is studying fashion design at ESMOD in Paris.... So, we are living half the year in L.A. and the other half in Paris. This is not unusual for us anyway, as Andre has clients in both countries.... I am very close to the twins; they phone me at least twice a week when we are not residing with them, as we do turn-about. They are close, so are in constant contact with each-other.

2001

January 27th

Unfortunately Junior, George W. Bush has just been sworn in as our 43rd President. God spare us all, I don't have a good feeling about this year.

February 4th

I have just read that the Rothschild mansion located at 18 Kensington Palace Gardens London, is on the market for eighty-five million pounds. Apparently, this is the most expensive residential property ever to go on sale in the U.K.... I was invited to a party there once, when I was a young model living in London, many years ago. I remember I took my flatmates Veronica and Alison with me. The mansion is Victorian in style, built in marble is 9,000 sq. feet in size and has underground parking for 20 cars. Nowadays it is joined to number 19 Kensington Place Gardens, so it is even larger.

March 10th

David Rockefeller had just published his memoirs and is quoted as saying....

"Some believe we are part of a secret cabal working against the best interests of the United States, characterising my family and me as 'Internationalists', conspiring with others around the world to build a more integrated, global political and economic structure, One-World if you will.... If that is the charge, then I stand guilty" .... David Rockefeller

He is the Chairman of the board for the Council of Foreign Relations, and is also a Bilderberg group member. These are the ones the 'White hats' know of; he could be in more.

But I prefer this quote:

"The price good men pay for indifference to public affairs is to be ruled by evil" .... Plato. Too true.

I have met with Carl Z again....

The 'White hats' believe that the Illuminati goal is to bankrupt the U.S. and reduce their productive might, plus the standard of living. Also, to weaken and impoverish the country, so that there are only a few in control.... They want to own 99% of the wealth, and to leave 1% for the rest of humanity.... And this is possible.... I must ask myself that question.... Am I now part of these elite, whose aim it is to dominate the world.... Probably, despite not planning to be, as by being married to Andre, I am now back- in the Rothschild- de Rothschild family fold. And we are a very wealthy and influential family.... I was always a wealthy woman anyway; I just didn't always accept it.

Jonathon has been provided for far more than me though. The Rothschilds have seen to that, as he needed wealth for his political ambitions, and it came two-fold.... First, he inherited money and increased it, then he married into it, as the Bundys are wealthy investment brokers also, like the Wests....Not that he needs his in-laws, money.... But Jonathon has refused to change his name, even though he found out at seventeen his true parentage.... He said Saul West had wanted him and gave him his name and he is close to both his 'West' uncles and their families... Even so, Jonathon is a Rothschild through and through, as his birth father is a de- Rothschild, and he has inherited some family traits from him. Plus, me as of course as I am also a Rothschild, whether I like it or not, even if I have always preferred my Smyth side.

Of course, 'West' is a far better surname for an American President than de Rothschild, when it comes to relating to the man in the street and look at the slogan's potential 'West is Best 'etcetera.

Poppa is right though, as he came through to me clairaudiently, and told me that not everything goes to plan, as the Illuminati have not counted on the rise of China in the 2000s. This is the century for China, as all great civilizations have had their time and fallen throughout history. Look at the Greeks and Romans, the Incas and Aztecs, England, and the European nations.... And the U.S. will fall from its top position.... In the 2020s the Yuan will be the world's leading currency. China will trade with Russia more, as by 2030 the U.S. will have lost its technological leading edge.... But to prevent this from happening the Illuminati will try to destroy the reputation of the Chinese on the world stage....

Poppa said China will get the blame for a deadly influenza type pandemic which will kill over five million people world-wide around 2020. This will also have a huge effect on the global economy and cause a major recession. Poppa said this is not like a lot of viruses deadly to humans that come from animals, this one is man-made.... But China will not handle the situation well and will come across as arrogant yet defensive and not admit it was their fault. *Maybe it wasn't, entirely? Maybe it was deliberately leaked from a lab in Wuhan by someone with an agenda.* Poppa also said Chinas aggressive take-over of Hong Kong, then later Taiwan, will also damage their global reputation and the latter could lead to a war with the U.S. and its allies.

Of course, this prediction came true about the pandemic. The world is still affected economically by this. But who really manufactured the covid 19 corona- virus? Wuhan in China where it originated, does have huge biochemical laboratories, but they also have wet markets selling live wild animals which is where some experts think the virus originated.... The 'White hats' however believe it was manufactured by the American branch of the Illuminati and introduced into Wuhan. Their goal being to destroy the Chinese economy and reputation. They also planned to destroy Donald Trump's credibility as President, but he's managed to do a lot of that by himself.

A lot of what Poppa channelled through me to the U.S. military in 1980 has come true, but they did not believe it then nor probably what he has predicted for the future. I suppose they couldn't really have prevented these things from happening, without a huge commitment of resources and alarming nations of people.... Which makes me wonder what the point of prophesies are then?

My assessor back then sent me a full written copy of what I had channelled, he thought I had a right to know, even though he was taking a personal risk giving it to me at the time. Of all the clandestine ways he could have given me this information, he simply posted it to me, no doubt with stamps previously purchased.... I received it a few weeks later and passed it to the 'White hats'.

Poppa's transcript:

The Illuminati exist.... They are an elitist group of extremely wealthy and influential families who rule the world.... They have been funding terrorist cells for decades, and this will only increase. These cells are made up of fanatics, usually young, indoctrinated males, who are enlisted to cause random acts of terror around the world.... The result being to have people living in fear, as it will be more dangerous to travel and to meet at large gatherings in the next thirty years. And they also are not beyond using chemical warfare. *Baba Vaga, the Bulgarian mystic who died in 1996 also predicted this, along with many other things that have come true like 9/11.*

In the U.S. there will be an epidemic of shootings at schools especially by random gunmen....These will be young men who have been alienated and indoctrinated, sometimes they are not even aware of this, as it is subliminal messaging through music and television screens.... *He may also have meant by personal computer screens, as of course they weren't invented then.*

The reason for this is to turn the U.S. into a more police state with tighter regulations and to make people even more fearful.... It has always been about control at the end of the day. Plus, there will be a major attack on U.S. soil, which will shock the free world and change security and overseas travel forever.... *Poppa was predicting the destruction of the world trade centre 9/11 which happened the year I finally wrote this in my journal; 20 years after I had also channelled it.*

But this misguided Illuminati-based plan will be the final downfall of the U.S. especially. That plus not making Russia their ally, as Russia will side with China economically and some middle eastern nations.... This cost to the U.S. plus their incessant warfare in distant lands will affect their economy and their share in the global economy will have halved by 2020.... *This also came true.*

Poppa also said that China will try to grow their way out of their problems. In the late 1990s they will switch from reform to development. This means excessive building and production with a bigger economy but not a strong enough foundation. Plus, in time their outflow of capital investment will weaken their currency but it will give Chinese goods an advantage. Soon everything will be made in China and exported around the world. And this will affect industries in all developed countries, not just the U.S....Even so, China will still have its problems with its communist government struggling to keep control of their wealthier better educated, better informed people. Hong Kong residents being one. China will not allow their independence or Taiwan which will result in a show of military power and could lead to a war with the U.S. and her allies in the South China sea.... Also, an influenza type virus will emerge from China and spread around the world causing a major pandemic. This will kill around 5 million people globally, stop international travel and cause a world- wide recession.... Until a vaccine is created around 2020.

Poppa also predicted the rise of Islamic extremist militant groups who will try to take woman back a thousand years by reinstalling Shari law in many Muslim countries. This will eventually cause the more moderate Muslims, tired of being persecuted along with the extremist ones, to eventually rise-up to resolve the problem, leading to an emergence of strong female Muslim leaders. *I especially hope this comes true.*

2001

October 30th

Unfortunately, Poppa's prediction came true on the September 11th, 2001, with four co-ordinated terrorist attacks. All involved hijacked passenger planes used like missiles, which caused the iconic world trade centre twin towers to eventually implode. Also destroyed were WTC buildings, 3 and 7, and the remaining three were severely damaged.

The Pentagon was also hit by another plane but sustained only partial damage to the west wing. And the fourth plane fortunately, never reached its target.... It kept being shown again and again on television.... The planes striking the twin towers, the panic that ensued with people jumping out of windows in desperation. It was sickening and unbelievable. Like a Bruce Willis movie, only this was real.... I feel that life as we know it may change forever.

The truth may never come out about 9/11, as with the assassination of J.F. Kennedy. But one thing is definite, there was a lot more to this than the world was told.... The prime suspect behind the attacks, was Osama Bin Laden, leader of al Qaeda, a militant Islamist network. He was a younger brother of Salem Bin Laden, one of George W. Bush's first business partners. After the attacks, 140 wealthy Saudis including Bin Laden family members were, unlike anyone else, cleared to leave the country.

In 1977 Salem and George W. were founders of the Arbusto Energy Oil Company, in the U.S. state of Texas. Bush also had his own drilling company Arbusto Energy, in Midland Texas. Saudi multi-millionaires, Texas oil men, the infamous BCCI bank and Bush were financially linked with the Bin Laden family... Until Salem was killed in a freak microlight accident near San Antonia, in 1988. Salem was also a close friend of the Saudi King Fahad.

Arbusto later became 'Bush Exploration'. In 1984 it neared financial collapse, so was merged with Spectrum Energy corp. friends of Bush Junior's father, George H. W. Bush; President at the time, who called in some favours.... Two months before Iraq invaded Kuwait in 1990 both Bushs sold two thirds of their Harken stock as they had insider knowledge.... Why wasn't the President impeached then, for insider trading?

James Howard Hatfield author of the controversial biography 'Fortunate son George W. Bush and the making of an American president' said, like his father, George W. Bush had also made his fortune in the oil business with the money of others. Hatfield was found dead at aged 43 on July 2001 of a prescription overdose, which the police declined to investigate. Bush senior was director of the C.I.A. in 1976 so maybe he called in some more favours.

The world Trade Centre and the Pentagon were attacked by supposed terrorists who had hijacked American and United airlines long haul passenger planes that carried a lot of fuel. A poll taken in 2006 showed that 42% of American citizens did not believe then what the government had told them.

Everyone in America remembers where they were that fateful day 9/11.... I tried frantically to get hold of Beth and she finally did call me about six hours after the planes struck. She said she was okay but obviously they were all in shock, as everyone around her seemed to know someone who was involved like a fireman or someone who was missing.... I asked her to please call me more often, but she said there was a much bigger picture now, than just her and me.... I didn't know to what she was referring, to the twin towers disaster, or the Illuminati and her place in it.

Not long after 9/11, another metaphoric bombshell hit our family; thank heavens Oma had passed. As I met up with Piers Huxley again and he had some rather unsettling and surprising news.

Piers was still with British Intelligence M16 and was in Washington with information about al Qaeda, we assumed. Due for retirement he had been resurrected because of his uncanny intuition which he had seemingly inherited from his father, Peter Huxley, who had also been with MI6; and his wife.

Piers asked me to gather as much of the family together as I could and arrived at our home with a small projector, a screen and a thin file.... He was charming and polite when he introduced himself. He then dropped a bombshell by offering up a convincing case that Clarence Reginald Smyth, was also, his grandfather.... He played film footage of Poppa, then of his father, when they were both young and uncannily alike, which I also confirmed, as I had met Peter.... Piers then produced his grandparent's marriage certificate and his father's birth certificate, which showed that his father was born four months after his grand- parents had married, and nine months after his mother and her parents were released from the P.O.W. camp in Berlin.... It appears that our Poppa had given Dulcie, his grandmother, a departing gift.... namely a baby.... And it was her wish that it was never revealed to our family, until after Clarence's wife had passed, she had said.

Needless-to-say the family were stunned.... Uncle William was the most upset, as he now realised that he was not Poppa's only son. And by all accounts Peter Huxley was a fine man and a brave one, who had had an amazing career in MI6, according to his son...? As there was no denying the likeness of Peter and indeed Piers to our late Poppa.... Apparently, Dulcie had told Peter when he was twenty -one, who his birth- father was.... Gordon Huxley, the father who had raised him was a good man but Peter had always had his suspicions apparently, as he looked nothing like either of his parents or his two younger sisters, nor was he like them in nature.... After he was told, Peter found out everything he could about Clarence R. Smyth and was not surprised to hear about his psychic abilities.... as he had a few quirks of his own.

Uncle William immediately thought that my mother also had a right to know she had a brother. And as Peter was now eighty-two and he and his twin sister were seventy-six, said they should go to England soon, to visit him.... Apparently Great Aunt Violet had known for years, as after Peter joined MI6, he tracked her down. She had kept the secret for decades, feeling it was not hers to reveal.... She had told Peter about me and that is why he sought me out, whilst I was living in London and coincidently his wife Elanora, was also a Rothschild....It was all so bizarre.... My intuition had really let me down on this one although I knew I had some sort of connection with the Huxley's, aside from the Rothschild one.

Piers Huxley was a fine man too, intelligent, articulate and he also had Poppa's charisma. He and his father were both freemasons, Piers said, like Poppa's father and grandfather, so he asked me why Poppa had never joined. Of course, Piers already knew that Poppa's father Geoffrey Smyth had worked for British Intelligence and that Poppa had passed on valuable information to them about the Nazis, just prior to WWII.

I told Piers that Poppa had known Martin Bormann, Rudolf Hess and met Hitler once, and that he had given Hitler and Hess, accurate predictions. Plus, I said, Poppa also knew Sir Winston Churchill and had given his chief bodyguard a list of probable attempts on his life. Therefore, possibly saving his life. I then told Piers that Sir Arthur Conan Doyle, himself a devoted spiritualist, had vouched for for Poppa's abilities when he and his father were arrested. Poppa was twelve years old at the time and he had inadvertently channelled top military designs for a school project.

Piers chuckled and said he and his father would love to hear more about Poppa. He then asked if he could read Poppa's diaries, as Great Aunt Violet had told him about them.... I was surprised at this and said "possibly" .... I wondered why great Aunt Violet had disclosed to him about Poppa's diaries, perhaps she had been a bit senile.... I decided I would have to think about whether I handed them over to the Huxley's.... They were certainly not getting his notebooks. Especially as Piers had admitted they were freemasons.... I never answered Piers as to why Poppa refused to join. And of course, I never mentioned the Illuminati or the 'white hats' as I wasn't sure if I could trust him yet.

Sophia

2016

I have to write down my thoughts about the poor choices we have been left with in this presidential race.... Mainly because they are two of the most unpopular candidates ever.... And for very good reasons being, Hilary, corrupt Clinton, Democrat, and Donald 'grab the pussy' Trump, Republican.

How on earth have we been left with these two....Where are all the decent candidates? Or is there no such thing, as every President has probably been put into office by one secret society or another. They are the real puppet masters here.... *Why did I not admit to myself then, that this is what had happened to my senator son.... Even though during this round he was eliminated fairly, early from the presidential race.*

The outgoing president, Barak Obama is charming and charismatic and was considered the most admired man in America for eleven consecutive years.... He is credited with pulling America back from a great recession, improving gay rights, and apparently, he granted more commutations than any other president to date. The same number in fact as the last thirteen presidents combined, during his terms. He had a 60% approval when he left office and has been voted the 12th favourite president. His biggest legacy though is probably his Patient Protection and Affordable Care Act.... Obamacare, amongst other things, and he represented America well on the world stage.

But I found Obama and his wife a bit hedonistic, they seemed to enjoy mixing with Hollywood celebrities, musicians and billionaires more than other world leaders.... At least everyone can settle down now for a few decades, as we have had an afro- American President, even if he was raised by his white mother and grandparents.

But what did he do for his own people? Who are in fact only 12.5 percent of the population...? Nothing....He certainly didn't help them with the Flint water controversy.... Or the Louisa floods, as he was too busy golfing with pro golfers and having photo calls I felt.

And the Clintons have had their time in office and their fair share of scandals.... A third of Bill Clinton's commutations, the majority of which were done on his last day in office, were for company fraud. As in the case of Marc Rich, who owed $48 million in tax and was accused of 51 counts of tax fraud. He was pardoned by Clinton of tax evasion, how despicable. And has everyone forgotten the 1990s Whitewater controversy....The dodgy real estate investments of Bill and Hilary Clinton and their associates, Jim and Susan Mc Dougal in the 'Whitewater Development Corporation' already? Which Clinton pardoned her of, plus that tax fraud scandal with the Clinton Foundation....Honestly!

And when Hilary Clinton was Secretary of State, she ordered US diplomats to spy on UN officials, and gather their fingerprints, iris scans, DNA, credit card details and computer passwords, which surely contravened the human rights of these US officials....to say the least. So imagine what sort of president she would make....

Suddam Hussein had no links to al Qaeda and was in fact hostile to them in his own country, nor did he have weapons of mass destruction, yet this resulted in the deaths of 50,000 combatants and 100,000 civilians.... Can her reckless war mongering be forgiven so easily.

Hilary Clinton has threatened military action against Iran on numerous occasions protecting the security and safety of Israel. Is she a Zionist? Indeed her daughter Chelsea married Marc Mezvinsky an investment banker for Goldman Sachs, whose father is the corrupt former politician Edward Mezvinsky, and who spent five years in a federal prison for fraud.....What circles do the Clintons mix in that allowed these young people to even meet?

And Hilary Clinton's presidential campaign ads with images of Osama Bin laden, Hurricane Katrina, and soldiers marching, plus other fear- provoking imagery, preying on our concern for our children is blatant propaganda.... Then there's her choice of staff, like Sandy Berger, as in 2005 Berger was convicted of theft of secret documents from national archives.... And Clinton herself falsified state-ments to the federal election commission, about a large donation to her 2000 senate campaign. Plus there have been cover-ups and lies on her part about receiving campaign funds and hiding emails from security.... Which should have everyone wondering, how many deals has there been to get her into power.... And how many scandals will it take before that power is taken away.... Finally her health care policy saw an increase in donations to her from health insurance and pharmaceutical companies, which is also questionable.

In a nut- shell she lacks principled integrity and is a liar and a propagandist. And this not even mentioning her husband Bill, the 42nd President, who was publicly accused of sexual misconduct by four women.... Plus, the Monica Lewinsky scandal which began as a sexual relationship with the then twenty-one-year-old white house intern and her forty-eight-year-old husband president, and lasted for over eighteen months, which he then lied about.... How many wives could sweep that worldwide public humiliation under the carpet for the sake of their own ambitions. Plus, she is and elitist and not in touch with regular people and this will go against her as she comes across as being better, smarter and superior....

Which brings me now to the other candidate Donald J. Trump, with his known Mafia ties and unscrupulous business dealings. Organised crime controlled the New York concrete business in the 1980s and Trump with his construction and casino businesses had dealings with them. And four times Trumps companies have entered bankruptcy, in fact, at one stage his hotel and casino business was $1.8 billion in debt. The Trump Taj Mahal and the Trump Plaza were eventually closed and he had $900 million in personal debt, even though his net worth has been quoted by Forbes this year at $4.5 billion.... Quote from Trump "This is a business thing, I've used the laws of this county to pare debt" .... Something doesn't quite add up here though, legally.

And he is famous for being a womaniser and a racist. He used illegal Polish emigrants on $5 per hour to tear down the famous Art deco Bonwit Teller store, to build his iconic Trump tower. And many were not even paid for their services, but instead threatened with deportation. Also, he and his father, were known to be racist about who they let into their buildings as tenants.

Plus there has been a raft of allegations of sexual harassment and misconduct by numerous woman from different places and eras. His quote: "grab the pussy and then you can do anything".

But unfortunately for the masses of underappreciated Americans his quote "punch the elite on the nose" and his combative hostile persona which they can relate to with their own anger and bitterness could win him the presidency.... Out of the two candidates I prefer Trump though, despite the fact that he is a bit of a lose canon, because I don't feel that he is part of the Illuminati.

His recent quote in Bluffton, South Carolina: "We (the U.S.) went after Iraq, we decimated the country, Iran is now taking over, but it wasn't the Iraqis. You will find out who really knocked down the World Trade Centre, because they (the Government) have the papers in there that are very secret, you may find it was the Saudi's okay, but you will find out"

Trump has promised to declassify this information if elected because 28 pages of the 2002 joint congressional intelligence inquiry of 9/11 has been withheld, on national security grounds, by George W. Bush.... Many politicians have tried but failed to get their release, and these redactions have yet to be reversed.... Why? Because they are about the relationship between the Bush Administration and the Saudis as Osama Bin Laden received money from the Saudi Arabian government.... Interestingly around the time this statement was said, by Trump, Jeb Bush pulled out of the race for the presidency.

June 20th

It seems an age since I have recorded any family news. But we all got together to celebrate my 70th birthday on June 10th. I decided on a catered party at home because it was also my Mother's ninety- first birthday. Sadly her twin brother, Uncle William had passed two years earlier. Some family came from overseas so we had a full house, as did Jonathon and Julia; it was all wonderful. Everyone was there from the family except for Beth who was missed by me. Jonathon tried to get her to attend he said, but I did at least receive a card from her a week later.

My Mom has been living with us for the past six years, just as Oma did. When Dad died she didn't want to stay in Zurich alone, as she was finding the winters too hard to bear. And Alexander, his wife Marguerite, their children and grandchildren are very good at flying over for the holidays to visit her.

Alexander has matured into a much nicer man, we get on well now. His accountant son, Alex junior, has followed him into the family bank and his daughter Claudia, has married a Vontobel, from anotherwealthy banking family.

Philip is quite eccentric and always seems to be a bit distracted. I suppose it's from all those years of taking drugs. He's also a bit deaf and has hearing aids, as does his wife Mitzi.... Philip still holds a special place in my heart though.

The extended family are all doing well. Christian's twin sons were both champion skiers and now run a Ski school and coach future Olympians. Both are married with children. Their Mother never remarried, but she does have a partner. Isobel's sons have taken professional paths, one is a doctor and the another a lawyer. Isobel's mother, my Aunt Katrine sadly died of cancer ten years ago.

July 16th

Poppa isn't the only prominent psychic dead or alive to make accurate predictions. Baba Vanga a blind Bulgarian peasant and mystic who died in 1996 aged eighty-five, had an accuracy rate of 85%, Poppas was 80%. She predicted 9/11 and also that the 44th President would be an African American. She predicted the rise of ISIS, and also Brexit.... As on the 23rd of June 2016, the UK voted to leave or remain in the European Union, and 51.9% voted to leave.... This Baba Vanga predicted will lead to a European economic collapse, late 2020. That, plus a pandemic, a corona virus from China which will affect the global economy as major countries around the world, will go into months of lockdown. And there will be more terrible tsunamis like the one which hit Indonesia in 2011 due to undersea volcanoes on the ring of fire, causing earthquakes in Asia, with much loss of life. There will also be an attempt on the Russian president Putin's life Baba Vanga said.

Baba Vanga also predicted that the world with end in the 51st century.... Let's hope she is wrong about that.

Edgar Cayce who died in 1945 made many accurate predictions that have come to pass and some are yet to happen. He predicted that humans will be able to expand their life span significantly and suggested organ replacement, and scientists are now growing organs from our own cells. He also predicted a gasless motor that is self-fuelled, with perpetual motion, this is also in development.... He also said strife will arise to keep the lands in Libya, Egypt, Turkey and Syria, and the Persian Gulf open, and the straits above Australia, in the Indian Ocean. Only the latter has yet to happen.

Cayce predicted that there will be a new level of spiritual consciousness. Records will be found to prove the existence of Atlantis, which will itself be found near Bimini in the Bahamas.... And he is the second renown psychic to predict that China will become the 'cradle of Christianity' and that the height of civilization will move west to the Chinese people. As they will progress even more in the 2020s.... Poppa predicted something similar.

Poppa also predicted 9/11, which would change national security forever and see many countries tightening their borders.... He said that a woman will come up to challenge Putin in Russia and that a young French male President will be ousted in favour of woman, and so he should, as he is an elitist and part of the Illuminati. He could see the French people rioting.

He also said that in the U.K. a woman prime minister will try but fail to bring together a Brexit deal. But Britain would eventually leave the E.U. and their timing would be significant. Plus a woman of Afro- American heritage and divorced, would marry into the British royal family and cause a major upset.... I remembered this, as I found it interesting what Poppa said about all these influential women.

Things don't sound too good for Europe though leading into the 2020s. Perhaps some strong female leaders do need to come forward. They also need to do something about the 40 million sex slaves in Europe, the highest now in the world. As I have said before, Poppa predicted that the 21st century would see a swing away from Communism towards Capitalism in Eastern Europe and Indochina. He said this would cause criminal gangs to rise- up to fill the power vacuum, which would also increase human trafficking, especially of young female sex slaves, which it did.... What a rotten world we live in.

I notice I expound my theories and get up on my political soap box but I never address the elephant in the room.... Which was, that my son had been selected by the most powerful cabal in the world, because of his Rothschild bloodline, inherited hypnotising oratory skills, and Zionist Jewish ancestry. Plus, his illegitimate Collins bloodline of course with its links to the occult; to be the leader of the free World.... And despite me knowing that this was my destiny from aged ten to be his mother and supposedly guarding myself against it.... I was still a powerless pawn in the Illuminati game.... I never stood a chance really.

2021

January 22nd

The President of the United States of America has just been sworn in for another four- year term. Donald J. Trump.... Everyone close to me has been in shock as to how my son Jonathon Clarence West came to lose this election.... But I know how it happened, and who was behind it even....

I hadn't spoken to Jonathon much since the elections last October, but the extended family got together for thanksgiving and he put on a brave face.... Jonathon told us then that he planned to run again, as politics are his life, and he truly believes he is fated to have the 'top job' one day, he said. I'm not so sure now, as Jonathon and his supporters have underestimated the power of the people, I feel.

It is hard for me to admit, that I have been played like a fool by every man I have ever loved, who I truly believed loved me back; except for Sam Winchester that is.... Perhaps, that is why I was chosen as 'The mother'.... Andre, and I are still together, we have reached an understanding, as we do suit each other, plus at my age, I may as well stick with the devil I know.... In all fairness to Andre, he was born a Rothschild male and was indoctrinated from a young age.

But the biggest surprise and definitely for me a life's-lesson, was the part played by Beth my estranged daughter, in all of this.... She has been wholly underestimated by so many including me.... As no one saw her coming....

I remember clearly the night of the election.... We had all been so confident at breakfast that Jonathon was going to win. He had supposedly run a clean campaign and done everything he could possibly do, to win the election.... He had worked tirelessly with his support team, which had paid off as he came out on top in the polls, and with all the debates, plus he had the popular vote.... We always knew the middle bible- belt states could be a problem for him, but no one had anticipated just how influential they could be.... As at 10 am on the day of voting, a political bomb exploded.... I was oblivious to it all, being at home alone in my study writing an introduction to my memoirs, to calm my nerves. And no-one thought to contact me.... Why didn't I know intuitively this was going to happen? As every polling station is these middle states was hit with scores of Christian anti-Jonathon West protestors....

The Protestors held slogans and distributed literature, but the most damning were the big screens being driven around on trucks, showing footage claiming that Jonathon was an anti- Christian Satan worshipper.... Apparently, he was part of an elitist Zionist cabal who had been manipulating the world economy and wars for over two hundred years. And whose plan it was to rule the world and abolish Christianity....They then proceeded to show damning evidence of this, of Jonathon speaking at Illuminati meetings to large groups of robed people, with the all-seeing eye insignia behind him....

And to cap it all off, this was also simultaneously televised in these states.... But it soon went nation-wide.

Not since the 9/11 plane strikes of the twin towers had anything had such an immediate impact on national television and radio.... The media were in a frenzy, scrambling to not miss out on this momentous story, one which so far no-one had stepped- up to take responsibility for.... And people did stop to watch and listen.... What's-more, there were scores of well-known Christian business people, writers, musicians and actors, endorsing this as fact, and they were all reading from the same script.... As of course, this played into the strong Christian belief, that the Anti- Christ would appear to try to gain ultimate power and intimating that Jonathon was him....

Of course, many voters thought it was rubbish and others an elaborate smear campaign and simply ignored it.... But enough didn't.... And some were so confused that they chose not to vote at all, as voting numbers were down significantly.... Obviously, it caused a huge amount of damage.... So much so that Jonathon lost the presidential election as Trump won by a slim majority.... After all quoting my son, "What makes America so great, is that everyone here has the right to freedom of speech" .... Well, that backfired on him didn't it.

That night, when Jonathon took to the stage with Julia to concede and to congratulate President Trump....I was in the wings with the rest of the family and his close supporters, and I saw their faces change into something reptilian.... First Jonathon's, then Julia's, as they were seething with rage and indignation.... This was a quirk that Poppa had, but I had never seen it before.... Panicked, I turned to find Andre and Laurent were the same, as was my brother Alexander, and Benjamin de Rothschild, Jonathon's, best friend. But blessedly not Philip, Oliver or Martine, who all gave me a concerned look just before I passed out....

I woke up in hospital where Andre had insisted, I be taken, and a young doctor told me that I was dehydrated. This had caused a sudden drop in my blood pressure which made me pass- out, plus the stress of the election of course, at my age.... But just to be on the safe side, they were running some tests, which so far had come back normal he said.

The hospital-staff were very kind. They all said they didn't believe a word of what was broadcast about my son and had all voted for him anyway and were sorry that he wasn't elected.... So, I decided to stay in hospital for a few days to rest as I was exhausted, plus I needed time by myself to think.... I was seventy-six years old and had a wonderful life with my husband who I still loved, plus our children and grandchildren of course.... What was I to do? I asked the family to leave me alone for a few days and thankfully they obliged. They also needed time to come to terms with what had just happened to Jonathon, indeed our whole family, in their own way.

On the third day of my stay, I had a surprise visitor.... My estranged daughter Beth, who I hadn't seen in person for over five years.... I hardly recognised Beth when she walked in, as she was slim and with her blonde highlights looked more like me now than Tom, plus she was more confident some-how....

Beth sat down next to the bed and grabbed my hand. She said she was sorry, and I noticed she was holding back tears.... So, I told her she had nothing to be sorry about.... Then to my surprise she pulled out a small detector from her handbag and checked the room thoroughly, for electronic devises, putting a finger up to her lips for me to remain silent.

Satisfied, what she told me next totally floored me, as she confessed that it was her.... She was the one who had done everything with-in her power, to stop Jonathon becoming the next President of the United States....Including secretly filming him at Illuminati meetings. And he never suspected a thing, she said, as he had completely trusted her, never doubting her loyalty to 'the Order'.... She then said she had been working for years gathering information and was secretly a member of the 'White hats' and had been for eight years.

I was flabbergasted, more-so that I had never suspected any of this. And hurt and confused. Beth told me she wanted me to know as she knew her life was now in danger, and it was only a matter of time before she too was eliminated, like her late father.... She then told me she loved me and was sorry that we were not able be close over the years.... As she knew from the age of sixteen, she said that she had to continue what her late father had started.... Which was to expose the Illuminati.... Beth also said this was the reason she had chosen not to have children, as she didn't want them to join 'the Order'. But sadly, her husband Brad divorced her because of this as he had wanted children who he now has with his new wife.

I remember I was so stunned that I didn't know what to say or even how I felt. But I did tell her who I'd seen the night of the election turn reptilian, to which she nodded...?

I then asked her what I should do now, and she answered "nothing" .... I said it may be too late as Andre already knows I am anti the Illuminati. But then realised, except for Beth, I had told no-one who I had seen election night turn reptilian.... Who would I tell anyway, except for members of the 'White hats' as I would never endanger Philip, or Oliver and Martine, by discussing any of this with them.... And no one in the family now, knows that I have met up with 'White hats' members and passed on valuable information, except for Beth obviously, as I have always kept this side of me from Andre.

I decided at that moment, even with my mind in a whirl, that I had to stay in my key position. Even if I wasn't very active as it was the only way I could stop my son from ever becoming President and to try and save my daughter's life....

Of course, Beth would never come forth publicly and admit that she was the main instigator of the smear campaign against her brother. With a group of Christian, anti-Illuminati-ists which is what they call themselves.... But quite frankly the American people have been fed so much fear, propaganda and conspiracy theories over the years. That many non-Christians also believe that a wealthy, powerful and elite group are trying to rule the world by any means they can.

Beth said that she didn't have much time, as someone was bound to work out who April Thom actually, was which is the name she now uses.... Thom after her father Thomas (Tom) Collins and April the month she had the epiphany which changed her life forever she said.... She has also had some plastic surgery done in Mexico six months ago, with fillers in her cheekbones and chin and had her hair lightened, she said. But this had backfired, as being two stone lighter, from becoming a gym addict she looked even more like me and Jonathon now.... Beth has also trained herself to speak with a deeper voice and a New York accent I'd noticed.

Before her physical transformation Jonathon thought she was living a reclusive life in Florida and emailed her occasionally, she said. But now like everyone else, he was probably looking for her, so she had left him a trail that led into South America, via Mexico....

I just realised that Jonathon could not tell me he had been in contact with his sister all these years, as I would have then known he was also a member of the Illuminati....This made me sad.... Also, Beth had insisted none of the 'White hats' members tell me she had joined, as one she had been dealing with knew me, she said, Carl Z., to which I just nodded.... I then asked what her 'White hats' name was and she said Sarah C., as mine was Maria R. As most choose a same gender grandparent's name, followed by the first initial of a surname of another grandparent.... She also said she had met a Clarence D., a very brave and active member who had gathered a lot of important evidence. But I knew him by his real name of course.... I remember whispering to her "Piers Huxley" to which she answered, "precisely."

March 3rd

After my stay in hospital, I returned home and life went back to normal, or so it seemed. Of course the family were all devastated that Jonathon had missed being elected. And were already rallying around him making plans for his next run, as Jonathon still had time at fifty-six.... Well, some of the family were anyway....

Philip and Mitzi are also retired like Andre and me. They spend most of their time travelling around the U.S., going to all the beautiful national parks and selected music gigs in their trusty Winnebago, with their dogs 'Pink' and 'Blue', miniature schnauzers. They usually avoid the extreme heat or cold anywhere and are happy in each-others company they say.... I envy them sometimes their carefree life.

Alexander at seventy-one is still on the board of the Rothschild and co bank and his son Alex is now the banks CEO. Alex jnr. also married a Rothschild relative, Nadine, and they have two children. Alexander's daughter Claudia divorced but re- married Pierre Duhamel from another prominent Swiss banking family and they have four children between them.... My dad would have been very happy with this banking dynasty....

Oliver and Martine are busily involved in their careers. Oliver like his father is an architect and father of three, Noah, Luca and Mia and he has taken over the de Rothschild architectural business which Luca hopes to join one day.

Martine has her own fashion house 'Maison de Fabien', with her husband and business partner Thierry Fabien. They are always very busy but still managed to find time to parent Bella and Odette identical twins, who at eighteen are both fashion students and sought- after models.

Beth, I have no idea about.... She could be living a life incognito, or she could also be on the run.... One way I can stay sane is to immerse myself in charitable works, so I and am now the president of Legal Aid Foundation L.A. and on the committee of the L.A. LGBT Centre....I have some credibility because of the years I spent working with the homeless and fundraising for charity, in New York. Plus as I have been twice widowed, a single parent and raised a blended family, I am accepted in most women's circles.... Even if I am a wealthy and influential de Rothschild, whose son narrowly missed becoming the President of the United States, who may also in some Christian circles, be considered the anti-Christ....

This is only one side of me though, my other persona is Sophia Smyth, psychic medium. As I sit and tune into people and give them spiritual guidance, I see about six clients a week and am booked out about ten months in advance.... I also still run my weekly healing circle.... So, I wear many hats still, one being a white one.

This is my life. I hope my beloved Poppa and Oma would be proud of me.

This was the end of my memoirs, or so I thought.... I knew I could never publish them anyway.

Post cap:

2023

June 16th

My life had gone back to its usual routine the past eighteen months. With Andre and I spending part of the year in France visiting Martine and family. Then holidaying on the French Riviera where we also have a group of friends and enjoy catching up with his brother Laurent and his lovely partner Gabriel.

When we are at home in L.A., I immerse myself in my charity work and psychic readings which I do from home and I try not to involve myself in politics anymore.... Although obviously the fall-out of Jonathon's confession of being part of an elitist cabal that he was born into, has been enormous and on-going.... One good thing that has come out of this is now information about these secret societies is coming out in every media outlet, radio, television, newspapers and magazines. And fortunately no one has tried to kill Jonathon, as- yet.... Beth, I am not so sure about.... But I 'feel' she is alright when I sit and tune into her, which I do every day in my meditation and ask for her protection....

I have just turned seventy-eight. Andre is seventy-seven and fortunately we are both in good health.... The rest of the family are also doing well. We are all just getting on with our lives and trying to stay away from the media.... The only one in our family who has been a bit lost is Oliver's son Noah, as he discovered drugs and partying at a young age, but now seems more focused. He is working as a trainee viticulturist on a Rothschild estate in Chamois, France. Andre's Cousin Pascal de Rothschild, got him the job.... Some factions of the Rothschild's just lead normal lives, not all are active Illuminati.

My mom died in May, just shy of her ninety-ninth birthday so there was a great turn out of family for the funeral. Of course, every one of her generation has passed now, she was the last one left.... We I did an add up my Poppa and Oma have to date 40 descendants, not bad from just two children. No wonder the world is so grossly over-populated, even though the Illuminati has recently tried to do something about that....

The family all know of Poppa's dalliance and of the Huxley's.... Piers followed their family trend and produced only one son Rodney, who in turn has only one son Nigel.... And they all resemble Poppa more than anyone on our-side does. Only the late Peter, Piers, Beth and I, have inherited his psychic abilities that I am aware of. At mom's funeral Jonathon asked me to call on him the following day as he needed to discuss something with me in private, he said.... I immediately thought of Beth and feared the worst....

I arrived by taxi at Jonathon's house promptly at 10 o'clock as requested, as I no longer drive. I was surprised when he then ushered me into his study and closed the door.... He said his office was more secure. Then he made me a coffee the way I like it and we settled down on the sofa. I wasn't sure if Julia was home but I assumed not.

If Beth had floored me eighteen months ago with what she had said.... What Jonathon then told me came as an even bigger surprise, if that was even possible.... As he told me that he had also been leading a double life, but only recently.... He said that like Tom and Beth, he also had an epiphany.... This occurred after he lost the election he said, when it was suggested to him that his sister should be disposed of, and it was expected that he would agree.... He said, this was when what he was part of became very real and personal for him, as he realised that his father Saul, and stepfather Tom, had been disposed of, just like this....

Jonathon said he decided then that he was no longer going to be a major player in any Illuminati game.... He did have a choice, even though he had been 'selected'.... His brave sister had shown him that.... He also decided then he said that he was going to use every means possible to expose them, the Illuminati, and the plan that he and Beth had hatched together.... Yes together, was so far working .... He said Julia was with them also as were the West's, who had never been a part of the Illuminati anyway.... Plus, he was also in contact with the 'White hats' he said.

I sat there stunned and then stated, confused, that I had seen him and Julia, plus Andre, Laurent, Alexander and Benjamin de Rothschild turn reptilian.... Meaning Illuminati, when he conceded to Trump on election night, just before I passed out.... Jonathon said that was correct, then, but not now and added that there were still a lot of the family who weren't Illuminati.

He then said, he did not ask to be born a Rothschild, that was the hand he was given, and he had no choice but to play it.... And he would have been a fool to reject them or go against them, he said. He had no choice but to join their secret societies, as this was the way business is done, through the Skull and Bones, the Bilderberg group, the freemasons, to name a few, plus the Illuminati.... The latter of which, he and Julia were still officially members of, plus her father, as the others were for men only.... Jonathon said the U.S. is not alone, England has its Freemasons, old Boys Clubs and other secret societies as does Europe. He also said that he has had a few meetings with Donald Trump, and although he doesn't agree with the way he carries on or all his politics at least Trump is nobody's puppet.... The Illuminati love him though, as he is getting the U.S. into even more debt with them and is upsetting a lot of people, especially the Chinese.

Jonathon then said that a lot of countries are still furious the Chinese. Not only due to the recent pandemic but also because of their bullying and military peacocking, which nearly started a war over Taiwan, which Trump managed to avert.... But then there is more to this, Jonathon said.... Why should the Chinese own up to something they didn't invent? or even distribute. It was the Illuminati, the elite few who control the world. They started this pandemic in China (Germ warfare) to get the world on its knees and to make it dependant on a vaccine that they own and distribute. This will further impact people's health and cause them to need more medication in the future, some for life, from the companies they own. Also, their plan is to destroy the world economy, and to get most countries into huge debt. Next, they will control the worlds resources, oil, coal, and there has already been shortages.

Jonathon doubts Trump will finish his term, due to his health, and thinks Mike Pence his Vice will soon be President. And he has a far better hair-do Jonathon said, then laughed.

Jonathon said after his epiphany he decided to do what President Kennedy wanted to do when he spoke about exposing these secret societies, which have no place in a free society. That was the real reason Kennedy was eliminated and his brother, who they feared would become the next President then. They also tried to eliminate Ronald Reagan and to put Bush senior in as the President earlier mainly to control the politics in the oil rich nations....

I said surely the Illuminati now realise that you have turned, and Beth, and your lives must be in danger.... He said Beth is gone and she was such a quiet mousey little thing that no one associates her with April Thom.... Plus, she was never in line to become the Grande Dame, that information was just fed to the 'White hats'.... He said Beth did show her abilities to 'the Order' at sixteen but was not selected by her grandmother.... After that she kept them hidden. Beth decided her grandmother was honouring her late son's wishes by not selecting her, Jonathon said, which made sense.... Maybe the old witch had one decent bone left in her body after all.

Jonathon told me that his political opponents were obviously carrying this on, as now that he had been exposed and were trying to eliminate him from public office.... But he said as a senator still, he is staying to complete the valuable work he started in housing the homeless. Only now he is being honest about his past associations by admitting to the societies he belonged to.... He has not mentioned the 'Illuminati' though but has admitted belonging to 'the Order', of which some people have assumed is the Freemasons.... Fortunately for Jonathon he has had no scandals, affairs, or dubious business dealings, which is more than can be said for most of his political opponents.... Although they have tried to invent some for him.

But what no one had reckoned on, especially the Illuminati, is what actually- happened.... Jonathon being exposed as being a member of an elite ruling cabal, with damning evidence.... As now every investigative journalist worth their weight, is out to find out as much as they can about these secret societies, the Rothschilds' and the other prominent families involved and what they have or have not been responsible for, over the last century at least.... Jonathon West as a story is gone, his birthright is of more interest now....

Jonathon said there is now a now a major witch hunt and people are taking this seriously. It is no longer seen as just sensationalist conspiracy theories. And people are talking, too many people are talking now to all be eliminated, because of the injustices they have suffered, or their loved ones. Jonathon said that he hasn't actually- admitted to or denied anything that these societies have been accused of doing, as he is artful in deflecting, like most politicians. Except he has vehemently denied being a Satanist.... So really my son has just been the catalyst, and all this thanks to his sister....

Accurate information has also finally come to light about the death of my two late husbands. The truth has always sat been between the main so-called respected newspapers and the sensationist tabloids anyway, as we all know....

I asked Jonathon why he and Beth hadn't trusted me, and he said that it was too dangerous for me to know anything.... And now April Thom is his new personal assistant he said....

With that April walked in the door and gave me a kiss....

I just sat and looked at them both, stunned.... I told them I had never been prouder of them as as I was now.... I also said that as their mother I feared for their safety....

Jonathon said with what had been exposed, his days as a senator were numbered but he had not revealed enough to be killed-off he hoped.... But obviously, he did employ 24hr security.... And as he was still a very wealthy man with a loving wife and family, what more does he need.

Beth said once this is over, she will enjoy creating a whole new life for herself. Possibly in Canada with a generous account that Jonathon has set up for her.... Jonathon said hopefully they will soon be yesterday's news, as there are other more powerful family dynasties are out there who are far more dangerous and far-reaching who need to be exposed....

I just hoped as their mother that they will both live long enough to enjoy their new lives.... But Poppa would have said this is but one incarnation and their job which was an important one and mine were now complete.

The End

Epilogue:

Piers

4th August 2024

Andre has given me all of Sophia's Diaries.... And Clarence's. He said he trusts me to do what is right with them. So, I am going to publish, all of them.... And to hell with the consequences....

Sadly, we buried our beloved Sophia on the 2nd of June, just shy of her 80th birthday... She was taken to hospital with a suspected heart attack on the 18th of May two days after hearing of the sudden death of her 60-year-old son Jonathon in a freak car accident. Apparently, he was pushed off the road at high speed by another car, but that car and driver were never found. The road conditions were good, it was late at night and on a quiet street and there were no witnesses. Of course, this was highly suspicious. I also knew Sophia's passing was highly suspicious as her heart attack the family were told was mild. But three days later for no apparent reason she died of a massive stroke.

Sophia has been to visit me since she passed, to say that her and Jonathon are reunited with loved ones and to assure me that Beth is safe, living out of the U.S. and will remain so. As with her gift for clairvoyance she can be warned. Sophia told me that her and Jonathon were murdered as a lesson for others....

Sophia said when she passed her Poppa and Oma greeted her, but not Jonathon. He was in a place under lights surrounded by loved ones, as the grief of the loved ones left behind was affecting him very much. Plus, as an atheist he was taking longer to process being dead than she was.

Sophia also said that when we pass-over we can be in more than one place at a time as many have jobs to do helping the souls still living like Oma who helps children that have passed.

17th December

Sophia had been to see me a twice in the last few months. She comes through clairaudiently, that is, I hear her. Sophia told me she is evolving quickly through the astral planes so has therefore spent a lot of time alone. But she does have a guide Runa, who is very beautiful and who emulates pure love she said. Her and Runa see each other as light beings with human features and when Runa is close it puts Sophia is a state of total Bliss she said.

Sophia said that after reuniting with loved ones, her life from birth to death was presented to her as a hologram. And she could play out the other paths she could have taken. But in the end, none of it mattered and there is no right or wrong, no judgement, just unconditional love and acceptance.

Sophia said pain is part of the human experience, as living in the limitations of human existence is painful at times. She told me that she hasn't met with Jonathon yet as he is still playing out all his preconceived ideas about death and working through his life's hologram, as he must learn to let go of ego. As a younger soul than hers Sophia thinks he will choose to reincarnate. But of course, he will have no memory of his former life.

Sophia said she has met some supreme light beings, as many stay to become part of the universe like we all do, in time, but some reincarnate to earth like Jesus, Mohammed, Mahatma Ghandi, the Dali Lama, and to a lesser extent our dear Poppa Clarence.

The End

'Sophia's Diaries' is the Third book in the Clarence R. Smyth trilogy.

Born on the first day of the new century 1900 in London, England, Clarence from a young age was a renowned psychic in the U.K. then later parts of Europe and the United States. Clarence had many adventures growing up and throughout his life and his accurate predictions had him being 'watched' by more than one interested party. He was asked many times to join a powerful cabal of elitists but he always refused, which nearly cost him his life. This third book also told in diary form, tells the story of his granddaughter Sophia Elizabeth Rothschild and her struggles, as she was not only similarly gifted but also born into one of these powerful families....

Clarence dies when Sophia is only sixteen, so she loses her mentor and protector. As Sophia like her famous grandfather has also been monitored all her life by the cabal. Guided by her deceased grandfather and her own intuition, Sophia tries to not be a pawn in their game, but she is powerless. And later she fears for her two eldest children who have also been selected for key roles in this powerful cabal, that some may call 'the Order', but more call the 'Illuminati'.

This book is a combination of historical facts, psychic predictions, spirituality and conspiracy theories and is an interesting and thought provoking read.